MYSTERIES *of* **MARTHA'S VINEYARD**

A Light in the Darkness
Like a Fish Out of Water
Adrift

MYSTERIES *of* MARTHA'S VINEYARD

Adrift

BETH ADAMS

Guideposts

New York

Mysteries of Martha's Vineyard is a trademark of Guideposts.

Published by Guideposts Books & Inspirational Media
110 William Street
New York, NY 10038
Guideposts.org

Cover and interior design by Müllerhaus
Cover illustration by Greg Copeland, represented by Deborah Wolfe, LTD.
Typeset by Aptara, Inc.

Printed and bound in the United States of America
10 9 8 7 6 5 4 3 2 1

Adrift

CHAPTER ONE

Priscilla was just climbing into her car when her phone rang. It sounded so foreign out here, on this spit of land surrounded by crashing waves, that it took her a moment to place the sound. Then she dug around in her purse to locate it before it stopped ringing. It was always buried under her wallet, keys, sunglasses—there it was. She pulled it out and looked at the screen. Gerald O'Bannon. She answered the call.

"Couldn't wait, huh?" Priscilla was on her way to meet Gerald at the Nautilus Café for lunch. He'd invited her, saying he had a favor to ask. She was glad for the opportunity to see him and had been looking forward to it.

"I'm afraid I'm going to be a bit late for lunch," Gerald said. She could hear some voices behind him and what sounded like metal banging on metal.

"Is everything all right?"

"Yes, it's fine. It's just—something came up at work, and it looks like it might take a while."

"Oh dear." Priscilla felt more than disappointment. Gerald was a captain at the Coast Guard station just up the road. She knew that if something had come up at work, it was serious. "Do you want to reschedule?"

"No. I mean, I'd still really like to have lunch, if you have time."

"I have time." Priscilla certainly kept busy since she had moved from a farm in Kansas to Martha's Vineyard a few months ago, but this lunch was the only thing she had on her calendar today. "Do you want me to meet you in an hour?"

"I'd love that, but I'm not sure exactly how long I'll be. How about this—could you come here? And then as soon as I get this squared away, we can drive over to the Nautilus together?"

"That sounds just fine," Priscilla said. She had only been inside the Coast Guard station briefly, but she'd thought it was fascinating to see what it was like inside a real military post way out here on the coast of this remote island. And, she had to admit, she was a little curious about what could have happened to delay him. It had to be something big, the way he sounded. "I'll be there shortly."

Priscilla tucked her phone back into her purse and set it on the passenger seat. As she started the engine, she looked up at the Misty Harbor Lighthouse, just a little way up the cliff from the keeper's cottage where she now lived. It stood tall and proud, guarding the craggy hillsides that gave way to the ocean below. Sometimes she still couldn't believe she lived here.

Priscilla backed the car around and pulled out onto the narrow old lane that led to the main road. Trees arched over the road. The first of the leaves were just starting to turn orange and gold. She couldn't wait for her first New England fall. Of course she'd seen plenty of trees change color back in Wheatfield, Kansas, but everyone said she hadn't seen anything like the riot of color she would witness here.

As she drove down the road, she passed small wooden houses, set right up next to the road, that had been here for centuries and cottages sided with weathered shingles. These homes were the kind of beautiful that didn't call attention to itself. Understated and classic. She loved this place. She passed barns faded to a soft gray and fences made of stones piled one on top of each other. She turned right at the Quaker graveyard that had tombstones dating back to the 1700s. That was another thing that was different from Kansas—the sense of history that permeated this island and the pride the islanders took in their past.

As she got farther from the heart of Misty Harbor, houses gave way to marshland, and finally she wound her way around the last bend and the bay opened up before her, blue churning water all the way to the horizon. Beyond that lay Cape Cod, she knew, but she couldn't see the mainland on this hazy morning. Off to the right was a road with a big white wooden sign that read US COAST GUARD.

She turned in and drove toward the stately white buildings that made up the station. The main building was three stories and topped by a cupola surrounded by a widow's walk. She saw several cars parked in the lot and more lined up in front of the white building that served as housing for the officers stationed here, but this area was quiet. She looked around and saw people in orange suits headed down the hill, moving toward the dock that lay just past the row of old weather-beaten fishing shacks. Priscilla started moving toward the action, and as she got closer, she saw what had gotten everyone so excited.

It was a building. A floating wooden building tied up at the dock.

As she got closer, she saw that it was a cabin of some sort. A houseboat, maybe? But what was it doing here? There were a couple of people who didn't look like they could be much out of their teens wearing the official Coast Guard dry suits, but they didn't pay her any mind as she walked down the catwalk toward the vessel.

"Hi there," Gerald called, seeing her as he stepped out onto the dock from the cabin. He was wearing an orange dry suit over his clothes, and he gestured for her to come closer.

"Hi." Priscilla now stood in front of the floating building, and she realized what it was. "Is that the houseboat that's been parked out in the marina?"

Until a few weeks ago, the only kinds of houseboats Priscilla was familiar with were the typical double-decker floating motorhomes that spewed out exhaust and leaked gasoline. People liked to take them out on the lakes during the summers back home. But this was nothing like that. This was a floating wooden cabin of sorts, built on a platform that surrounded the tiny home. It was covered in wooden shingles and had a sliding door that led from the platform to the inside. It was kind of like those houseboats in *Sleepless in Seattle*, only newer and with less rain.

"That's right," Gerald said. "This is the one that's been moored over in the harbor. The one that's been causing so much uproar around here."

Priscilla nodded. She'd read in the newspaper about the furor this boat had caused when it appeared in the marina a few weeks back. No one seemed to know anything about the man who had taken up residence on the harbor, and he didn't seem inclined to come ashore and introduce himself. And some people in Tisbury and the surrounding communities, it seemed, did not like the idea of a houseboat being parked out in the harbor. It ruined the view or something. Priscilla had seen the headlines, but she hadn't really paid that much attention to the story. She didn't see what the fuss was about. A boat was a boat, right? She could see the marina from the top of the lighthouse, and it hadn't bothered her to have it there.

"Interesting." She stepped closer. Up close, she could see that it was very well constructed with solid wood siding and neatly painted white trim. "But what's it doing here?"

Gerald let out a sigh. "I wish I knew." Then he stepped off the dock and onto the houseboat's deck.

"Captain O'Bannon," came a call from inside. Gerald turned toward the door and peered inside. "Can you come check this out?"

He smiled at Priscilla and held up a finger, asking her to wait. Priscilla stepped onto the houseboat's deck and watched as Gerald stepped in through the open sliding glass door. He crossed the small space and hunched over something on a small table, across from a young man in the Coast Guard uniform. Priscilla had met him before. Seeley? She thought that was his name.

Priscilla stood outside the door for a moment, feeling awkward. Should she just hang out out here? She'd thought he was just going to duck in for a moment, but he was now in discussion with the other Coast Guard officer. The platform the boat rested on bobbed up and down, and the air carried the salty, briny tang of the sea.

Priscilla waited a few more minutes, but Gerald didn't come back out. She peered through the door and saw that it was just a small space, and it was only Gerald and Seeley in there right now.

She made a decision. She hadn't exactly been invited inside, but no one had asked her to stay out either. She stepped through the open sliding glass door. No one seemed to notice. Both Gerald and Seeley were focused on something on the counter.

"The police are on their way," Seeley was saying. "I'm sure they'll run tests—fingerprints, UV scans, the works. But if we can get this unlocked before they get here..."

"Yes. Good. Focus on that," Gerald said. Then he added, "Thanks."

He turned and saw Priscilla standing inside the boat, and she was certain he was going to kick her out, but he didn't. "Be careful there," was all he said, indicating a wet patch on the floor.

"Thanks."

She looked around. So this was a houseboat. It was small—not more than ten feet by twelve feet, she guessed, but it was cunningly designed. Directly across from the glass door was a table, which she could see folded down into a bench when not in use. Priscilla and her late husband Gary had gone on a trip to Yellowstone in an RV many years ago, and it had the same feature, but this was built out of solid, handsome cherry. The table was crookedly hanging off its hinges now, and the blue-and-white-striped fabric that had lined the bench had been sliced open.

The front wall held a few cabinets and a narrow electric stove. The cabinets and drawers had all been yanked open, and cans of coffee and beans had spilled out onto the counter. Milk leaked out of the open door of the minifridge. Next to that was a door that led to the smallest bathroom she'd ever seen. A single bed was pushed up against the far wall, blankets strewn over the floor, the mattress sliced open. A dog bed was propped on its side next to the mattress, and it had also been sliced through. Most of the remainder of the small space was given over to a table and an easel and chair. Tubes of oil paints had been knocked onto the floor, and a shelf that held canvases in various stages had been knocked over, the canvases tossed this way and that.

"What happened here?" Priscilla asked. It looked like it had been ransacked.

Gerald let out a slow breath. "We got a call from Almeida Charier this morning," he said. Priscilla nodded. She had met Almeida, who drove one of the ferryboats that went back and forth to the mainland. "She was driving the first boat out this morning, and she spotted the houseboat floating in the shipping channel, headed out to sea."

"It was just floating? No one was driving it?"

Gerald shook his head. "These houseboats don't have motors. There's no way to drive them. They just float."

"So how did it get out there?" Priscilla tried to wrap her head around this. "And what happened to the guy who was living here?"

He shrugged. "That's what we're trying to find out. My crew towed it back here, but there's no sign of the man who was living here."

A feeling of dread washed over her. Judging by the state of this place, whatever had happened, it could not be good.

"Somebody was looking for something," she said, indicating the opened cabinets and sliced upholstery.

"Looks like it," Gerald said. "But we don't have the slightest clue what."

"Who was he?" Priscilla wandered into the kitchen area and peered in the open cabinets. Some coffee, a tin of sugar, coffee filters. A half-empty box of granola bars and a few packages of beef jerky.

"We don't know that either." Gerald sighed and turned to Seeley.

Priscilla studied the canvases that were strewn around. They all seemed to be abstract paintings with lots of patterns repeated over and over but no discernible bigger shape. Not Priscilla's taste but interesting in their own way, she supposed. The whole space had the oily, mineral smell of turpentine.

She pointed to the dog bed. "He had a dog, right? I remember reading that in the paper. What happened to the dog?"

Gerald just shrugged. "No idea. Any luck, Seeley?"

"No. It's password protected."

Priscilla noticed that he was hunched over a small silver laptop computer. He must be trying to get inside.

How odd, she thought. Someone had gone to a lot of trouble trying to find something in here. But whatever it was, it wasn't the guy's laptop. She would have thought that would be the most valuable thing on this boat.

She turned back toward the open cabinets in the kitchen. What had the person been looking for?

She crouched down and peered in the open lower cabinet. The pans it had contained were now scattered across the floor, and only a couple of spare lids remained inside. A few large-handled knives from the butcher block were splayed across the counter. Maybe one was used to slash open the furniture?

Someone had come on this boat looking for something. She wondered what it was and whether they had found it. They certainly had done their best. The guy who'd been living here must have done a good job of hiding it. Whatever it was.

She thought for a moment. If she had been hiding something on this boat, where would she have put it?

She didn't even have to think. She knew exactly where she'd always hidden important things. The same place her grandmother had hidden the farm's papers when her grandfather threatened to sell in the darkest days of the Great Depression. The same place Priscilla's mother had also hidden her cash. Where Priscilla always kept spare cash, just in case. In the last place anyone would ever look: taped to the underside of the silverware drawer.

Still crouched on the floor, Priscilla looked up.

"Gerald?" she called. "I think I found something."

CHAPTER TWO

W hat is it?" Gerald was bent over the laptop, still trying to figure out the password and unlock it. He looked over at Priscilla, straightened up, and blinked. He seemed surprised and more than a little confused to find Priscilla crouched on the floor in the kitchen.

"It looks like a key."

"What?" Both Gerald and Seeley were looking at her now, brows furrowed. Seeley was adjusting the frames of his glasses.

"Underneath this drawer." She pointed up. "There's a key taped under here."

Gerald crossed the small space in a few strides and crouched down next to her. "What in the world?" He narrowed his eyes. "How did you find this?"

"Women's intuition," she said. It was easier than explaining the real answer.

He looked at her. The look on his face said that he didn't know how to respond. She decided to help him out and pointed up again.

He pulled a small flashlight off his belt and pointed it at the underside of the drawer. The key had a squarish head and was a silver color. "You didn't touch it, did you?"

"No. I haven't touched a thing."

"Good. When the police get here, I'm sure they'll want to dust for fingerprints."

"Speak of the devil," Seeley said.

Priscilla turned and saw two officers striding down the catwalk toward the houseboat. She recognized one of them, a woman she'd met when Priscilla had reported a break-in at her house a few months back. April Brown, she thought. Behind Officer Brown was a young officer she'd never met before. Both wore the deep blue uniform of the Tisbury police department.

"Wow," the female officer said, stepping inside the sliding glass door. "This is it, huh?"

Gerald stood. "Officer Brown. Officer Holmes."

Officer Brown looked around, taking in the small space, while Officer Holmes, who had thick, dark, curly hair and olive skin, was already taking notes on a small pad of paper.

"When did the call come in?" Holmes asked.

But Officer Brown had noticed Priscilla, and though she nodded at her, she indicated that her partner should hold off, and he stopped.

"Ms. Grant. Nice to see you again." Officer Brown was younger than Priscilla, probably in her midforties, if Priscilla had to guess. She had shoulder-length brown hair and a kind face, but there was a no-nonsense tone in her voice. She turned to Gerald. "Is she here in some official capacity?"

Priscilla got the message loud and clear. She was in the way. A civilian, she probably shouldn't have been allowed on the boat—no doubt an active crime scene—in the first place. But she hoped all would be forgiven when it came out what she'd discovered.

"I was just on my way out," she said, straightening up.

"Thank you, Priscilla," Gerald said. "Why don't you wait back at the station? I'll be done here in a few minutes."

Both police officers nodded at her as she made her way out. Priscilla knew she could be frustrated about being so unceremoniously dismissed, but her mind was racing. She couldn't believe what she'd just seen, and questions kept jogging back and forth in her mind as she walked past the fishing shanties and up the hill to the station. Who was the man who had been on that houseboat? What had happened to him?

Judging by what she'd seen, there was a good chance he was in trouble. As she walked, Priscilla whispered a prayer that God would protect the mystery man, whoever and wherever he was. Whoever had broken in to that houseboat wasn't messing around, and now the man was missing. She prayed that God would lead them to answers before it was too late.

CHAPTER THREE

Priscilla and Gerald entered the Nautilus Café, a newer restaurant overlooking the fishing wharfs in Tisbury. The restaurant, owned by Tobin Worthington, a Boston restaurateur who'd grown tired of the rat race and moved here full-time, was known for fresh salads and delicious and interesting sandwiches. The wooden interior, accented with nautical touches like anchors and fishing nets, was warm and inviting. But the real attractions here were the picture windows that overlooked docks where the fishermen unloaded their catch. It was fascinating to watch them heft their hauls out of the back of the trawlers and wheel them to the seafood market just down the way. In the summer, you had to get here early to snag a table by the window, but in late September, it was mostly locals, and Priscilla smiled at Pastor Katie Rona, who was eating with Eldora Williams, and then at her cousin Trudy and her husband Dan Galvin.

"Priscilla!" Trudy hopped up and came over to her. Priscilla had just seen Trudy a few days ago, but she acted like it had been years. Trudy was always bright and bubbly, and she sometimes reminded Priscilla of a puppy, ever upbeat and sometimes tripping over herself trying to get her words out. "It's good to see you. What are you doing here? Oh!" She noticed who Priscilla had come in with. "I won't interrupt. I just wanted to say hi."

"I'm glad you did," Priscilla said.

She saw that Dan was looking down at his burger. Trudy's husband was her opposite. Quiet and reserved and quirky to the core, he was a scientist at the Woods Hole Oceanographic Institution and studied sea life all day. He had strong cheekbones and a kind smile, but he could be a bit awkward in social situations. Trudy sometimes joked that she didn't know how she'd ended up marrying a nerd, and Priscilla had to admit she'd wondered the same thing. She supposed opposites really did attract.

"Tell Dan I said hello."

"I'll see you soon," Trudy said and waved before heading back to her table.

Priscilla and Gerald settled in at a table by the big wall of windows. A boat had just pulled up to the dock, and two men in waders had started unloading crates of what Priscilla guessed were crabs. She looked over her menu, but Gerald just set his down.

"What are you going to get?" she asked.

"Fried scallops," he said. "Best thing on the menu."

Priscilla smiled. That did sound good, but she was in the mood for something a bit lighter. "I'll have the broiled cod. And an iced tea."

Their waitress appeared, and they placed their orders. She set a basket of bread down and assured them their food would be out soon. In the meantime, Priscilla had a thousand questions.

"So. What's the big deal with this houseboat?" she asked. As soon as she said it, she realized how ridiculous that sounded. "I mean, aside from the obvious. Pretend what we saw today didn't happen. What was it about this houseboat that had people so up in arms?"

Their waitress brought an iced tea for Priscilla and a Coke for Gerald and then quickly disappeared. Gerald took a sip and settled his napkin in his lap before he answered. "It's hard to explain if you don't spend a lot of time around boats, I guess."

Priscilla nodded. By now she'd gotten used to feeling like an outsider, to not understanding the nuances of the culture around her new home. But that didn't mean she wasn't willing to try.

"People around here…Well, they like things to stay the way they are, I guess. Change can be scary."

"Yes, I've picked up on that." She ripped off the end of her straw wrapper.

"I guess the idea of someone living in the harbor was upsetting to some people."

"But people live on their boats all the time, right?" She hadn't been on many boats in her life, but she knew that over the summer, the harbor had been filled with sailboats from all over the world, and the owners slept in them. They went from place to place and ventured out to see the sights, but they lived on their boats, she was pretty sure.

"True, I guess. But there's a difference between sleeping and cooking on a sailboat and parking a houseboat in the harbor."

"How so?" She cocked her head. "You can live on either one, right? Both kinds of boats can have kitchens and beds and bathrooms. Isn't it really just the shape of the boat that's different?"

Gerald hesitated and then nodded. "In some sense, I guess you're right. It's just that..."

He was searching for the right words. Priscilla had an idea she knew what he was trying to say.

"It's that sailboats are classy and houseboats are not," she offered. The people who'd come off those sailboats in the harbor were mostly wealthy, from what she could tell. When she'd seen them around town in the summer, the men had worn pristine V-neck sweaters, boat shoes, and pink shorts that for some reason everyone was okay with because they called the color "Nantucket Red." The women were fit and slim and had frosted hair and designer jeans. She knew there was a kind of cachet about having a sailboat. It made you think of the Kennedys and seafood salad at the yacht club.

A houseboat on the other hand...

"Some people around here have grown up with sailing culture," he said. "They're used to seeing a certain kind of boat moored in the harbor. And the houseboat, to them, represents a different kind of lifestyle creeping in, and that makes them uncomfortable. I'm not saying they're right. I'm just explaining what has some people so upset."

Priscilla plunked her straw into her iced tea. She understood what he was getting at. "Have there ever been houseboats here before?"

"Not in Misty Harbor, no." He played with the paper he'd taken off his own straw. "There's a famous houseboat community over in Woods Hole. That's Cape Cod. There are several dozen houseboats moored off the coast there every summer, and they've been there for years."

She nodded. Woods Hole was one of the places where you caught the ferry to Martha's Vineyard. She'd seen the houseboats from the ferry but hadn't realized what she was looking at.

"But they're somewhat controversial. It all started because housing prices were so high that people couldn't afford to stay on the mainland, especially when prices skyrocket during the season. So they started simply building houses on the water and parking them in the harbor. For the cost of renting a mooring, you had a place to stay all summer."

The opposition to the houseboats was becoming more clear. It was about money, as most things ultimately were. Martha's Vineyard was an island, with a finite amount of land. If people started finding other places to live, it could devalue the properties on the island.

"But as the group of boats in Woods Hole grew, people became concerned."

"About their property values."

"Not just about that. Also about the kind of people who were spending the summer out there."

Money and class then. It was about the differences between people who could afford to have a permanent place in one of the most expensive real-estate markets in the country, and those who couldn't.

"It became something of a party culture. Loud music, lots of drinking, that sort of thing. Anyway, the town of Woods Hole eventually passed a law banning any more houseboats from setting up off the shore. The ones already there were grandfathered in, but no more could be built. So there are a few dozen that spend the winter on Eel Pond, where they're protected from the currents and rough water of the winter storms, and every summer get towed out to the water off Woods Hole."

"And people on Martha's Vineyard are upset because they don't want this to become another Woods Hole."

"*Some* people on Martha's Vineyard are upset. It's a small group actually, but a vocal one."

She'd go back and read the newspaper articles about this. There had seemed to be plenty of people upset when that boat appeared in the harbor.

"Is the boat you found one of the boats from Woods Hole?"

"No. That's a very well-known group of boats, and this is not one of them."

She took a packet of sugar from the dish on the table and stirred it into her iced tea. "This may be a ridiculous question, but I've always wondered this. Remember, I come from a landlocked state."

He smiled.

"If that man was living on the houseboat, how did he get back and forth to land?"

"Not a ridiculous question. The answer is, he didn't, at least not very often. But when he did, it was the same way people get to land when they have a sailboat moored in the harbor. Some people have a smaller boat they pull behind them when they sail, but most use the mooring companies' launch services."

"The what?"

"The moorings are all owned by a few private companies. Well, except for the ones owned by the town, but those are only available for short-term use. For a longer stay, you have to rent a mooring from one of the private companies that operate in the harbor."

"Like reserving a parking space?"

"Or a campground. Same idea, I guess. Anyway, the mooring companies have launches—small boats—that ferry people from their moored boats to the dock."

"Ah. Okay." She used her straw to stir the ice in her glass. "Another question. You said people live on these houseboats in the summer. But it's past summer."

"Yes. That's part of what makes this all so unusual. The houseboat showed up in our harbor just after Labor Day. By that point, most of the Woods Hole houseboats are put up for the winter."

"So why would this man start living on one then?"

"I don't know." Now he was rolling the wrapper from his straw into a ball. "But from what I saw, this boat was well-made. And as you saw, it was wired for electricity, which not all of them are. There must be a generator onboard somewhere. I suspect that with a space heater, he could have lived out there for at least another month before the fall weather really set in and made it uncomfortable."

Priscilla thought about that and decided he was probably right. The boat she'd seen wouldn't be much fun in winter, but it could be downright cozy this time of year. Well, before it had been upended anyway.

"You said the Woods Hole boats are towed into place. The boat we saw doesn't have a motor. Would it have been towed there too?"

Gerald nodded. "It surely had to have been. We don't know by whom or when, though. We'll be looking into this."

"We? Will the Coast Guard be investigating? Why did the police come along then?"

"It's kind of a gray area as far as jurisdiction goes. Since whatever happened took place on the water and since we discovered the boat, the Coast Guard is involved. But the police have more expertise when it comes to missing persons cases. That's not really the kind of thing we do. So basically, we'll be investigating what happened together."

"Huh." Priscilla leaned back as the young waitress set a plate down in front of her. The fish and the side of french fries were too good to pass up. She reached for the bottle of ketchup at the edge of the table and gently tapped the end of the bottle. "Okay, so what do you think happened on that boat?" She set down the bottle and dragged a french fry through the ketchup.

Gerald had speared one of his scallops, but he stopped with it halfway to his mouth. "I sure wish I knew."

She popped the fry into her mouth and chewed for a minute. "I guess the first question is, who was that man?"

Gerald nodded, chewing.

"But it can't be that hard to find out, right? Don't all boats have to be registered? They have numbers on the front, right?"

Gerald nodded, swallowed, and dabbed his mouth with his napkin. "The bow. Yes, all boats with motors have to be registered before they can be used on a waterway in Massachusetts. There's just one problem in this case."

Priscilla saw it right away. "The houseboat doesn't have a motor."

"We've put in a call to the Boat, Off-Highway Vehicle, and Snowmobile Registration Bureau."

"Catchy name."

He smiled. "It pretty much tells it like it is, I suppose. Anyway, we'll see if by some miracle the boat was registered after all, but I'm guessing we're not going to find much."

"Okay." She ate another french fry and thought. "Well, someone has to know who he is. He must have paid someone to be able to park in the marina, right?"

"He must have paid for the mooring, yes."

"Well then." This was going to be easy. "Just ask them who he is."

"We've already got officers on it," Gerald said.

Oh. Of course they'd already thought of that. Well, that just meant it had been a good idea. There had to be some other way to find out who he was and what happened. She thought over what she knew for sure. Someone had been on that boat, and now he was gone. The boat, which had been parked—moored—at the harbor had been set adrift.

"Do you think he was kidnapped?"

Gerald shrugged. "I don't know."

"Was it a robbery gone wrong?"

"I couldn't say." His tone was even, but he seemed more amused than anything by her questions.

"*Hmm.*" She took another bite and chewed, thinking. She pictured the inside of that boat. If it had been the middle of the night when someone boarded it, for whatever reason, the man would probably have been asleep in the bed. But surely he'd woken up. "Why didn't he call for help?"

"I don't know."

"Would a cell phone work in the marina?"

"I would expect so. It's not so far from shore. I would imagine you could get coverage in the harbor. Mine typically picks up a signal there. But the police are trying to get access to his cell records as we speak. We'll know more when we get ahold of them."

Gerald was smiling at her, like he was enjoying her questions. A small part of her—a very small part of her that she tried to ignore—whispered that he thought it was cute that she was trying to play detective. But that wasn't like the Gerald she knew. He was a kind and gentle man. And she was just trying to make sense of what she'd seen. Besides, even if the Coast Guard and the police were working together to solve this, who was to say that she wouldn't come up with something they hadn't thought of? She decided to keep at it.

"What about a distress signal? Isn't that what people do on boats when they're in trouble?"

Gerald nodded. "Sometimes. But the Coast Guard didn't receive any distress signals last night."

She took a sip of her tea. "How does that work?"

"You mean, how would you call for Coast Guard help?"

"Exactly. All this boating stuff is new to me. I assume I wouldn't just pick up a phone and call for the Coast Guard, but I don't actually have the slightest clue what I would do."

"Well, hopefully you wouldn't be in a situation where you'd need to do anything." His eyes met hers over the rim of his glass.

"Humor me. I'm trying to understand here. Do boats have, like, I don't know, flares? They always set off flares in the movies."

"What movies are you watching?"

"I don't know. Boat movies."

"Boat movies, huh?" He was laughing again. "All right." He set down his glass. "Well, those boat movies you seem to love get it partly right. Yes, many boats do have flares as part of their emergency kit. Setting off flares would be a good way to let someone know your location. The problem is someone has to be watching for the flare to go off."

"What if you set off a bunch in a row?"

"If someone were out there to see them, that would be a sure sign that something was wrong. Setting off a flare is a pretty universal distress signal. But your best bet would be to use a marine radio to call for help so someone was already searching for your location."

"So how would I make a distress call?"

Gerald laughed. "I sure hope you'd never need to. But every boat should be equipped with a marine radio. It's basically like an oversized walkie-talkie. There are many different channels you can use to talk to other vessels in the area."

"Like a CB radio?"

"Yes. Like that." He moved his straw around in his glass, and the ice tinkled gently. "Channel sixteen is the designated station for 'hailing and distress.' If you were in trouble, you would tune to channel sixteen and state the name of the vessel and your location, and then say the word *mayday* three times to indicate there is a serious problem."

She took all this in. People said *mayday* a lot in movies too. "Would a houseboat have flares or a marine radio?"

"I didn't see anything like that. But then again, that houseboat isn't supposed to cruise. Under normal circumstances, it needs to be towed from place to place, and I'd imagine the boat doing the towing would have emergency supplies."

"'Under normal circumstances.' You mean, when it's not simply set adrift."

"Exactly."

"What did he even look like? Did anyone ever see him?" she asked.

"We have conflicting reports. Some people reported that the man had brown hair, others blond. No one seems to have any idea how old he was."

He took another bite of scallops, and Priscilla dug into her cod as well. It was fresh and flaky. As she chewed, she thought through everything she'd learned. And she thought about something else. Something she remembered. Was it possible . . .

"You're not letting it go, are you?" Again, Gerald seemed more amused than anything.

"I'm thinking."

"Well, I can't argue with that. And I have to admit, you've put a couple of puzzles together since you've been here. But I assure you that between the police and the Coast Guard, we can solve this one."

Without her help. He didn't have to say that part. It was implied.

Just then Marigold Townsend came in, and Gerald and Priscilla both waved as she sat down at a table in the corner.

"I'm certain you can." But she still had questions. And why shouldn't she ask them? What could it hurt if she satisfied her own curiosity about the missing man? "I was wondering about his dog."

"What about his dog?"

She picked up another fry. "You said people reported that he had a dog. I read that too. What kind of dog was it?"

"Best guess from reports is that it was a golden retriever or yellow Lab. We're checking to see if anyone knows more than that."

She nodded. Those were popular dogs and well-loved. "I was thinking about Jake. I can't imagine he would stay quiet if someone broke into my home at night and started flipping tables over." In fact, that was part of why she'd adopted him when she'd moved to Martha's Vineyard. Well, that and the fact that the little scamp was so darn lovable she couldn't resist.

"No, I imagine he wouldn't. But that area is deserted at this time of year. There are still a few boats out in the marina, but no one else was living on the water. For all we know, the dog could have been barking like mad. But there's no one around to hear anything."

"But you're going to ask anyway, right?"

"Of course."

She nodded, but something was still bothering her. "So what happened to the dog?"

"I would imagine the same thing that happened to the man who was there. Hopefully, they're safe and sound somewhere."

She popped the fry in her mouth and thought some more. As they'd been talking, she'd thought of something. Something she hadn't really put together until just now. Should she say it? It was so unformed, so vague. Would it be helpful at all? She decided to just go ahead and see how he reacted.

"You know, I heard something last night."

"Oh?"

"The thing is, I could have sworn I heard a dog barking. It was around three, and I had woken up and couldn't get back to sleep."

He nodded, and she went on.

"I was lying in bed, and I could have sworn I heard a dog barking. I remember it because it struck me as really odd. Jake heard it too. He perked right up."

"Priscilla...," Gerald began. He set down his fork and wiped his fingers on his napkin. "I don't doubt that you heard something. But there's no way you could have heard a dog barking in the harbor from your house."

Priscilla's house—and the Misty Harbor Lighthouse—sat on a spit of land that stuck out above the town. From her house, all she could really see were trees and water, but if she went up into the lighthouse, she could see down to the harbor and the town to the east, and the bay and mainland beyond to the west. As the crow flew, it wasn't far to the harbor, really. But he was right. The distance was too great to have heard a dog barking.

"That's the thing. The sound wasn't coming from the direction of the harbor. It was coming from the other side. The west. The Sound side."

"*Hmm.*" Gerald looked dubious. And maybe it did seem a tad too convenient that she'd heard a dog just when one had gone missing. But she knew what she'd heard. "If that were true, and if it were the same dog, that would mean the dog had gone around Bailey Point and was heading up-island. To the west."

She nodded. That was what she'd been thinking as well.

"The working theory right now is that if the man survived whatever happened on that boat, he was taken back to the mainland."

"Survived?" A chilling thought came to her. He couldn't mean . . .

"We're all hopeful that he was taken somewhere and we can track him down. But you should know they'll be dragging the harbor this afternoon, just to make sure."

He meant there was a chance the man was dead and lying at the bottom of the harbor. Priscilla couldn't believe it.

"I mean, that's the worst-case scenario, and we just need to be sure," Gerald continued quickly. "But if he did survive—and we're hopeful he did—then in all likelihood, he was taken back to the mainland. So we're focusing our energies there."

Priscilla was too stunned to argue. Maybe she'd been naive. Of course it was possible that this was more than a missing person case. It was probably evidence that she really was an amateur that she hadn't even considered that possibility. But still...

"I can see that I've upset you. I'm sorry about that."

"You didn't upset me," she said. It wasn't him who had done this.

"All I'm saying is that it's very unlikely you heard a dog barking from the west side of Bailey Point." He used the tines of his fork to cut a scallop. "The wind does strange things with sound, especially where you are. Maybe you heard a neighbor's dog, and the wind made it seem like it was coming from the direction of the water."

"Maybe." But even as she said it, she had doubts. It sure had sounded like the dog had been out on the water.

"Let's talk about something more pleasant," Gerald said. "I actually invited you to lunch because I want to ask you something."

Priscilla had almost forgotten that he'd invited her to lunch. She'd gotten so wrapped up in the mystery that she hadn't remembered why they were here. "Ask away."

Gerald took a sip through his straw and then looked at her. "I was actually hoping to ask for your help with something. I noticed that you do some sewing."

She nodded. She wasn't a professional by any means, but she could handle herself with a sewing machine. She'd made most of her daughter Rachel's clothes when she was young, and sometimes she'd make a dress or some special garment, though it was usually simpler and cheaper to just buy clothes nowadays. She'd made a few things for the cottage since she'd been here—curtains for her bedroom and new cushions for the dining room chairs.

"I enjoy sewing." Where was he going with this?

"Well, you know Aggie is having another baby this winter."

Priscilla nodded. Aggie was Gerald's daughter who lived in town. She had a little boy named Max and was expecting her second in January.

"She's having a girl this time. And—I don't know. Maybe that's making me sentimental. It's hard to imagine my little girl is having her own little girl, you know?"

Priscilla couldn't imagine how it must feel. Though she wanted to. She not-so-secretly wished that Rachel would find a good man and settle down and have some children for Priscilla to spoil. But that was a wish for some other time.

"I was going through the basement the other day, and I found some old bags of Aggie's clothes. My first thought was that she might want them for her little girl, but then I realized they're probably out of style. I don't know. People dress their kids like little adults these days, don't they?"

"Yes, they often do." She'd been surprised to see little boys in fedoras and vests and little girls in skinny jeans and Lilly Pulitzer dresses all over the island this summer. She couldn't imagine spending that much money on clothes kids would grow out of so quickly.

"But I was thinking, maybe it would be nice if I took her old clothes and made them into a quilt. Like, for the baby." His cheeks had turned the slightest bit pink. It was pretty endearing.

"Oh, Gerald. That's a lovely idea. That would be such a meaningful gift. I'm sure she'd love that."

"I hope so. I don't know. Her mom has always been better at knowing what to get her. But I thought she might like this."

Priscilla knew that Gerald and his wife—Aggie's mom—had been divorced for many years and that his ex lived in Virginia. She didn't know much else about that situation and had never had occasion to ask.

"I think she'll love it. And I'd be happy to help you make it."

"Thank you. I really appreciate it."

"Of course. I'm flattered you asked. Why don't I come by tomorrow and take a look at what you have, and we can go from there?"

"That would be great."

This would be fun. She loved a good project. In her mind, she started thinking through quilt patterns and decorative stitches and imagining the different fabrics they might be able to incorporate. For a moment, she even forgot about the missing man and the missing dog.

Just for a moment. Then, once she'd remembered them, she couldn't get them out of her head.

CHAPTER FOUR

After lunch Priscilla went home and tried to focus on making dinner. Her cousin Joan—one of three cousins who lived on Martha's Vineyard and with whom Priscilla had been reunited when she'd moved here—was coming over for dinner, and she was making lentil soup and trying a new recipe for stuffed acorn squash. She wanted to get the bulk of the prep work out of the way before her guest arrived. But as she stood in the kitchen chopping walnuts for the stuffing, her mind kept drifting back to what she had seen on that houseboat. What had happened there? Where was the man who had lived there? Was he—she couldn't even bring herself to think it. He was out there somewhere. He had to be. And someone out there had to know where.

Finally, she decided it couldn't hurt to take a little break from her cooking. A pot of wild rice was bubbling on the stove, and she turned the flame down then went into the garage and dug through her recycling bin. She hadn't taken her stack of newspapers to the center in a few weeks, and she sifted through glossy ads, unread sports pages, and weeks-old local news before she finally found what she was looking for. There. Last Wednesday's edition of the *Vineyard Gazette* had a picture of the houseboat on the bottom of the front page. "Selectmen's Meeting Turns Contentious over Houseboat in Harbor," the headline read. She'd skimmed this article but hadn't really paid much attention, and she sat down at the kitchen table and read it properly now. Jake sat down at her feet and rested his chin on her lap. She patted his head as she read.

Tuesday's meeting of the Tisbury Board of Selectmen turned unexpectedly ugly when a motion was introduced to bar houseboats from the marina. The meeting, which was open to the public, was held at the Town Hall and was sparsely attended, but the motion attracted a lot of attention and generated much discussion.

The motion was introduced by Frank Ripley, longtime member of the Board of Selectmen, who insisted that the harbor could not be allowed to "become like that mess over in Woods Hole." Pressed further, he admitted he thought houseboats were "ugly" and ruined the idyllic view of the harbor.

The motion was met with resistance from other members of the public, who see houseboats as a possible way to ease the island's affordable housing crisis. Tracy Buschman, a leader of the homeless shelter run by Faith Fellowship in Tisbury, said, "We need to consider all options for helping people get back on their feet." Another member of the public, Sheila Weller, insisted that, "rich old men can't make rules that put their own property values above the good of the community." The meeting devolved into a shouting match until Ginger Stewart, Chairman of the Board of Selectmen, was able to restore order.

There is currently one houseboat docked in the harbor. Neither the owner nor a representative from Lloyd and Fisher, the private company that owns the mooring, was present at the meeting.

Well, that was interesting, Priscilla thought. She had met Frank Ripley briefly at a Labor Day party thrown by her cousin Gail, and he seemed like a genial enough guy. But it sounded like he wanted the houseboat gone. Still, he was probably a decade older than she was. She had a hard time imagining him doing the kind of damage she'd seen in the houseboat just to get rid of the guy.

Who was "the guy"? That's what she kept coming back to. No one seemed to know who he was. How was that possible? *Someone* had to know or have a record of who the man in the boat was. He'd been living in the harbor for almost two weeks. Surely someone had learned something about him—even just his name—in that time.

She reread the article. The company that owned the mooring was called Lloyd and Fisher. Surely they had a record of the guy's name. Gerald had said they would be talking to them and that between the police and the Coast Guard, they would solve this. Well, she was sure they would. But that didn't mean she couldn't do her best to make sense of what she'd seen too, did it? It wouldn't hurt just to ask a couple of questions.

Priscilla pushed herself out of the chair. She wouldn't be able to stop thinking about this until she at least tried. And she had several hours before Joan would be coming over. She could run down to the marina and just see what she could find out.

Jake looked up at her hopefully.

"Sorry, boy. We'll go for a walk a little later." He turned away and wandered into the living room, settling down next to the couch. She turned off the stove, grabbed her jacket, and headed out.

The short drive down Water Street to the harbor, past the shops and stalls that made this such a vibrant community, went much faster than it would have just a few weeks ago. She had been told the tourists would trickle off in the next few weeks, but they mostly appeared on the weekends now, and on this Friday in late September, she didn't have to worry about crowds on the sidewalks or circling the blocks to find a parking spot. She pulled into one of the spots in the lot that ran along the waterfront then stepped out and turned to study the marina.

The marina was basically a big U shape, with most of the buildings—shops, restaurants, and offices—near the bend. Along this side of the harbor was a small park, and across the way were the bigger buildings and large docks that serviced the ferries that ran back and forth to the mainland. Long rows of docks stuck out into the water. Boat slips, she thought those were called. A few boats were still tied up at their slips, but most were already gone for the winter.

She looked out over the water beyond the docks and saw a few boats tied up at those bobbing ball things. Those must be the moorings. She'd never known what they were called. From here it just looked like a big batch of them with no discernible pattern.

How did people on the boats know where to go when they wanted to park? Or moor, she meant.

The newspaper had said the houseboat was moored with a private company called Lloyd and Fisher. She pulled up the map feature on her phone, and a moment later she saw exactly where the office for Lloyd and Fisher was. It was just a few storefronts down Union Street, right off Water. It only took a few moments for her to stride past the cafés, boutiques, and designer handbag stores that lined this section of town. She found the office in a narrow building with a large plate-glass window on the first floor. The second and third floors were given over to apartments—vacation rentals, no doubt. She stepped inside the small office and found cherry floors and stark white walls hung with one large mirror in an ornate gilt frame. There was a table at the back of the small space, where a man sat staring at the screen of a sleek silver computer.

"Hello?" Priscilla closed the door behind her and crossed the room in a few steps. The man looked up at her but, not recognizing her, looked back down. Well. That was not how people behaved back in Kansas. Undaunted, Priscilla pressed on. "I was hoping I could ask you a quick question."

He looked up again, his hand on his mouse. His eyes telegraphed boredom. He wore fitted pants and a vest over a long-sleeved shirt and had a bow tie around his neck.

"I was hoping I could find out the name of someone who had a boat moored with your company."

"I'm sorry, but I can't tell you that. Here at Lloyd and Fisher, we pride ourselves on discretion."

Well, they certainly didn't pride themselves on customer service. "Yes, but this one is something of a special case, so I was hoping you might be able to help me. I'm trying to find out the name of the gentleman who was living in the houseboat out in the marina. You may have heard that he's—"

"Are you with the police?" He had some kind of accent that she couldn't place.

"No, but I—"

"I'll tell you what I told the police officer who was here earlier and what I told the Coast Guard officer who was here before that. Here at Lloyd and Fisher, we value the privacy of our clients above all. We do not reveal information about our guests without a court order."

After listening to him a bit more, she was starting to wonder if the accent was real at all. She tried to keep calm and attempted another tactic.

"Maybe you don't understand." She put on her most charming homespun Midwestern accent. "A man is missing, and we're trying to find out who he is so we can locate him."

"I heard," was all the man said. "And I do wish I could help. But I'm afraid our regulations prevent me from releasing client information—to anyone—unless ordered to do so by the courts." He gave her a smile—a tight, forced smile—that she saw right through.

She could see charm wasn't getting her anywhere. Nevertheless, she persisted. "Do you have security cameras?"

His false smile didn't falter. "I'm afraid I'm really not at liberty to say," he said. "Unless you are in possession of a court order."

Priscilla took that as a yes. But it didn't mean she would be getting to take a look at the footage anytime soon.

"If there is anything you could—"

"I'm afraid I can't."

Priscilla could see she wasn't going to get anywhere here. She thanked him and then turned and walked out. Well. That had been less than useful. She should head back home and get going on dinner. But first she walked out to the waterfront and gazed over the harbor.

Water lapped against the hulls of the few boats still docked there, and the soft sound of waves pressing against the wooden pier was soothing. It was calm and peaceful here. She looked out toward where the houseboat had been tied up. Moored. What would it be like to live like that, out there on the water? Why would someone choose to live there?

Who are you? Priscilla asked. *What happened to you?*

She turned and headed back, but before she climbed into her car, she made a quick stop at Candy Lane Confectionery.

"Well, hello there," Candy said. She smiled at Priscilla over the display case. "I haven't seen you in a few days. I was starting to get worried."

"I was trying to stay away, but who am I kidding?" She gazed down at the goodies displayed behind the glass. There were flaky croissants piled up next to buttery scones and muffins topped with a crumb topping to die for. There were piles of gorgeously frosted cookies and rich pastries glistening with glaze.

"What can I get for you?" Candy asked.

"Oh, I'll take some cookies, and a cream puff for Joan." She knew cream puffs were her cousin's favorite.

"Coming right up." Candy used wax paper to pick her treats from the case and slipped them in a small box.

After she'd paid, Priscilla climbed back into her car and headed home. She set the treats in the refrigerator and turned the heat back up under the soup. This mystery was puzzling, but for now she had other things to focus on.

That evening after they'd enjoyed the lentil soup and stuffed squash and devoured the desserts, Joan helped Priscilla clean up the kitchen. Priscilla had been thrilled to meet all three of her cousins—Joan, Trudy, and Gail—when she'd arrived on Martha's Vineyard, but she'd quickly felt a special connection with Joan. She loved Trudy's effervescent, optimistic personality and Gail's nurturing, caring nature. But Joan had a sense of calm, quiet strength that Priscilla found appealing. And the fact that Joan was also single and lived alone meant they had another thing in common and often spent the evenings together here or at Joan's sweet cottage. Tonight they'd enjoyed a leisurely meal, and Joan had chatted about the budding relationship between their uncle Hugh and Marigold Townsend, and she'd told a funny story about Trudy breaking into song at the bank the week before.

"Oh, goodness, I can't believe I didn't think to bring this up before," Joan said. She was helping clean up the kitchen while

Priscilla loaded the dishes into the dishwasher. "You'll never guess the crazy story I heard when I was at the grocery store today."

"What's that?" But Priscilla had a feeling she knew.

"You know that guy who was living on that houseboat in the marina?" Joan used a spoon to scrape the leftover soup into a glass storage container.

"Yes. Is this about how the houseboat turned up floating in the harbor this morning, with no sign of the guy?"

"You knew?" Joan snapped the lid on.

"Yes. Funny story, actually." She told Joan about her day's adventures. Joan's eyes looked like they were about to bug out of her head.

"Wait, what?" Joan set down the soup. "You were actually *on* the houseboat?"

"Yes."

"And you didn't think to mention this until now?"

"We were discussing other things."

"What was it like?" Joan put the pot next to the sink, and Priscilla rinsed it then set it into the warm water.

"It was... Well, it was trashed."

"Oh my goodness. Tell me everything you know. Everyone in town is talking about this."

Priscilla dunked the pot and started to scrub. She told Joan about how the houseboat had been upended, like someone was searching for something. She told her about the fact that whoever the guy was, he'd been painting, and about how they'd found the key.

"I can't believe you were there." Joan sprayed the counter with cleaner and shook her head. "Does this mean you're going to try to solve this mystery too?" She gave Priscilla a knowing look.

"I might see what I can find out," she said. "The first question, of course, is who was he?"

"*Hmm.*" Joan used a rag to wipe down the counter and thought for a moment. "Someone has to know that."

"I'm sure someone does," Priscilla said. "But it seems no one in town even got a good look at him, let alone knew his name."

Joan set down the rag and leaned back against the counter. "You know, I saw him in town one time, right after that houseboat showed up."

"You did?"

"Yep. At Ortmann's." The locally owned grocery store.

"Really." Priscilla rinsed the pot and set it on the drying rack. "How do you know it was him?"

"I saw him in the launch as I was heading into the market. You know, the one that brings people to shore?"

Priscilla nodded as if everyone naturally knew what a launch was.

"There aren't very many boats in the harbor right now, so when I saw it out there, I noticed it. That blond kid the girls fawn over all summer was driving it. You know, the real creepy one who smiles at everyone?"

Priscilla laughed. "He's creepy because he smiles too much?"

"No, the smiling is separate from the creepiness. His eyes dart around too much, like he's always looking around to see if there's anyone better nearby. Anyway, maybe it's just me. I've never actually talked to the guy."

Priscilla didn't even know what to say to this. Joan sometimes had the strangest ways of characterizing people. She just laughed.

"So you saw the mystery man in the launch with the creepy guy." The dishwasher was partly open, and she opened it the rest of the way. "And then you saw him in the store?"

"Yep. I ran into him in the cereal aisle. He was wearing the same tan coat I'd seen in the launch, so I knew it was him."

"What kind of cereal was he buying?" Priscilla took the dishwasher soap out of the cabinet beneath the sink and squirted some into the compartment in the dishwasher door.

"Raisin Bran." Joan stuck out her tongue. She had a well-known disdain for raisins. "So you know there's something wrong with him."

"Maybe he's a *cereal* killer."

Joan laughed. "I set you up for that one." She froze. "Wait. Do you think he really is?"

"I don't know. I hope not. No. There's no way."

"No one has turned up dead, I guess."

"Making it less likely he's a serial killer." Priscilla pushed the dishwasher closed. A soft hum filled the air as the machine started. "But it doesn't change the fact that I need to figure out who he is."

"Do you think knowing what kind of cereal he likes will help you track him down?"

Priscilla laughed again. "Unlikely. But you never know." She dried her hands on the dishrag. "But you know what might help? Knowing what he looked like. Any chance you noticed that?"

Joan thought for a moment. "He had brownish-blondish hair. It was hard to say. Maybe light brown but with some gray?"

"How old was he?"

"I didn't study him all that long. I didn't want to get a reputation for being creepy too. But if I had to guess, I'd say midfifties."

That could describe a good chunk of the men on this island.

"He was tall, I think. I don't know. Honestly, the main thing that comes to mind when I think of him is the word *sad*."

"Sad?" Priscilla hadn't expected that.

"Or troubled somehow. I don't know. It was just a sense. But that's what I felt."

"Sad how?"

"I don't know. I didn't analyze it. I didn't realize it was going to matter. I just grabbed my Lucky Charms and went."

"Please tell me you didn't buy Lucky Charms."

Joan sighed. "Sadly, I didn't. I fear my Lucky Charms days are far behind me. I just wanted you to think I was more fun than I really am. I bought Wheat Chex."

"That sounds more likely." Priscilla straightened the dish towel on the handle of the dishwasher. "And you're plenty of fun just the way you are."

"Thanks."

After she and Joan finished straightening up, they went out onto the patio and had a cup of chamomile tea in the Adirondack chairs. They watched as the last light of the day disappeared from the sky and the stars started to appear. The light from the lighthouse spun far above. The conversation moved on to other topics, but after Joan headed home, and after Priscilla finished getting ready for bed and crawled under the covers—even then, she couldn't stop thinking about the missing man.

Jake hopped on the bed and curled up next to her, defying her once again, and she couldn't help but think about the dog she'd heard the previous night. Gerald had said the wind had been playing tricks on her. But Priscilla wasn't so sure.

In the morning, she would find out more.

CHAPTER FIVE

The next morning after a cup of strong coffee and some quiet time with the Lord, Priscilla read through the morning's headlines. She knew not many people still got a physical newspaper these days, but she found the habit of reading the paper kept her informed and grounded in the world. The missing man and the houseboat were front-page news, and she read the article carefully, looking for clues she'd missed the day before, but there was nothing new. Either nothing new had turned up in the investigation or they weren't sharing it with the press.

After she'd cleaned up her breakfast, she fed Jake and climbed into her car for the short trip to town. It was a perfect fall day, with a clear, cerulean sky, a few high puffy white clouds, and a nip in the air. Sweater weather. Her favorite time of year.

Back home in Kansas, it would almost be harvest time, she reflected as she drove toward town. When all the year's labor came to fruition. The earth gave up its fruit, and the combine ran nearly all day and into the night. More than once Priscilla had brought dinner and a thermos of coffee out to the fields as the sun set so Gary and the seasonal workers could keep going just a little while longer. It was always a race to get the corn in before the first frost.

It was strange to be so far removed from that this year. Gary was gone, and the farm was in the process of being sold. She felt a pang of sorrow at all that had changed, all that she'd lost.

Then again, she'd gained so much, she thought as she rounded the last bend and the little town of Tisbury lay spread out before her. The charming old fishing village, the harbor, the lighthouse high up on the cliff behind her—it was stunning. All those years on the farm, she'd never imagined she'd end up living next to a lighthouse on Martha's Vineyard, and she couldn't have found any place she loved more. God knew what He had been doing bringing her here. This place was a balm to her soul.

She parked in the small lot in front of the white clapboard police building. Even the police stations were charming around here, she thought as she stepped inside. She walked into a small lobby with wooden floors and soft beige walls and moved toward the desk. A woman with heavy-framed glasses looked up from her computer screen as Priscilla approached. A brass name plate on her desk said *Gabrielle Grimes*.

"Hello, I'm Priscilla Grant," she said. Gabrielle nodded, waiting for her to go on. She was probably in her late thirties, Priscilla guessed, and wore a no-nonsense button-down. "I'd like to speak with Officer Brown or Officer Holmes, please."

"What is this regarding?"

"It's about the houseboat they were investigating yesterday," Priscilla said. "I saw them at the scene," she added, hoping that might help this woman take her seriously.

"Why don't you have a seat? I'll see if they're available," Gabrielle said.

Priscilla thanked her and took a seat in one of the padded chairs that ran along the wall by the door. She pulled her book out of her purse—she never traveled without one—and started to read. She loved to read novels, especially mystery novels, but she'd always had a special place in her heart for biographies. She'd checked this biography of Dorothy Sayers out of the library last week and was enjoying it thoroughly. Priscilla had read many of her Lord Peter Wimsey mysteries but had never realized she'd been a contemporary of C. S. Lewis and J. R. R. Tolkien and had been part of the infamous Inklings.

"Ms. Grant?"

Priscilla looked up. She'd been so absorbed in the cobbled streets of Oxford that she'd forgotten where she really was. Officer Brown was standing in front of her.

"Why don't you come on back?"

Priscilla tucked her book back into her purse and followed the police officer past the front desk, through a set of doors, and down a short hallway to a small room. There was a table in the middle of the room, and Priscilla sat on one side while Officer Brown sat down on the other.

"Can I get you any coffee? Tea? Water?" She had already placed a paper cup of coffee and a yellow legal pad at her place.

"No thank you, Officer Brown. I'm fine."

"So." She uncapped the pen lying on the pad. She was thin, and her uniform hung a little loose on her. "Gabrielle said you wanted to talk to me about the boat you saw yesterday?"

"Yes. I was talking to Gerald afterward—"

"It was pretty unusual for Captain O'Bannon to allow you onto the crime scene. Was there a reason for that?"

"Oh." Priscilla hadn't expected she would be questioned here. Wasn't she the one who had come in to volunteer her help? "I meant no harm. I was simply supposed to meet Gerald for lunch, and since he was running late, I met him there. I didn't realize it was a crime scene at the time, and he probably just wasn't thinking straight. I doubt the Coast Guard has dealt with many situations like this one."

Officer Brown looked dubious, but she nodded and indicated Priscilla should go on.

"I promise, I didn't touch a thing." The officer nodded again, so Priscilla decided to get to the point. "I wanted to tell you that I was woken up late Thursday night, around three, and I heard a dog barking."

Now Officer Brown just looked confused. Priscilla rushed to explain.

"I live out on Bailey Point. By the lighthouse? I live in the old keeper's cottage."

Officer Brown's face relaxed a bit at this, but she still waited to see what Priscilla would say.

"I was lying awake in bed, and I heard a dog out on the water. I thought it was strange at the time, which is why it stands out. But now I'm wondering if it might have been the dog that vanished with the man on the boat."

"Did you actually see the dog?" She took a swig of her coffee.

"No." Priscilla knew it lowered the credibility of her evidence, but it was the truth. "I wish now I'd gotten out of bed to look out the window, but I haven't turned on my heat yet, and my bed was so cozy..."

Officer Brown made a note on the legal pad. "This would make the position of the dog to the west of Tisbury." She drew a rough sketch of the island, with Bailey Point at the top and Woods Hole, labeled *CC* for Cape Cod, above it. Down to the right were the towns of Oak Bluffs and Edgartown, and to the left was the bulk of the island, West Tisbury, Chilmark, and Aquinnah, and the Sound. At the far side was land, which she labeled *RI*, for Rhode Island.

"Yes, that's right."

"That would mean the dog was in a boat headed west through the Vineyard Sound," Officer Brown said, tracing her pen left along the north shore of the island.

"I couldn't really say which way the boat was going. But that's the direction I heard the sound coming from."

She made another note on the paper. "That's interesting."

"Interesting?" The way she said it, it sounded like she meant *useless*.

"The evidence we have so far indicates that the man on the boat was most likely taken back to Woods Hole," Officer Brown said.

"What evidence is that?"

The woman gave her a smile. "I'm afraid I'm not at liberty to say."

Priscilla nodded. Maybe they had found his cell phone records, or perhaps a camera on the mainland had picked something up. In any case, she could see she wasn't going to get the police officer to tell her more about that. "Of course. But I assume this means they didn't find anything in the harbor?"

Officer Brown's smile faltered. "I guess Gerald must have told you about dredging the harbor too."

Priscilla nodded.

"We found something in the harbor, but it was not a body, thank goodness."

"That's great news," Priscilla said and then paused. She decided to press her luck. "Any chance you'll tell me what you found?"

Officer Brown laughed a little. "I admire your tenacity. But no, I'm afraid I'm not at liberty to say."

A man stuck his head into the office. "Brown. Anything on that key?"

"Not yet, Chief. We're still looking."

Priscilla hadn't met the police chief before, but she guessed this must be him. He was tall and had thick brown hair and a strong local accent.

"Good." And with that, he disappeared.

Priscilla tried to figure out how to get more information from Officer Brown. She wore a gold wedding band and a ring wrapped with tiny diamonds next to it. Her nails were painted a very light pink, so subtle you wouldn't see it if you weren't looking. Beneath the hard exterior, there was softness.

"What about the laptop? Any luck getting into that?"

"It's password protected. Our team is running software to try to crack the passcode."

"It's probably his birthday. Isn't everyone's password their birthday?"

Officer Brown laughed. "If we knew his birthday, we'd probably try that. So far we haven't been able to turn that up."

Interesting. She hadn't said that they couldn't find his birthday because they didn't know who he was. Had they figured out his name, just not his birth date?

"Any luck finding out who he was?"

Officer Brown hesitated and then said, "I can't share that with you."

She hadn't said no. She had a name. She had to have a name.

Priscilla nodded and then sat back in her chair, thinking. Officer Brown picked up the coffee and took a sip. A moment later, Priscilla spoke. "You're married, Officer Brown?"

"Yes, ma'am. Nineteen years."

"That's wonderful. What does your husband do?"

"He runs a business installing and maintaining pools."

"No doubt a big job around here."

"For parts of the year, sure." She held the coffee cup a moment more then set it down.

"Any kids?"

"Two boys. Teenagers. Lord help me." She laughed softly. She was loosening up. Relaxing. Just what Priscilla hoped for.

"I've been there. I had a girl, which is different, but these are tough years no matter what. But so magical. It's amazing to see them become who they were meant to be."

The officer nodded but didn't answer.

"I was married to my husband for nearly forty years. He passed away earlier this year. I lived on a farm in Kansas for most of my life. This island is all new to me. It's wonderful but so very different."

"You're a Latham though, right? Didn't you inherit Marjorie's lighthouse?"

"That's right."

"So this island is in your blood, whether you lived here or not."

"I suppose that's true. In some ways it feels like where I was always meant to be."

They were both quiet again. For a moment, the only noise was the hum of the fluorescent overhead lights.

Then Priscilla spoke again. "Look, I know I technically have no business asking this stuff. I'm not police, and I'm not Coast Guard. But I can't help feeling like maybe if I'd done something differently Thursday night, things might be different."

Officer Brown nodded but didn't say anything.

"I'm personally invested, I guess you might say."

"I'm glad to hear it, Ms. Grant. And if you have any more leads, please don't hesitate to bring them to us."

"I won't." The officer knew something more. How did Priscilla get her to spill it? She only had one idea. It seemed nuts, but lacking any other sane ideas, it was all she had. "You know, several years ago, I joined a website called Ancestry.com. Have you heard of it?"

"Yeah. It's one of those sites where you can trace your family history, right?"

"Exactly. You can build your family tree and all that. I was working on finding out more about my father's side of the family. He was turning seventy, and I wanted to give him a gift that would be meaningful. So I spent a lot of time and put together a whole family tree going back six generations, all the way back to Scotland and Germany. One really interesting thing about the site is that there are so many people registered that when you search for a name, there's a good chance you'll turn up a lot of information about a person. Not just who their family is, but birthday, where they were born, etc. It's really helpful. I mean, it's all based on public records, but a lot of times you don't know where to find that sort of thing, and this makes it easy. So if you're looking for his birth date, you might want to try searching there."

"We have official means of gathering such information," Officer Brown said. But still, even as she spoke, she wrote something down on her pad. Priscilla leaned forward and squinted. She could barely make it out, but she thought it said, *Search Ancestry. com for Bart Flask.*

"I'm sure you do," Priscilla said. She couldn't help the smile that was spreading across her face. "But it never hurts to ask."

CHAPTER SIX

Bart Flask. That had to be his name. Priscilla ran the name through her mind as she drove home, Officer Brown's card tucked into her purse. The name wasn't familiar to her, but it couldn't be all that hard to find out more about him now that she knew who he was.

As soon as she got home, Priscilla settled in on the couch with her laptop and pulled up a search window. Jake settled down beside her, and she patted him then turned to her search.

The first thing she did was run a basic Internet search for the name Bart Flask. The first result was a white pages listing for 240 people, but when she clicked on it, none of them were actually named Bart Flask, but some close variation. She moved on to the next link. There was a social media page for a Bart Flask in Australia, and a LinkedIn page for a banker in Dallas. Some high school kid in San Jose. An ad for a silver hip flask. None of them seemed right. Joan had said he was probably in his fifties. Even with those broad parameters, nothing she turned up looked right.

Bart. Maybe short for Bartholomew? She tried again, searching for that name, and got a few more results, but none turned up much of anything. No newspaper articles, no records, nothing.

The only thing that seemed even remotely plausible was a man named Bartholomew who had been born in the 1960s, but judging by the last name Yoder and the city of birth listed as Lancaster, Pennsylvania, she was pretty certain he was Amish. He didn't seem like the right man.

She tried the search again, adding the qualifier *artist*. Were the paintings he'd been making a clue in all this? Priscilla wished she'd taken a picture of them while she was on the houseboat. She tried to picture them now, but they mostly just looked like a bunch of spilled paint to her. If there was some secret message hidden in the paintings, she was missing it. She looked down at the screen now and saw that adding *artist* to the search had only returned fewer results.

Well. Priscilla hadn't been lying when she'd said ancestry websites could be great sources of information. She went to one that she'd used before, which seemed to have way more information about people than seemed necessary. She typed in his name, hit Return, and held her breath.

Three results popped up. The three she'd already found. The teenager was out, she knew that. The guy in Australia seemed unlikely. The banker from Dallas was really the only plausible option. She clicked on him, and his recent known addresses were listed at the bottom of the page. She copied the most recent one, and it only took a moment with a reverse phone number look-up site to find a number for him.

"Here goes nothing, Jake," she said, reaching for her cell phone, which was on the coffee table in front of her. Jake lifted his head and then, perhaps realizing there was no food on offer, settled back down with a sigh.

She dialed the number listed on the screen and listened as it rang. It rang once, twice, three times. Then she was connected to his voice mail. The man had a deep voice rounded out with a soft Texas accent. After the beep, she left a somewhat rambling voice mail introducing herself and asking him to please call her. She hung up feeling dubious. If someone left her a message like that, she was pretty sure she wouldn't call back. Oh well. She'd just have to wait and see.

She turned back to her search screen, and her fingers hovered over the keyboard. If only she knew anything about him—a place of birth, a birth date, anything. If the guy in Dallas wasn't her guy, she wasn't sure what she'd do.

She'd set aside the question of his identity for now. One question that had been nagging at her was how that boat had gotten into the harbor in the first place. Gerald had said it didn't have a motor; it needed to be towed from place to place. Someone had obviously towed it to its mooring. Someone had to know where it had come from.

Priscilla didn't know where to look, so she started, once again, with a basic Web search for "where to get houseboat Martha's Vineyard."

A few articles about the Woods Hole houseboat community came up, and a website for selling and renting houseboats around the country. She clicked on that, searched by state, and realized these were all the motorized double-decker kind she was used to seeing back home. Had Bart Flask owned the houseboat? Or was he just renting it? Maybe he'd had it for a long time? But it had looked brand new to her.

On a hunch, Priscilla searched for "houseboat builder." The first link that popped up was the site for a craftsman who built, the site claimed, "unique, sophisticated floating homes." The site was sleek, with lots of close-ups of interesting textures and shots of vibrant sunsets. The pictures on the main homepage looked a lot like the boat that had been floating in the harbor. Lots of glass and wood shingles and clean lines.

She clicked on the page about the builder. He was named Ethan McCall, and he'd started out as a contractor building homes on land but had become interested in the tiny-house movement that seemed to be all the rage these days on HGTV. He'd recently transitioned to building "small, sustainable, well-crafted homes on water." There was a picture of the builder. He wore a flannel shirt and had a beard, much as she'd suspected.

She clicked over to the page that listed the boats he had for sale. There were four listed, at prices that seemed lower than what Priscilla would have expected. Around the same price as a mid-range car. That wasn't cheap, of course, but it was cheap for a house. She remembered what the newspaper article had said about these boats being an option for affordable housing. It was possible, she thought.

She clicked on the first houseboat for sale and saw that it was about the same size as the one she'd seen yesterday but configured differently. Still, it had the same finishes in the tiny kitchen and the same retractable table. This had to be the guy who'd built the one in the harbor.

She clicked back to the page of boats for sale. The one she'd seen wasn't listed. But then, why would it be? It wasn't for sale. Still, this had to be where Bart had bought it. Priscilla clicked over to the contact page and saw that Ethan McCall worked out of New Bedford, Massachusetts. A thrill of excitement went through her. This was him!

She retrieved her phone and dialed the contact number listed on the page.

"Hello?"

"Hi. My name is Priscilla Grant, and I'm hoping to find out about one of your boats that I believe was recently sold."

"Oh yeah? Which one?"

Which one? How was she supposed to describe it? "It was one big room with sliding glass doors and a folding table."

He laughed. "Well, ma'am, that could be just about any of them. How recently was it sold?" He had a slow, lazy manner of speaking, but he wasn't unkind.

"I can't say for sure, but I would guess a few weeks ago. It ended up in Martha's Vineyard."

"Ah. Yep. I know the one."

"You do?" Her heart soared. "Can you tell me anything about the guy who bought it?"

"Not really, I'm afraid. I don't know much about him."

"Did you meet him at all?"

"Oh yeah. I towed the boat to the harbor for him. Nice harbor. Real pretty."

"You towed it there? How does that work?"

She could imagine him shrugging as he answered. "I tie the houseboat up behind my boat and tow it. Like you'd tow a car but on water."

"That must be a big boat."

"It's got a powerful engine."

"Do you usually tow the houseboats into place for the new owners?"

"Unless they have a boat of their own that can do the job, sure."

"Do you have any idea how long he planned to stay there? Or what he would do with the houseboat when he needed it moved again?"

"I asked him about that, but he didn't seem real sure," Ethan said.

"What do you mean?"

"He didn't seem to quite know what his plan was. That was fine with me. I gave him my card and told him to call me if he needed anything."

"This man you met. Was his name Bart Flask?" Priscilla asked.

"Seems to me you don't need to ask me questions. You already know the answers."

"Did you ever meet him in person?"

"Briefly. He was waiting for me in Martha's Vineyard when I towed the boat there."

"What did he look like?"

"I don't know. Average middle-aged white dude, I guess. I didn't really study him. He gave me the cash, and I took it and left. He had a cool dog with him."

Priscilla heard this, but her mind was stuck on something he'd just said. "Did you say he paid cash for the boat?"

"That's right."

"Like, actual dollar bills?"

"Yep."

"But...," Priscilla sputtered. "I saw the prices on your website. He gave you all that money in cash?"

"Yep. I'll take it any way I can get it."

Priscilla tried to process this. That was a lot of money to carry around. Why would he pay cash? Was it so that he didn't leave a paper trail? And how did he get all that cash in the first place?

"Did he tell you what he did for a living? Or what he intended to do on the boat?"

"No, ma'am. He wasn't real chatty, and I don't tend to ask."

Priscilla tried to think. What else would he be able to tell her? "Is there anything that stood out to you about him? Anything that made him memorable?"

"Honestly, not really."

Priscilla could see she wasn't going to get any further here. She thanked him for his help and hung up. She rolled her neck, trying to loosen the muscles that had suddenly grown tight. At least she knew how the boat had gotten to the harbor now. Not that it got her any closer to finding out what had happened Thursday night. She closed her eyes and tried to imagine it.

Her mother had always said she had a great imagination. That was what came of growing up on an isolated farm, she supposed. She hadn't had many playmates, so she'd had to invent them. She'd whiled away hours on the front porch as a child, dreaming up friends and adventures. She tried to harness that imagination now and think about possible scenarios.

Maybe Bart was a bank robber, hiding out with his haul on the houseboat, and...the bank official had come for him? That didn't seem likely.

Okay then. He was a lonely artist, just looking for some peace, and a fan who couldn't wait for his next painting had tracked him down and broken in to get his hands on it, and something had gone wrong.

But no, the paintings were still in the boat. That didn't seem likely either.

"What happened to you, Bart Flask?" she whispered.

Maybe she was being too fanciful. Maybe he was just a guy who needed a place to stay, and this was the most affordable option. All along, she'd been assuming something bad had happened to him. Maybe he'd just grown tired of houseboat living and set the boat adrift. But no—what about the upturned furniture? If he had just walked away, he'd gone to a lot of trouble to make sure people thought there was foul play involved.

Was that it then? Had he faked his disappearance? Maybe he was trying to outrun a checkered past and this was the only way to escape?

Priscilla sighed. The trouble was, there was no way to know. Each scenario she came up with was as plausible—or implausible—as the next. She could sit here and daydream all day. But what did she really know? Not much of anything.

She thought for a minute then got up and found the newspaper article she'd read yesterday. The one that detailed the fight over the houseboat being moored in the harbor.

The only thing she really knew for sure, she realized, was that at least one person really wanted the houseboat gone. Maybe it made sense to pay Frank Ripley a visit.

CHAPTER SEVEN

It wasn't difficult to find out where Frank Ripley lived. Gail knew everyone in town, it seemed, and provided Priscilla with, if not an address exactly, at least a location. A few minutes later, she hopped in her car and did her best to follow Gail's instructions. She drove past the ice cream shop and turned left on Meetinghouse Road then drove past the cemetery "where there's the plaque for that old sea captain," turned right at the light just past the farm with the self-serve farm stand, and went till she got to the place where the road forked off to the right. Half a mile down that road, at the edge of the cranberry bog, she found the blue-and-white house Gail had promised would be there.

There was a car in the driveway. Priscilla took a deep breath, grabbed the box of cookies she'd picked up from Candy Lane's, and pushed herself out of the car. Maybe it was the Midwesterner in her, but she couldn't bring herself to show up empty-handed, even to a place she hadn't been invited. She walked up the crushed-shell path, past beautifully maintained rosebushes that still had some blossoms clinging to the stems, and up the front step. The house was a two-story farmhouse-style wooden affair, with brass lanterns flanking the entrance and a nautical knocker on the door. Who even used knockers these days? The house was on a large piece of land and set on a rise, so it had a great view of the cranberry bog behind it and the Sound beyond that. There was a separate garage and what looked like a fenced-in pool. She thought of Officer Brown's husband. Pool maintenance was certainly not a bad business to be in, not around these parts.

She rang the doorbell and waited. A moment later, the door was opened by a man with gray hair and a neatly trimmed beard. He wore khakis and a button-down shirt that strained over his belly.

"Hello?" He peered at her through thick-framed glasses.

"Hi. You must be Frank Ripley. I'm Priscilla Grant. I recently moved into the keeper's cottage over by Misty Harbor Lighthouse."

"Oh. Marjorie's niece then."

"Yes, that's right." She held out the box of cookies.

He nodded and opened the door a bit wider.

"I'm sorry to bother you, but I wondered if I could talk to you for a minute."

He didn't say anything for a moment, just looked her up and down, and then sighed and pulled the door open. "I guess you might as well come in."

Well. She had dropped in on him with no warning, she reminded herself as she stepped inside. The entryway was high, with a wooden staircase that curved up toward the second floor where big windows let in a lot of light. To the right was a formal dining room, and to the left a living room. The doorway ahead led to the kitchen, which had dark wood cabinets and granite counters. He led her into the living room, where two couches faced each other in front of a roaring gas fireplace.

"This is lovely," Priscilla said, holding out the box from Candy's bakery again. "Here, I thought I'd bring something sweet. It's my way of saying thanks for letting me barge in like this." She kept her voice breezy and light.

He didn't answer, but he set the box on a side table and gestured that she should sit on one of the couches. She could see a biography of the Wright brothers facedown on the other couch. She'd interrupted his reading.

"That's a good one," she said, pointing to the biography. "I read it last year."

"The writer is very good." He groaned as he lowered himself down. "So. How do you like living at a lighthouse? Marjorie loved it. Said up in that lighthouse she felt closer to God. But it always seemed kind of strange to me. A relic of another time."

"It is something of a relic," Priscilla said, "but then, I do love history. It's exciting to me to be right here in the middle of it."

"That's true. Where do you come from again?"

"Kansas." She realized she was sitting with her ankles crossed and her hands gathered neatly in her lap. Something about this man made her feel like she had to be on her best behavior. "So this is very different."

"I suppose it is." He adjusted one of the blue-and-gold pillows behind him. "How about your cousins? They don't mind that you got the house?"

"They don't seem to. They've been lovely. Getting to know them has been one of the best things about moving here."

He nodded again. He seemed to be waiting for her to say something. She realized he was no doubt wondering what she was doing here.

"Thank you for taking the time to talk with me, and I'm sorry to drop in unannounced like this. I understand you're on the Board of Selectmen in Tisbury."

"Yes. Have been for years."

"Oh good. I was hoping to ask you a few questions about something that happened at the most recent meeting."

"Yes?"

She tried to figure out how to phrase this. A fire danced over the ceramic logs in the fireplace. It was pretty, and no doubt convenient, but it lacked the smell and the feel of a real wood fire.

"I'm hoping to learn more about the houseboat that was in the marina. I understand there was some discussion about it."

"What about it?"

"I got the impression that you were quite adamantly opposed to the houseboat mooring in the marina." She hoped she'd used that word right. "And I wondered if you could tell me why."

"You read the article in the paper then?"

She nodded.

"Well, it wasn't unfair. I do think houseboats are ugly, and they don't belong here in Tisbury. And if you let one in, pretty soon it's a floating trailer park out there in the marina."

She tried not to let those words bother her. Priscilla had known many lovely people who kept well-tended homes in mobile home parks. He'd probably never even seen a trailer park in real life, she realized. There was nothing like that around here. Whatever stereotypes he had were baseless.

"Did you ever talk to the man on the boat about it?"

"Nope. Don't even know his name. Never even saw him up close, just glimpses of him and that dog on the boat now and then."

"But you felt sure he was going to turn the marina into a trailer park."

"I didn't say he personally was going to. Just that once you open the door, it's difficult to close it again. So it was better to get him out of here before anyone else got any ideas."

"Did he ever respond, in any way, to the news that you hoped to bar his boat from the harbor?"

"Not as far as I know."

Interesting. She wondered if Bart Flask had even heard. If he hadn't come ashore very often—and it sure seemed that he hadn't—then it was possible he didn't even realize the future of his boat had been debated. Why would anyone choose to live so close to a community, she wondered, yet stay intentionally apart from it?

She wanted to ask Frank why he felt so adamant about this and whether he believed his property value would be adversely affected, but she realized she probably knew the answers, and she needed to focus on what she'd come here to learn.

"I don't know if you heard, but the houseboat was found drifting in the harbor yesterday morning, and there's no sign of the man who'd been living there."

"I did hear that. It's in the newspaper." His voice was wary.

"I guess I just wanted to ask whether you knew anything about the man or where he might have gone."

He looked up at her from under the rim of his glasses. "What are you suggesting exactly?"

"Nothing," she said quickly. "I'm not suggesting anything. I'm just asking what you might know, since you seem to be very well-connected in this town." In her experience, making men feel like you really valued their expertise was a good way to get them on your side.

"What I know is this," he said. "I know that I had nothing to do with that boat disappearing, and I know nothing about the man. If you believe otherwise—"

"I don't believe anything," she insisted. "Just trying to learn. I'm new and just trying to figure this all out."

He stared at her for a minute. Was she crazy, or had he gotten unnecessarily upset over her questions? It sure seemed like his response was outsized. Had she hit a nerve? His lip was twitching, and the way his forehead furrowed, she could see that this was not going to get any better.

"I sure do appreciate your talking with me," she said, standing. That had not gone as well as she'd hoped. She turned and started for the door. He groaned as he pushed himself up to follow her. "Thank you for your time. And you sure do have a lovely place here."

He didn't say anything, just held the door open for her as she stepped out.

"Nice to meet you!" she called, forcing her voice to take on a brightness she didn't feel.

Well. That had gone badly. Why had he gotten so upset so quickly? Was it because she had pushed too hard, too soon? Or did he react so strongly because he had something to hide? She couldn't be sure. She just knew she hadn't made a friend in Frank Ripley today. Hopefully the cookies would help erase any bad taste she'd left in his mouth.

She puzzled over the encounter as she drove home. She wanted to find out more about Frank Ripley. Was his response today typical, or was there some reason he'd reacted as strongly as he had? She'd do some asking around, she decided. The interaction had only made her more suspicious that he knew something he wasn't saying.

CHAPTER EIGHT

Back at her house, Priscilla ate lunch and took Jake for a walk along the beach, laughing at the way he chased seagulls but ran from the waves. The sun shone brightly, reflecting off the water in a thousand tiny sparkles, and the sand was soft and warm despite the briny breeze. It was a glorious fall day, and she spent some time praying, thanking God for this new start and this new life. Then when Jake was worn out, they returned to the cottage, and she made herself a mug of tea while Jake lay down in his bed.

She headed into the small dugout basement—which she'd discovered shortly after she'd arrived actually contained a tunnel that ran out to the beach—and dug through the boxes she still hadn't unpacked yet. She found her sewing machine buried in one at the back, and she pulled it out and set it up in the spare bedroom. Plugging it in and threading the machine was like talking to an old friend she hadn't seen in many years. She spent some time setting up her spools of thread and organizing the boxes of trimmings and accessories, dreaming about what she might make after Gerald's quilt.

Then after a dinner of leftover stuffed squash, she headed to Gerald's house. He lived just outside of Tisbury in a neighborhood of older homes near the beach. She had been to his house a few times before, so she easily found the two-story home covered with weathered shingles and hung with blue shutters. She stepped out and walked up to the door, balancing another box from Candy's on her hip. Nothing wrong with keeping a local business going, she thought. Besides, she hadn't even gotten to try any of the cookies she'd taken to Frank Ripley.

"Hello, Priscilla," Gerald said, pulling the door open. "Come in."

She followed him in through the wood-floored entryway and into the living room. The room was painted a soft beige, and he had a long blue couch and several nice side tables. On the wall were pictures of old sailing ships, and he had a model ship on a table behind the couch. There were plastic bins set on the coffee table, and Priscilla could see that they were filled with pink and purple clothing.

"So this is it." Gerald pointed to the bins. "I haven't gone through any of this in years, so I don't know what we're going to find. But hopefully there'll be something we can use."

"I'm sure there will be." She handed him the box of pastries, and he set it on a side table and returned a moment later with small plates and napkins. She sat down on the couch and gently tugged the lid off one of the bins. "It's so nice that you kept all of these."

"Yeah. Well, I guess technically it was Cathy who kept them. She was good about things like that. Keeping everything neat and organized."

Priscilla knew that Cathy was the name of Gerald's ex-wife. She didn't know much about her, but knew that she lived in Virginia now. "Well, it's nice that she did that."

"Yes. I'm grateful now." He took the lid off another bin and set it aside. He pulled out a red-and-white striped cotton dress and smiled.

"That's really cute," Priscilla said.

"Aggie hated this dress." He laughed. "Hated most dresses, truthfully. We'd force her into one every Sunday, but for the most part, she was happy to roam around in shorts and T-shirts. She was such a tomboy. She wanted to do everything Ian did."

Priscilla knew that was the name of Gerald's son, though she didn't know much about him. She thought he lived somewhere far away—California maybe?

"Girls often do want to be like their big brothers." Priscilla smiled. "What's she like now?"

"Oh, she's wonderful. Smart, talented, kind." His face shone with pride, and it warmed her heart. "She's a lawyer. Or was, until Max was born. Now she stays home with him. She married Nick, a teacher. He's so good to her."

"She sounds wonderful." She pulled out a set of pink shorts and a T-shirt with an ice cream cone on it. It was really cute. In her head, Priscilla was creating piles. She'd sort the clothes by color and then by fabric and see what kind of quilt design would work best for the materials they had.

"She is. She's really something special." Gerald adored his daughter, that much was clear. He pulled out a smocked pink dress, which Aggie must have worn when she was no more than three. He held it up and bit his bottom lip.

"That's a beautiful dress," Priscilla said.

"Easter," he said simply.

She nodded. Her own daughter Rachel had had a dress very similar when she was young.

"Are you sure Aggie wouldn't want these clothes for her little girl?" Priscilla asked. She set the shorts and T-shirt aside and pulled out half a dozen tank tops in varying colors. They were in good shape. They could certainly still be used.

"No. I asked if she wanted any of this, and she said she'd rather pick out her own clothes for her daughter," he said. "She's kind of particular. Did I mention that? I think I might have forgotten to mention that."

Priscilla laughed. Her daughter was like that too.

He looked at the Easter dress again. "But maybe I'll set a few things aside and ask again, just in case."

"I think that's a good idea." She smiled and held up a pink jumper. "This one is really cute."

"I think Cathy bought that for her," he said, smiling. "She was really into all this stuff."

"It's impressive how much she saved."

"Yeah. We have all of Ian's clothes tucked away too. I think she was hoping there would be more kids coming at some point, so she held on to a lot of things."

"Oh." Priscilla felt like she'd stepped in it. She knew this was a sensitive area for a lot of people. "I—I'm sorry."

"No. Don't be. It is what it is. Truth is, we probably could have had more kids. There was no physical reason we couldn't, at least not that we know of. It was more..." He trailed off. He set the

Easter dress aside and pulled out a tiny pink-and-white winter coat. "Those were difficult years."

Priscilla nodded. "Having young children is demanding in so many ways."

"We got married young. We didn't know what we were getting into. We were in love and thought our faith meant we were invincible. But I was working too much. I was trying to build a career here. I probably left her to handle most of the parenting on her own. I know she felt that way, anyway, and she probably wasn't wrong."

He set the coat aside. Priscilla continued to take clothes out of the bin, but Gerald looked like he wanted to say more, so she stayed quiet.

"Cathy never settled in to Martha's Vineyard. She grew up in a big family in Texas, and the isolation and the winters really got to her. Back then you didn't have the Internet to help you stay connected, and she had a rough time with that. And I'm sure having me off at the station most of the time didn't help."

"I'm sure you were doing the best you could," Priscilla said.

"I thought I was at the time. Now I'm not so sure. We fought a lot. She was always complaining that I didn't help enough, that I didn't do anything around the house. I saw it as nagging. Now I can see that she probably had a point. I thought that because I was the one bringing in the money, she should be responsible for most of what happened at home. That seems silly now."

It wasn't an uncommon attitude, she knew. The division of labor hadn't been so sharp out on the farm, but it was a regular enough mind-set.

"When did you separate?" she asked gently.

"Oh, twenty-some years ago. She went to a high school reunion and reconnected with some guy. At the time, all I could see was that she was cheating on me. I was too mad at her to be able to see my own part in it. It's probably not fair to say I drove her to it, but I certainly didn't make it easy for her."

Priscilla nodded. In the end, Cathy had made her own decisions. But relationships relied on having both people invested. "Aggie and Ian were young then."

"Yep. Ian was ten and Aggie was only eight, and suddenly their family was torn apart and they moved to Texas. Took a huge chunk of my heart with them." He reached into the bin and pulled out a soft purple nightgown. He bit his bottom lip again.

"Did they come back and visit?"

He didn't answer for a moment. He seemed to be fighting back tears. But then he set the nightgown aside and said, "Yes, of course. Technically we shared custody. But Texas and Martha's Vineyard are not exactly next door." He continued to look down at the nightgown. "I missed them like crazy. This place felt so empty without them."

Priscilla wasn't sure if he was talking about the kids or all of them. Possibly both.

"Anyway, I think Cathy kept all this stuff in case we needed it. But we never did. After she left, I couldn't face any of it, so it's all stayed down there for decades."

"And it's a good thing too," Priscilla said. "We have a lot to work with here, and Aggie is going to love the quilt."

"You think so?"

Priscilla nodded. "I don't see how she couldn't."

"I know it's too late to be there for Aggie, but I want to do better with my grandchildren."

"It's not too late for Aggie," Priscilla said gently. "Girls always need their dads, even when they get big and pretend they don't. And I'm sure she'll see how much love you're putting into this quilt." She touched his arm. "Thank you for sharing that."

He looked at her, and the fog he'd been in seemed to lift some. "Thanks for helping me. I fear I haven't done much sorting yet."

"We can take as much time as you'd like. And there's dessert whenever you're ready."

He looked down at the bins of clothes and then nodded. "Maybe we can take a dessert break and then get back to this."

"That sounds good to me."

They would really dive in and sort the clothes by color after they ate. A little sugar would help fuel their decision-making, she was sure. In the meantime, she was grateful to have been able to see a side of Gerald she'd never seen before. She was enjoying getting to know him. That was all she was willing to admit at this point, but she was excited to see where their friendship would lead.

CHAPTER NINE

The next day, Priscilla soaked in the hymns and the preaching at Faith Fellowship Church. The red brick church was simple but well-maintained, and Priscilla loved the historic wooden pews—each tagged with a brass nameplate that said who had donated the money for the pew a hundred years ago—and the simple white walls. This church had been built as a Congregational church before Kansas was even a state, and though that initial congregation had given the building up years ago, she loved the feeling of history, of being grounded in something bigger and older than herself she always felt here.

She sat next to her cousin Gail and her father Hugh, and she loved hearing how Hugh belted out the songs slightly off-key. What he lacked in skill he more than made up for in passion.

After church, she followed them to the Fellowship Hall, where she grabbed a cup of coffee. She looked around the room. She was starting to recognize a lot of the faces she saw here each week. She saw Pastor Katie Rona across the room, and Mildred Pearson was talking with Tilly Snyder.

"Well, hello there, Priscilla."

Priscilla turned to see Ida Lee Jones standing in front of her. She had a plate with a slice of pumpkin bread in one hand and a cup of coffee in the other. Ida Lee—or Ida, as she preferred to be called—was a waitress at the Marshland Diner, and Priscilla had met her soon after she'd arrived on Martha's Vineyard.

"Hi there. How is everything?"

"Oh, just fine," Ida said. "Things have slowed down some at the diner now that the tourists have mostly gone. That's not a bad thing. How's the garden?"

Ida had helped her aunt Marjorie with the yard work as she got up in years and had helped Priscilla design and develop the cottage's garden as well since she'd arrived.

"I have to admit, I haven't been paying as much attention to it as I should," Priscilla said. "I've been too busy enjoying the season." But now that Ida mentioned it, the hedges by the road were getting a bit overgrown, and she hadn't deadheaded the flowers in quite some time.

"Well, let me know if you want me to come on by and help out," Ida said. She picked up a cracker with a wedge of cheese on it and popped it in her mouth. "Have you heard about this whole houseboat thing?"

"Yes. It's been all over the news." Priscilla decided not to say anything about having been on the boat just yet. The front page of the newspaper this morning had another story about the boat and the missing owner. There had been no new details included in the article—not even the name Bart Flask, which the police must be trying to keep quiet—but the story was obviously capturing a lot of attention on the island. "It's crazy, isn't it? No one seems to have even talked to him in all the time he was here, and they know almost nothing about him."

"You know what's funny? Randy actually did meet him."

"What? Really?" Priscilla had met Ida's husband Randy briefly at church a few weeks back. He'd seemed like a nice guy. She looked around now but didn't see him.

"What does your husband do?" Did she know this?

"He's an electrician. He got a call from the boat. The guy's generator was on the fritz, and he needed someone to take a look at it ASAP. So Randy went out and met the guy and fixed his generator."

"Wow. When was this?" Priscilla couldn't believe it. Someone really had met Bart after all!

"It must have been a week ago? A little over, I guess, because he was late getting home Friday night, and I was upset because that was my only night off from the diner."

"Wow." Priscilla looked around. "Is he here? I'd love to talk to him about it."

Ida Lee leveled her gaze. "You know, I heard a rumor that you were good at solving mysteries. Are you working on solving this one too?"

"Not in any official capacity." Priscilla smiled. "I'm just curious, is all."

Ida gave her a devious grin. "That's a yes. In that case, hang tight. I think he's still in the sanctuary. I'll go find him."

She dashed off, and Priscilla stood in place, nursing her cup of coffee. All around the Fellowship Hall, people were chatting and laughing. Cheryl Finnegan, who ran the children's ministry, was chatting with Bruce Gore, who headed up the choir that performed for special services. Priscilla thought she might volunteer for the Christmas choir. She was a decent mezzo-soprano and had often been in the choir back in Kansas, and she liked that this one didn't require weekly rehearsals.

"Oh good, you're still here." Ida returned with her husband Randy right behind her. "Randy, you remember Priscilla?"

"Of course." Randy was tall and lanky with graying dark hair that touched his collar. "Good to see you again."

"You as well."

"My wife tells me you want to know about the man in that houseboat."

"I think the whole island wants to know about the man in that houseboat." Priscilla laughed. "But I am particularly interested."

"Because you're going to find out what happened to him." He was smiling, and he seemed like he genuinely believed she would. Could she?

"Most likely the police or the Coast Guard will do that." She was starting to feel ridiculous, acting like she would be able to solve this thing. The two mysteries she'd solved so far had just been about history, objects that had some significance for her family. Neither of those were about a missing person, and neither had involved the police or the military. "But I do have fun trying to put the pieces together," she finished because she didn't know what else to say.

"Well, I hope you figure it out before the police do. Give them some competition." Randy laughed. "Here's what I know. I got a call Friday afternoon a week ago. The guy said he was on a houseboat out in the marina, and his generator had stopped working. He wondered if I could come right away. Well, of course I did, and not just because that meant I could charge the rush fee." He winked, and Priscilla smiled.

"I have to admit I hadn't actually done a generator on a boat before. Most of the electricity on boats I've seen is powered by the engine and a battery. But I've installed plenty of generators—the power does go out pretty regularly during storms here. So I said sure, I'd take a look."

Priscilla wondered whether her house had a generator. She'd have to look into that. She'd hate to be all alone without power during a winter storm.

"When I got there, the guy introduced himself as Bart, and he showed me the small opening that led to where the electric was."

"What was he like?"

Randy thought for a moment. "Quiet. He didn't say much. Probably my age or a little older, and he had grayish brown hair."

"Did you notice anything else about him?" You could tell so much about a person by noticing the small details, like what they were wearing and how their clothes fit and whether they bit their nails.

"I didn't pick up on anything else. I'm sorry about that," Randy said. "I was mostly interested in the boat. I'd never been on one like that before. It was like something out of one of those tiny-house shows Ida is always watching."

"You watch them too," his wife said. "Don't blame this on me."

He laughed. "Anyway, everything was built in and designed to take up as little room as possible. It was pretty neat." He was holding a paper cup of coffee, and he took a sip now. "He was a painter, I could tell that. He had all these canvases stacked up and set around the room, and he was working on one on an easel."

"Could you tell anything about him from his work?"

Randy shrugged. "I'm hardly an art critic. Alls I know is that most of it wasn't to my taste. All kinds of abstract nonsense. This modern stuff doesn't make sense to me."

It hadn't made sense to Priscilla either. But again, she had to wonder if there was some clue in the paintings she'd missed. Were they more than just abstract pictures? Was there some message hidden in them? Priscilla didn't know how to figure that out.

"Was there anything else that stuck out to you?" Priscilla asked.

He thought for a moment and then said, "He had a dog. A golden retriever, I think."

"What was it like?"

"It was a sweet dog. Well cared for, and he obeyed when Bart told him to stay back. I petted him, and he nuzzled my hand. It was pretty cute."

"You said he?"

"I guess it was a boy because he was wearing a tag that said Hawthorne, and that's what Bart called him. But I guess I don't know for sure."

"Interesting." Hawthorne. What kind of a name for a dog was that?

"I'm racking my brain, but I can't think of anything else that might be useful. I found the problem with the generator. A part needed replacing, and luckily I had one with me, so I got him fixed up and headed out."

"Did he pay you?"

Randy nodded. "In cash. You don't always see that, not for jobs like this."

"Was it..." She tried to figure out how to phrase this politely. "Do jobs like that typically cost a lot?"

"They're not cheap, I'll say that. It's a specialized skill."

"Of course. It's a major job too."

"Exactly."

So he'd had a large amount of cash onboard the boat. Could that have been the reason for whatever happened to him? A robbery gone wrong? But then, what about the laptop that had been left behind?

"If you think of anything else that might be relevant, could you let me know?"

"Of course."

She thanked him, and then he and Ida Lee apologized and said Ida had to get to her shift at the diner. She said goodbye, and Priscilla moved off to find someone else to talk to. Before she'd gone more than a few feet, her niece Sara appeared beside her.

"Priscilla. I have been dying to talk to you."

"Hi, Sara." Sara wasn't technically her niece. She was Gail's daughter, which made her...a second cousin twice removed? Priscilla didn't have patience for keeping things like that straight. Sara was in her late thirties and tall, with shoulder-length brown hair and sky-blue eyes. She was outgoing and funny and knew more about books than anyone Priscilla knew. Priscilla knew she'd lived in New York for many years, working in publishing, but she'd missed home, so now she owned and ran a bookstore over in Edgartown. "Mom tells me you're looking into the man who disappeared. The one on the houseboat."

"Sort of." She hadn't told Gail about this, but she wasn't surprised that she'd heard. Joan had no doubt spilled the beans. And now Sara knew because, well, news traveled fast in a small town.

"I have a theory about where he is," Sara said.

"Oh?" She had Priscilla's attention now. "What's that?"

"My neighbors across the street are strictly summer people. Oh, maybe they'll come out for a holiday weekend sometimes, but they are never here in late September."

Priscilla nodded. The population of Martha's Vineyard swelled in the summer, and there were plenty of houses that stayed vacant the rest of the year. She couldn't imagine having enough money that you could simply not use a house for nine months, but in the few months she'd been here, she'd already seen many homes shuttered for the season.

"Well, Friday afternoon I stopped at home after taking Andrew to his lacrosse game to drop off his stuff before I headed back to the store, and something about that house seemed off. Something had moved or something. I later figured out that the mail that had been building up in the mailbox the past few weeks—just junk mail, I assume—had been brought in, but that didn't occur to me until much later. Anyway, it wasn't until later that I was sure because there was a light on inside the house. And get this—that night, I heard a dog bark. I went out to investigate, and there was definitely a dog barking inside that house."

"Wait. You think the man who was living on the houseboat is inside your neighbor's house?"

"The timing is a bit suspicious, don't you think? The houseboat gets cut loose, the man goes missing, and that same day someone shows up in a house that's supposed to be empty? The house that's never had anyone in it at this time of year?"

It was suspicious timing, Priscilla had to agree. But there were any number of possible explanations, and an extremely fortunate coincidence if it were true.

"Did you try getting ahold of your neighbors? Maybe they rented the house out."

"I tried calling, but no one picked up. I don't know them all that well. He's some fancy banker in New York, and she does some kind of sales job that involves traveling all over the world. But we're friendly, and I have their home number. But they've never rented it out before. Why would they now, at this time of year? And the day after the man goes missing? Come on. The timing is too crazy."

"It is definitely possible." Priscilla wasn't as convinced as Sara was, but she had to admit it was a possibility. Stranger things had happened.

"Should I call the police?"

"I don't know about that." If the person in the house was supposed to be there, it would be a nasty surprise for the cops to show up. Plus, she knew the police and the Coast Guard believed Bart had gone—or been taken—off the island. They were not likely to look into this. But if Priscilla was right, if she had indeed heard the dog barking where she thought she had, it was distinctly possible that he was still on the island somewhere. Why not in Edgartown? Though, wouldn't the boat have been headed to the east if he'd ended up in Edgartown? But then, maybe the boat had unloaded somewhere else and he'd been driven to Edgartown.

"I'd say keep an eye on it," Priscilla said. "See if you can catch a glimpse of whoever is there. And keep trying to get ahold of your neighbors. There may be a perfectly logical explanation for why someone is in their house."

"But if there's not..."

"If there's not, definitely let me know."

"Got it." Sara saluted, like Priscilla was a chief or something.

Priscilla laughed, and after chatting with a few more people, she headed home. The drive home was beautiful, but as she ate her lunch of tomato soup and a grilled cheese sandwich, she couldn't help feeling a little sad. Sundays after church had always been family time. Even after Rachel moved out on her own, Priscilla and Gary had always made a point of spending some time together, browsing through shops or even just watching the game together on the couch. Priscilla didn't care much for sports, but Gary had been a loyal Chiefs fan, and she liked snuggling up with him under a blanket on a cold winter day. Today she cleaned up the kitchen, feeling a little lonely.

She had planned to spend the afternoon going through her quilt books to select some patterns to show Gerald. But as she stared down a solitary afternoon and saw the beautiful autumn sunshine streaming in through the windows, she was suddenly itching to get out. She would only get melancholy if she stayed in here all afternoon. Sitting around moping wasn't going to help anyone.

She picked up the phone and dialed Joan. "Hey there. Do you have any plans for the afternoon?"

"Just transitioning my closet to my winter wardrobe. Certainly nothing I wouldn't love to be distracted from."

Goodness. Transitioning her closet? Was this a thing people did around here?

"Would you like to come with me to do some reconnaissance?"

"That sounds official."

"It's not. Sara gave me a lead this morning that probably won't go anywhere. But I thought I might as well check it out anyway."

"Sounds like a plan. Where are we headed?"

"Edgartown."

"Oh good. Can we swing by my favorite yarn store while we're over there? I want to pick up some yarn for Christmas presents."

It wasn't even October. Priscilla hadn't even started thinking about Christmas yet. "That would be fine."

"Great. Want to pick me up in a little bit?"

"I'll see you soon."

Half an hour later, Priscilla and Joan were in Priscilla's car. Edgartown was a beautiful historic village filled with gorgeous period homes and shops, inns, and restaurants. It had a stately feel, and Priscilla loved strolling down the narrow streets and peeking into little boutiques. But today they were on a mission. Priscilla had called Sara to let her know they were coming to check out her neighbor's home, and though Sara was at the bookstore, she said they were welcome to use her house as a base and told them how to figure out which house she meant. They parked in the driveway of Sara and Milton's white Greek Revival home and easily found the shingled two-story directly across the street. Its broad front porch wrapped around the house, and a driveway led to the separate garage. Boxy hedges along the property line were perfectly manicured but low enough that they could see over them.

"That's the one," Priscilla said. The driveway was empty. They didn't see any movement inside, but the house was set back a little way from the road, so it would have been hard to tell.

"Do we just go up and knock on the door?" Joan asked. She held her hand up to shade her eyes, squinting at the house. It was a beautiful block, shaded by large oaks and maple trees and lined with well-kept homes. This area had a number of old sea captains' homes, large and imposing, as well as newer construction, but each of the houses along this stretch was tastefully painted and tended.

"I'm not sure." If she was being totally honest, Priscilla hadn't really thought this through. What would they do? Go up and peek in the windows? Not unless they wanted the neighbors to call the police. "I guess so," she said hesitantly.

Joan nodded and started across the street. She was just going to go for it? Just like that? Priscilla sighed and then hurried to catch up.

She caught up to Joan on the porch. In the sun it was warm, but here in the shade there was a distinct bite in the air.

"Did you see that?" Joan was standing perfectly still, looking at the front window.

"See what?"

"That curtain moved."

"Are you sure?"

"I'm sure. I saw it move."

Priscilla looked at the curtain, but it didn't move again. "Okay. Let's see if whoever it is answers the door."

She pulled open the screen door and rapped on the hunter-green wooden front door. The only response was the bark of a dog inside the house. Priscilla's heart raced. There really was a dog inside! Was this the dog they were looking for? She couldn't tell anything about the breed by listening to him. They waited a minute, and then she tried again. More barking. After the third rap on the door, she stepped back and waited. They heard a thud and then footsteps. The dog's barking suddenly sounded farther away.

"What was that?" Joan asked.

"I don't know." They waited another moment, hearing more footsteps, and the dog's barking got quieter. Someone was carrying the dog upstairs.

"Is that..."

"There's definitely someone inside," Priscilla said. She knocked on the door. The footsteps had stopped, and the barking was fainter but still there. She knocked again. "Bart?" she called.

"Bart?" Joan turned to her. "Who's Bart?"

Priscilla remembered now that his name had not been made public. Well, she would explain later. Right now she needed him to come to the door.

"Bart? If you're in there, we just want to help," she called.

But there was no sound. No more movement. No more footsteps.

"Someone is definitely inside," Priscilla said. She shook her head and moved off the porch then stood on the front lawn and looked up at the house.

"Someone is," Joan agreed. "Now we just have to figure out if it's the missing man."

"And what on earth he's doing in there."

CHAPTER TEN

Priscilla was just pulling the lasagna out of the oven when the doorbell rang. Gerald was right on time. She'd invited him over to look through her quilt books to pick out a few patterns he might like to use for Aggie's quilt, and since he was coming over anyway, she figured the polite thing to do was to feed him. She set the lasagna on the counter, took off her oven mitts, smoothed down her hair, and headed for the door.

"Hi there." Gerald stood on the porch in a button-down and sweater, holding a bouquet of fresh white dahlias and golden spider mums.

"Hello. It's good to see you." She'd spent a good chunk of the day searching for any mention of Bart Flask anywhere—property records, birth or death records, articles in trade publications, 5K times, anything—but she had gotten nowhere. She was starting to wonder how this man had managed to keep his online presence so minimal. She might drive out to the property records office in Edgartown and see if there were any records of him there.

But right now she focused on Gerald. She didn't usually get to see him so often, but since Aggie's quilt would take a fair amount of time to cut and piece and sew together, she wanted to get started as soon as possible. You never knew when a baby might arrive.

She stepped back so he could come in, and he handed her the flowers.

"These are lovely."

"You're cooking dinner, so flowers are the least I could do."

"I'm glad to do it." She led him into the kitchen and set the flowers on the counter. "How was your day?"

"Oh. Fine." He sighed as he took a seat at one of the stools at the kitchen counter. "Frustrating."

"How so?" She opened a cabinet and pulled down a glass vase.

He shifted on his stool and then sighed again. "We can't find anything on this guy."

"On Bart Flask?"

He narrowed his eyes. "How did you know his name?"

Priscilla held the vase under the faucet and started the water. "Lucky guess?" she said, shrugging.

He watched her for a moment.

"I've been asking around," she said. "Just to see what I could find out about him. Which so far isn't much." She shut off the water and set the vase on the table.

"Who told you the name Bart Flask?" There was some look in his face that she couldn't read.

"No one told me. I figured it out." She carefully unwrapped the paper from around the flowers. "These smell wonderful."

Truthfully, they didn't smell like much of anything, but she was trying to distract him.

"How did you figure it out?"

Priscilla took kitchen scissors out of the drawer and began trimming the ends off the stems. She didn't want to get Officer Brown in trouble, especially since she'd tried so hard to make sure not to tell Priscilla anything.

"I used my feminine wiles," she said. She needed to change the subject. "And guess what else I learned?"

"I'm afraid to ask."

There was a teasing tone in his voice, but there was also truth in what he'd said. Priscilla plowed ahead anyway. "My niece Sara mentioned that one of her neighbors' houses is supposed to be empty, but she thought there was someone in it. I went to check it out, and she's right. There's definitely someone inside, and whoever it was didn't want to be found."

"What?" He narrowed his eyes. "How are you sure there's someone inside?"

"Joan and I went there. We heard footsteps inside the house, but no one came to the door. They took in the mail too. And Sara swears her neighbors are only here in the summer, but someone is in that house who shouldn't be. And they have a dog. *And* whoever it was arrived sometime in the night Thursday."

She expected to see excitement on his face. She'd just handed him a big clue! But instead there was something like consternation. He didn't answer her for a moment. Wait, was he mad? He looked a little upset. But why would he be mad? She wasn't inter-fering in anything. Just asking questions.

"Priscilla, I need to ask you to stay out of this," Gerald said soberly. "If the person in that house really had been involved in this, you could have been in some real trouble." He shifted in his seat. "Fortunately, we're pretty sure the guy is off the island, so I think you were safe, but you could have been in real danger."

"What makes you so sure he's off the island?" Priscilla asked. "Did his phone records show that or something?"

"No." He blew out a breath. "No, his phone records show exactly what we expected. Nothing since Thursday night."

"He turned his phone off?"

"Not exactly." A pause, and then he continued. "We found it in the harbor, right where the houseboat was moored. Or one we're fairly certain was his. Which explains why it hasn't been used."

That must be what Officer Brown had been referring to then. "So whoever attacked him threw the phone overboard."

"Or he did it himself. It's impossible to say at this point." He shifted in his seat. There was a pause, and then he said, "Someone saw him in Hyannis."

"What?"

"You asked why we were so sure he's off the island. It's because a gas station attendant in Hyannis reported seeing a man that matched his description Friday morning."

"From what I can tell, his description matches most of the men in this area—yourself included," Priscilla said.

"It's a first-person sighting," he said. "We have to take it seriously. And I'm not supposed to have told you that, so please don't get me in trouble."

Priscilla wasn't sure she would take the memory of one person as reason to stop looking on the island, but what did she know?

"Have they found what that key opens? Or gotten into the laptop?"

"Why are you so curious about all this?" he asked.

"I don't know. It's not that common that something like this happens. And I know the man might be in danger. I just can't help trying to figure out what might have happened to him. Maybe I can find him, wherever he is."

"Priscilla." He let out a long breath. "I know you've had fun solving a couple of small mysteries since you've been here, but this isn't like those."

Small mysteries? Priscilla tried not to be offended. Maybe they were small to him, but they had both been complex and involved a lot of moving pieces. She'd solved a mystery that had evaded people for centuries, for goodness' sake.

He must have seen the hurt on her face because he immediately said, "That came out wrong. What I meant was, it isn't safe for you to be poking around in this. At best this is a missing persons case. But there is strong evidence that it's more than that—kidnapping, coercion, maybe even murder. Someone knows what happened to that guy"—he shook his head—"to Bart. And that person is still at large and most likely doesn't want to be found. Please, leave this to the professionals. Both the Coast Guard and the police are working on this case. Together we'll figure out what happened. But this is too big for civilians to be involved." He looked up at her. The look in his eyes was more pleading now. "Even civilians who are very good at solving mysteries," he added. "It's not safe. I just want you to be protected."

Was she imagining the tenderness in his eyes?

"Will you promise me you won't keep trying to solve this mystery?" he asked.

Priscilla hesitated. She wanted to stay safe. She really did. And she wanted to make him happy. But she couldn't deny that his words still stung.

"I promise I won't interfere with the police and Coast Guard investigation," she said. There. That was close enough to what he'd asked for. She picked up the flowers and placed them in the vase.

He hesitated again. Priscilla arranged the flowers, keeping her eyes focused on the blooms so she didn't give anything away.

"All right," he finally said. "Thank you." If he'd noticed she hadn't promised not to investigate, he didn't say so. He must have seen the hurt on her face because he let out a long breath and then said, "We did find something interesting."

"Oh?" It was an olive branch, and she knew it. She tried to swallow her pride and accept it.

"Fingerprints. We found fingerprints in the boat that belong to someone here in town."

"Really?" That was interesting. Not a bad olive branch at all. And well chosen since, as he well knew, one she couldn't do much to investigate herself.

"I can't tell you who, of course."

"Of course." She felt more disappointed than she'd expected.

"But I can tell you that it's someone we're very interested in."

"Why?"

"Let's just say they've made their opinion on houseboats clear."

"Oh." Priscilla knew who he meant. "Frank Ripley?"

At first his eyes registered surprise, and then that quickly shifted. "The newspaper." He nodded.

"He told me he'd never been on the boat though," Priscilla said. "He said he didn't even know the guy's name."

There was a moment of quiet, and then he said, "I guess I shouldn't be surprised to hear that you've talked with Frank Ripley."

"I said I wouldn't interfere going forward," Priscilla said. "But I talked to him before, and he swore he didn't even know what the guy looked like."

"Well, if that's the case, he should have a heck of a time explaining how his fingerprints got on the kitchen knife we found in the houseboat."

"Wait. Are you serious?"

"I am. But remember, you're going to leave the investigating to the professionals, right?"

"Of course," Priscilla said. She mostly meant it too. "But how did they match them to his prints? They had his fingerprints on file?"

"He's a retired schoolteacher." He shrugged. "Their prints are on file. Now what is it that smells so wonderful over there?" He craned his neck toward the dish on the counter.

"Lasagna," Priscilla said. "With butternut squash and sage. I hope you're hungry."

"It smells wonderful."

"I hope you like it. It should give you the strength to sort through books of quilt patterns with me."

"Well, I know nothing about quilt patterns, so I'll need all the strength I can get."

Priscilla gestured for him to move to the table, but even as she did so, her mind was running in circles. Frank Ripley's fingerprints on a kitchen knife? The one used to rip open the furniture? The one used to...

Priscilla couldn't believe it. The biggest clue so far! And she'd just promised she wouldn't interfere with the police and Coast Guard. Well, she wouldn't interfere. But that didn't mean she couldn't ask a few questions here and there.

After they'd eaten, they cleared off the table, and Priscilla spread her quilt books and magazines across it.

"Wow. That's quite a lot of quilts."

"We don't have to look through every one," Priscilla said. "But I thought you might want to flip through some and get a sense of what sort of pattern you'd like to use."

"I was thinking just a basic design. Like, squares."

"You've just described dozens of quilt patterns." She laughed. "And even with the most basic design, it's how you arrange the colors that really matters. You can totally change the look of a pattern by gradiating the colors versus scattering different tones evenly. I want to see what you're drawn to."

Once again he looked uncertain, but he nodded.

"Here. Why don't you start with this one?" Priscilla handed him a book for beginners. It showed a dozen or so basic quilt patterns with full-color illustrations. He started flipping through the pages. Priscilla turned to a couple of quilting magazines she'd collected over the years and started marking pages she thought had interesting quilts.

"How's Rachel doing?" Gerald asked as he looked down at a log cabin quilt.

"She's all right." Actually Priscilla hadn't talked to her in a few days. She should call her. "Last I heard she was busy at work, just like always." Rachel was a project manager for a telecommunications firm in Kansas City, and she loved her work and seemed to let it take over her life, in Priscilla's humble opinion. "I wish she'd work less and spend more time connecting with other people, but I learned long ago not to try to tell her what to do."

"That's smart," Gerald said, smiling. "That's the thing about kids growing up. You can't tell them what to do anymore. They become their own people, and you just have to let them be who they are."

"It's sad but true," Priscilla said. Naturally, she was proud of Rachel. She sometimes couldn't believe her little baby had turned into this bold, independent woman. But sometimes she missed being able to guide her a bit more.

"Did you ever want more kids?" Gerald asked as he turned the page. "A little brother or sister for Rachel?"

Priscilla didn't answer right away. There was a time in her life when just the very question would have sent her into tears. So much pain and disappointment and loss were wrapped up in those innocent words, and she was glad she was able to feel a little distance now. But she still took a moment to compose herself before she answered.

"Very much so," she said.

"Oh." Gerald could see he'd said the wrong thing, and there was a slight panicked look in his eyes.

"It's all right," she said, and she realized that maybe for the first time in her life, it was true. Her life now felt so far away from this struggle that it gave her space she'd never felt before. "I don't mind talking about it." She was surprised to say it and mean it.

Gerald visibly relaxed, and she continued.

"We tried for years to have more children," she said. She flipped the page of the magazine gently. "The doctors couldn't find anything wrong, but it just didn't happen. Well, it happened a few times, but we lost those babies very early on, before anyone really knew about them."

"I'm sorry," Gerald said.

"Thank you." She nodded. "It was a long time ago."

It had been a long time ago, but that still didn't lessen the pain of loss. She'd been so excited when she'd found out she was pregnant, already filled with so many dreams for her tiny speck of a child, and then the awfulness of realizing what was happening when she lost them was almost too much to bear. It had happened twice after Rachel, and those awful long nights crying in the bathroom were some of the worst times of her life.

"I know Rachel would have loved a sibling," she said. "And I wish more than anything we could have given her that. But we were grateful for her. We had one wonderful child we adored, though we would have loved to fill the farmhouse with little voices, and believed that God had a plan for us, so we tried to just trust."

"It's not always easy to trust, is it?"

"No." Priscilla thought back to those long nights, those long mornings where she hadn't wanted to get out of bed. Where she'd wanted to just lie there and mourn, but she couldn't because she had a farm to run and because no one else in the world besides Gary knew what had happened. "It isn't. But Gary did his best to pull me through those times. He always had this deep faith that never wavered. Even when I was doubting God and having a hard time showing up at church because I was mad at Him, Gary would always remind me that God wanted the best for us and we would be safe as long as we trusted Him."

Even now after Gary was gone, she still sometimes marveled at the depth of his faith. He'd never once doubted, even as he lay in bed all those months, withering away from pancreatic cancer. He'd been her rock, her steady partner. He'd spent his life on a farm, and he always said he could see God's hand in the sprouting of a seed or the everyday miracle of milking a cow. He saw God's hand in the daily life of the farm and saw His nature in the rhythms of the seasons. The cycle of life, death, and rebirth—planting, harvesting, and resting—was a yearly reminder to him of the wonder of God.

"He sounds like a wonderful person."

"He was." Priscilla didn't say more. She didn't know if she could. This grief was still fresh. But she was surprised to find that it hurt just a tiny bit less than usual tonight.

"I like this one," Gerald said, pointing at a Flying Geese pattern. Bless him for trying to change the subject. So awkward and so sweet.

"That is a nice one." She gave him a sticky note to mark the page.

Talking about all of this—the miscarriages, Gary, the farm—it all hurt a tiny bit less than it used to. Was it because of this place, her new life here on Martha's Vineyard? She thought that was certainly part of it. Kansas felt like a world away from here, and the hurts and disappointments of her life there—even the really big, difficult ones—felt far away.

But she thought it was probably also a little bit because of the man sitting across from her too. Having Gerald here helped. It was startling, and a little bit thrilling, to realize that. She didn't know if their friendship would ever turn to anything more, but for now she was grateful that Gerald was a part of her new life.

CHAPTER ELEVEN

Tuesday morning dawned cloudy and cool. A blanket of clouds hung low in the sky, and the air had a distinct bite. Priscilla wrapped a flannel robe around her and put on her slippers.

She headed into the kitchen and started the coffee then moved toward the big sliding glass door that led out to the yard. The sea was rough today, whipped into whitecaps by the wind. On clear days, she could see all the way to the mainland, but today all she could see were clouds.

While the coffee was brewing, Priscilla ran out and got the newspaper and saw that the missing man was still front-page news. The paper reported that the police had a suspect in custody. Frank Ripley then.

She sat down with her coffee and a bowl of maple cinnamon oatmeal and thought through her plan for the day. First off, she wanted to find out how Frank Ripley's fingerprints had gotten onto those kitchen knives. But how would she do that? It sounded like he was in police custody. And even if he wasn't, she'd promised she wouldn't interfere. Well, maybe now that they had Frank locked up, there would be no need to interfere. Maybe he would simply explain what had happened, and this would all be wrapped up today.

But something about it didn't sit right with Priscilla. She'd thought Frank could be a suspect too, but after talking to him, she wasn't so sure. He'd reacted badly to her questions, but she had a hard time imagining the older man wielding a kitchen knife and attacking Bart. He could barely sit down without groaning. Was he guilty? If so, what had he done with Bart? And what about the dog? Were they really on the mainland?

Priscilla couldn't say for sure, but something in her didn't believe it was that simple. She had promised not to interfere, but she hadn't promised to stop asking questions.

She decided to find out whatever she could about the owners of the house she and Joan had visited on Sunday. Someone had been inside. If it was Bart, she wanted to know why he'd picked that house and figure out how to get him to come out. She also planned to look into the piece of information she'd picked up from Randy on Sunday: the dog's name, Hawthorne. There had to be some way to track the dog down or at least find out more about his owner based on that name.

But first, she needed to spend some time with the Lord. She opened her Bible and read from Colossians: "My goal is that they may be encouraged in heart and united in love, so that they may have the full riches of complete understanding, in order that they may know the mystery of God, namely, Christ, in whom are hidden all the treasures of wisdom and knowledge." She read through the verses then read them again. She wanted the riches of complete understanding, not just about this mystery but about God. *Focus on Christ*, the verses said. She needed that reminder.

After she'd spent some time in prayer, Priscilla cleaned up the kitchen and got dressed. When she came back into the kitchen, she saw that her phone, which had been on the kitchen counter, was beeping. She had a new voice mail. How had she missed the call? Then she realized that she'd turned the ringer off before bed last night and hadn't turned it back on this morning. She looked at the screen and saw an unfamiliar number. She listened to the message.

"Hello, Priscilla." She recognized that Texas twang in the voice. This was the Bart Flask she'd contacted in Texas. "I'm afraid I don't know anything about a houseboat or a dog. I work in finance here in Texas, and as much as I would love to visit Martha's Vineyard, I am afraid I have never been there. I'm sorry I can't be more help, but I hope you find what you're looking for."

Well, that was disappointing. But she wasn't sure what she'd expected. Even if he was the man from the houseboat, would he just come out and admit to it? That Bart had disappeared, either by his own choice or against his will, and he was unlikely to come out and admit his identity to her.

The next thing to do was to find out what she could about the people who owned the house across from Sara's. She had talked with Sara last night, and Sara had been happy enough to pass along the names and phone number of the people who owned the house. She hadn't heard back from her neighbors, which seemed odd to Priscilla. If a neighbor called and said someone was in your house who shouldn't be, wouldn't you pay attention to that?

Well, she would see what she could find out. Priscilla typed the name Adam Phillips into her browser. She pulled up a page on his company's website that listed his title, experience, and qualifications. According to the bio, he was a senior vice president at a major bank, had two Ivy League degrees, had been in management for twenty years, liked to travel, and split his time between New York and Martha's Vineyard. Priscilla knew the bio was meant to sound impressive, but she found herself more irritated than impressed. She did some more research but didn't come up with much that would help her find any connection between this man and Bart Flask. Next, she searched for the name Catherine Phillips, the man's wife.

This brought her to a bio of Catherine at the pharmaceutical company where she worked and also several articles she had been cited in. Priscilla also found her social media page, which was full of perfectly airbrushed shots of Catherine and Adam and their daughter Amber. The shots showed them at the beach or on vacation in France or skiing in the Alps. If the goal was to show off how wonderful their lives were, it succeeded. Priscilla felt a pang of envy, seeing how happy this family was and the amazing adventures they got to have. But even though she scrolled past pages of photos, she still didn't find anything that would link them to Bart, and nothing that might explain who was hiding out in their house.

Priscilla hesitated. Sara had given her their home phone number with a Manhattan area code. She wanted to speak with them, to find out what they might know. But she tried to picture what they might think when they got her call. She didn't know them and had no real business asking what was going on at their house.

Still, she couldn't leave this stone unturned. She dialed the number and held her breath. The line rang and rang again. She was almost relieved when the call went to voice mail.

"Hello, my name is Priscilla Grant, and I live on Martha's Vineyard. I have a question about your house in Edgartown, and I'd appreciate it if you'd give me a call." She left her phone number and then hung up. She just had to wait for them to call her back, she supposed.

Next, she turned to the dog. Hawthorne. Was he the dog inside the Phillipses' house? As Priscilla had been lying in bed last night thinking through all this, she'd had an idea. When she'd gotten Jake, she'd had a microchip inserted in his ear that would track his location. Many dog owners did this nowadays—it was almost painless and meant you could always find your dog if it were lost. She wasn't sure exactly how it all worked, but if there was some way to search for a particular dog by name...

She pulled up a new browser window and searched for *missing dog chip registry*. She found a site where you could type in the number on a missing pet's microchip and find out the name of the owner, but she didn't know Hawthorne's number or if he even had one. Come to think of it, she didn't know Jake's number. Her understanding of how it all worked was a bit shaky, but she thought a veterinarian had to be involved in reading the chip. She didn't have enough information to do anything else on this site.

She did find a few sites where you could search for found dogs in your local area. She searched the sites that came up, but there was nothing from the past two weeks in this area, and nothing that looked anything like the golden retriever Randy had reported. No dogs named Hawthorne. She was getting nowhere.

Priscilla wasn't sure if a local registry of microchipped dogs existed, and her research wasn't pulling up anything that clarified that. But she knew where she could find out. She set her laptop aside, pushed herself off the sofa, and grabbed her coat.

A few minutes later, she was walking to the Southside Veterinary Clinic, where she'd brought Jake when she'd first adopted him. The squat brick building was outside of the main commercial district of town and much more modern than most, though it was still nicely designed, with a cupola on top and pediments over the doors. She stepped inside the glass front door and greeted the receptionist, Robin, a heavyset woman about Priscilla's age.

"Hi there, Ms. Grant." Robin smiled. "No Jake today?"

There was a woman waiting in one of the seats along the wall. She was clearly pregnant and had a cat in a carrier on the seat next to her. Priscilla smiled, and the woman rubbed her belly and smiled back.

"Not today, thankfully. I mean, I'm sure he'd love to see you all, but I'm just here with a question today."

"Of course. What can we help you with?"

"I was hoping I could ask Dr. Morris about tracking a dog's microchip."

"Oh dear. Is Jake all right?"

"He's just fine, thank you. This is more like a hypothetical question, and one I couldn't figure out the answer to on my own. I figured it was best to come straight to the people who would know."

"Well, I'm sure someone here can help you with that." She looked down at the computer in front of her. "Dr. Morris is in the middle of a surgery right now, so I'm afraid it will be some time before he could come out and answer your questions, but I believe Mara is free. She's a tech, and I'm sure she could answer your questions. Would that work?"

"Sure. That would be great."

"Wonderful. Have a seat, and I'll see if she's free."

Priscilla took a seat next to the pregnant woman and gave her a smile. The cat in the carrier hissed.

"Oh hush, Rainbow Sprinkles," she said, sticking her fingers through the grate of the carrier door. Then she shook her head. "I never should have let my two-year-old name the cat."

Priscilla laughed. "Well, I suppose it could have been worse. When my daughter was two, she was into worms and spiders."

The woman shuddered. "Yes, I suppose it could be worse."

Priscilla smiled, and their eyes met. This woman was still in the thick of it, and she had no idea how much she would miss these days soon.

"Ms. Grant?"

Priscilla looked up when a tech she recognized called her name. She had shoulder-length black hair and a wide smile. Priscilla gave the pregnant woman one last smile, and then she hurried toward the door. "Thank you so much for taking the time," she said.

"It's no problem." Mara ushered her through the door and into a small exam room. "Robin tells me you're interested in learning how the microchip trackers work."

"Exactly." She looked around the small room, which was dominated by a metal exam table. Mara gestured that she should sit in the small plastic chair next to the door. Mara sat in a swivel chair in front of a computer.

"It's pretty simple, really. If Jake were to turn up somewhere and no one knew to whom he belonged, he could be taken to any vet clinic, and the vet would use one of these"—she held up what looked like a scanner gun—"and they could scan his chip. The scanner would bring up his number and the phone number of the registry he is connected with."

"Who maintains this registry?"

"Each chip manufacturer maintains their own registry of pets tagged with their products."

"Oh. So there isn't one big universal database where every pet's information is found?"

"No, unfortunately. That would be simpler. But the registries are pretty easy to use. The vet would then call the appropriate registry and give the pet's chip number, and the owner's information would be pulled up."

Priscilla had imagined that scanning the chip would bring up the owner's phone number directly. She was glad, for her own privacy, that it didn't, though it sure would make things simpler here.

"What if you didn't have the dog with you? Could you search for the dog based on the chip number?"

"Some chips have GPS capability but not all."

Priscilla thought for a moment. "What if all you had was the owner's name? Could you find out where the dog was based on that?"

Mara thought for a moment. "I'm sure someone could. Maybe the registry would give that information to the police if needed, assuming the dog had a GPS chip. But that seems like a pretty big invasion of privacy in general, which is probably why they don't let that information out freely."

"What if you searched for the dog's name?"

"Same problem, I'm afraid."

Priscilla understood that. She didn't want people to be able to look up her name and find her exact location while she was out walking Jake. But it did dash her hopes for finding Bart Flask based on the dog's microchip.

"Thank you for your help," she said, standing.

"Let me know if you have any more questions," Mara said.

Priscilla promised she would then stopped at the front desk and bought a new bone for Jake on her way out.

A few minutes later, she was back in her car and considering her next move. She wasn't willing to give up on the idea of finding Bart Flask through Hawthorne. It was one of the few pieces of information she had about the mystery man. But how else could she track him down?

Hawthorne. What a strange name for a dog. Then again, she supposed Jake could be considered a strange name for a dog by some, though lots of pet owners were giving their dogs human names these days. But Hawthorne? The only context Priscilla had for that name was Nathaniel Hawthorne, the author of *The Scarlet Letter* and other vaguely creepy stories set in New England. Why would Bart have named his dog after an author? Maybe Bart was an English professor, specializing in American classics? Could she find a list of English professors somewhere? Or maybe the name was significant for some reason. Priscilla realized she didn't really know very much about Nathaniel Hawthorne. Perhaps if she found out more about him, she'd see some connection she'd missed before.

Priscilla started the car and drove back toward the heart of Tisbury. She knew exactly where to head next.

CHAPTER TWELVE

Priscilla took a deep breath as she stepped inside the familiar library. She loved the smell of ink and paper and time and whatever it was that gave libraries that wonderful scent. She looked around. The high-ceilinged room was bright and airy, and the wood floors and rosewood shelving made the space feel solid and historic. The first floor contained the checkout desk, computer terminals, and online catalog terminals front and center, with the local history and children's areas to each side. Study carrels were scattered throughout the space. The sections Priscilla needed might be on the second floor.

"Hi, Priscilla."

Priscilla saw that Clara Lopez, the head librarian, was waving at her from the checkout counter. The painting of Llewellyn and Elodie Latham, who had donated the money that initially funded the library, hung above.

"Hi there." She smiled at her friend. Clara had helped her uncover some of her family's past when she'd just moved to the island, and Priscilla had come to appreciate her warmth and friendliness as well as her knowledge of the island and its history.

"You look lost," Clara said.

"Just uncertain." Priscilla walked toward the counter. "I'm interested in finding out more about Nathaniel Hawthorne."

"Ah. One of our favorite local authors. He's beloved around these parts." Clara wore a long skirt and a silky blouse, and her dark hair was pulled back into a low ponytail.

"He's local?" Priscilla thought it was funny that Clara was talking about him like he was still alive.

"Well, Boston. And Salem. Concord. Really, all of Eastern Massachusetts. Which makes him a hometown hero." She came around the counter. "Come on. You know where the biographies are. I'm sure we have a few about him."

"I do indeed. Thank you." Priscilla went up a flight of wooden stairs to the second floor and into the section for biographies. It only took her a moment to locate a few on Nathaniel Hawthorne.

Priscilla grasped the books and settled in at one of the carrels. She picked up the least intimidating biography first and skimmed the table of contents. Might as well start at the beginning, she decided. She skimmed the first few chapters and learned a great deal about the author. She'd thought he had written his books in Puritan times, since that was when *The Scarlet Letter* was set, but it turned out he wasn't born until 1804, and he grew up in Salem, Massachusetts. No wonder his stories were so creepy. One of his ancestors had been a judge during the Salem witch trials—one of the darker periods of American history, but a fascinating one. Hawthorne worked at the Custom House in Boston, where he wrote some of his early works. He was friends with the likes of Ralph Waldo Emerson and Herman Melville, and—

"How's it going?"

Priscilla looked up. It took her a moment to remember she was in the library in Martha's Vineyard, not an old farmhouse in the Berkshires. Clara stood in front of her, looking at her expectantly. She had no idea how much time had passed since she'd sat down, but if Clara had come up to check on her, she assumed it had been more than a few minutes.

"I'll take that blank stare to mean you're totally absorbed."

"It's fascinating," Priscilla said. She used a scrap of paper to mark her page. "But I'm not sure it's getting me any closer to finding the answers I'm looking for."

"Maybe I can help. What are you trying to find out?"

Priscilla paused for a moment. She could trust Clara to keep this quiet, she realized. If you couldn't trust a librarian with information, whom could you trust?

"I'm doing some research into that man who lived on the houseboat. The one who disappeared."

Clara's eyes widened, and she nodded and gestured for Priscilla to go on.

"His name was Bart Flask, but I haven't been able to turn up anything useful about him. I've found out his dog—the one that disappeared that same night—was named Hawthorne, and I was hoping I could learn something about Nathaniel Hawthorne that would give me some insight into who the man was or what he was like."

"Huh." Clara rested her elbow on the carrel and was quiet for a minute.

"Is there anything obvious about Nathaniel Hawthorne that I'm missing? Some reference to one of his books or something?"

Clara didn't say anything for a moment. Priscilla wasn't sure what to think. Then, finally, Clara shook her head. "No, I can't see anything obvious that would explain why this man would name his dog after the writer. I suppose there are all kinds of reasons people do things like that. Maybe he's just a big fan of Hester Prynne."

Priscilla recognized that as the name of the heroine in *The Scarlet Letter*—a Puritan woman who gets pregnant outside of marriage and is forced to wear a red *A* on her clothing, the mark of her adultery. But Clara looked like she wanted to say something else, so Priscilla waited, giving Clara a minute to think.

"What strikes me, actually, is not the name of the dog but the name of the man," Clara finally said.

"What do you mean?"

"It's an odd name, isn't it? Bart Flask?" She said each of the names carefully.

"Yes, I suppose it is."

"I haven't heard the name Flask too many times."

"No, I suppose you're right. I haven't either." She wasn't sure where Clara was going with this, but she could see Clara was thinking through something.

"The only instance I can think of, in fact, is the third mate of the *Pequod*."

Priscilla stared at Clara. Was that supposed to make sense? What was the *Pequod*?

"*Moby-Dick*. Don't tell me you've never read *Moby-Dick*. You can't live on Martha's Vineyard and not know *Moby-Dick*."

Priscilla felt a wave of shame hit her, but then she saw that Clara was laughing, and she realized Clara was teasing her.

"Sorry. I have to confess I haven't. It always seemed so...long. And...well, whaley."

Clara let out a laugh. "Yes, I suppose you learn more than anyone ever needs to know about whales by reading that book. But really, it's wonderful. Totally fascinating, and such an interesting way to learn about the history of this island."

"It takes place here?"

"Well, technically they set off from Nantucket, not Martha's Vineyard, and travel around the world. Have you been to the Melville House in Edgartown? The man Captain Ahab was modeled after supposedly lived at 80 Water Street. You should check it out. Anyway, his mates are from nearby as well: Starbuck is from Nantucket, and Flask is from Martha's Vineyard."

"Interesting." Could it just be a coincidence? A random fluke that this man who moved to a boat off Martha's Vineyard happened to share a name with a literary character from here? Looking at Clara's face, she was beginning to doubt it.

"Bart is an interesting name too."

"I thought it was probably short for Bartholomew."

Clara nodded. "Not as uncommon as Flask, but not especially common either, not anymore anyway."

"I found a few Bartholomews online, but none who looked like the right guy." Priscilla laughed. "Are there any Bartholomews in *Moby-Dick*?"

Clara smiled. "No. But there is a famous Bartholomew around these parts. Bartholomew Gosnold. He's the explorer who first discovered Martha's Vineyard."

Priscilla couldn't believe it. "You're serious?"

Clara grimaced and nodded.

Priscilla let out a long breath. "Well, I guess there goes that idea."

"You don't know for sure Bart Flask is a fake name," Clara said. But the look on her face said what Priscilla was thinking. It had to be a made-up name. The man on the houseboat had registered with the marina under the names of two people known for their association with Martha's Vineyard.

She was back to square one.

"I need to tell the police," she said.

"Yep," Clara said. "You probably do."

CHAPTER THIRTEEN

Priscilla pulled out the business card Officer Brown had given to her as soon as she got back to her car.

"Come on, come on, pick up," she said under her breath. Her first response had been to call Gerald to let him know what she'd found out, but after his warning to stay out of it, Priscilla had decided it might be better to start with the police.

"Officer Brown." Priscilla recognized the voice of the police-woman who had talked with her before.

"Hi, this is Priscilla Grant. I'm calling because I've learned something about Bart Flask that I think you might be interested in."

"Oh yeah? What's that?" If she was surprised that Priscilla knew the man's name, she didn't say so. Maybe Gerald had let them know the secret was out.

"Are you at the station?"

"I'm at the courthouse now, but I'm on my way back. How about I meet you there in ten minutes?"

"I'll see you then."

Priscilla was a few minutes early, but when she walked into the station, she was ushered back toward the same small room where she'd chatted with Officer Brown before. The police officer walked in a few moments later with her yellow legal pad in one hand and a cup of coffee in the other.

"Would you like some water? Coffee?" the officer asked. She was wearing the dark blue uniform of the Tisbury police force, her shirt neatly tucked into her pants and her shoes polished. But as she was sitting down, Priscilla noticed that her belt buckle, mostly covered by her shirt, was decorated with the smallest line of rhinestones.

"I'd love some herbal tea, if you have any," Priscilla said.

The officer laughed, but not in a mean way. "I've been trying to get them to stock anything but this sludge for years." She gestured at her paper cup. "I'm afraid herbal tea would be too far out for the guys around here."

Priscilla laughed. "In that case, I think I'm good."

"All right then." Officer Brown looked up at her. "You said you had some information on our missing boater?"

"Bart Flask." Priscilla nodded. "That's what you've been calling him, right?"

The officer nodded uncertainly.

"That's the name he used when he registered at the marina, right?"

The officer nodded again. "I'm not even going to ask how you knew that."

"It's better that way," Priscilla agreed. "Anyway, I'm afraid that's not his real name."

"What do you mean?"

Priscilla quickly explained the references to *Moby-Dick* and the explorer who discovered Martha's Vineyard.

Officer Brown let out a low whistle. "Are you sure?"

"I guess there is a very slim chance that could be his real name and the references to Martha's Vineyard are just coincidental," Priscilla said, but she was pretty sure her skepticism was evident in her voice. "But I'm guessing you haven't been able to turn up much under that name."

The police officer sighed this time, and then she shook her head.

"The newspaper said you had a suspect in custody. Has he told you anything about Bart Flask?"

"I'm not at liberty to say."

"He told me he didn't know the man and had never been on the boat."

Officer Brown's eyebrows rose. "You talked to him?"

"A few days ago. Just informally, of course. A friendly visit. The topic of the boat came up."

"Of course it did." Officer Brown shook her head.

"How about the laptop? Have you been able to get into that yet? Or what about the key? Any idea what that opens?"

Officer Brown laughed. "You're just full of questions, aren't you?"

"I *was* the one who found the key," Priscilla reminded her, hoping that would count for something.

"I remember." The woman took a sip of her coffee and grimaced. "I'm afraid I'm not allowed to tell you anything about an open investigation though."

Priscilla nodded and started to rise.

"I'm not allowed to tell you anything," the woman said again. "Don't get me wrong, I sure do appreciate the tip about the name Bart Flask. But even if there was any news to tell you, I couldn't pass it along."

Priscilla hesitated. "Are you saying…"

"I'm not saying anything," the policewoman said. "I'm just saying that even if there was any news about the key or the computer, I wouldn't be allowed to tell you about it."

Priscilla felt a slow smile creep across her face. "I understand perfectly." Officer Brown was telling her there was no news on either of those fronts. She was saying it without saying it: they hadn't gotten into the laptop, nor had they discovered what the key belonged to.

"I can say that we have gotten ahold of some evidence that we're hopeful will lead to more answers soon."

"But let me guess. You can't tell me what it is." Priscilla wondered what it could be. Was she talking about the fingerprints on the knife? Another sighting of the man?

"That's correct." The officer smiled like they were sharing a private joke. "Thank you for your time." She escorted Priscilla back to the front of the station, and as Priscilla was about to walk out the door, she heard Officer Brown already on her phone: "Holmes? That's not his real name. Flask is a fake name."

Priscilla smiled as she walked out into the sunlight. She wasn't any closer to finding out what had happened to the man, but she was still one step ahead of the police, and she had to admit that felt good.

CHAPTER FOURTEEN

The sun was setting as Priscilla made her way to Gerald's that evening. The days were getting shorter, and the sun was setting a few minutes earlier each day, but the dusky twilight cast the roads and yards in an almost ethereal glow. She wouldn't be at Gerald's long—she had a meeting at church to talk about getting the homeless shelter up and running for the season. She was just going to swing by his place and pick up the clothes they had decided to use for the quilt. The night before, Gerald had selected a Starflower quilt pattern from the books they'd reviewed, and Priscilla was ready to start working on the quilt. Since the sewing machine and all of her supplies were at her place, it made sense for her to have the fabric at her home as well.

She stood on the front porch and rang the doorbell. She waited, but there didn't seem to be any movement inside. Was he here? His black SUV was in the driveway. The lights were on. She tried again and waited, but there was still no answer. That was strange.

She pulled her phone out of her purse and dialed his number. It rang and rang, and he didn't pick up. Maybe something was wrong. He'd been expecting her, and she knew he was here. Priscilla hesitated then took a deep breath and pushed open the front door.

"Gerald?" She stepped into the foyer and looked around. The lights were on in the kitchen and the living room. "Gerald, are you here?"

There was no answer. She was starting to get worried. Had he fallen? Was he hurt? She stepped into the living room, but he wasn't there. Then she moved toward the kitchen. Thank goodness, there he was. Hunched over a laptop, staring at something on the screen. What in the world? He still didn't seem to hear her or notice her. She saw that he was looking at some grainy black-and-white video.

"Gerald?" she said loudly and stepped into the kitchen.

Gerald jumped in his chair, and his hand flew to his heart. "Priscilla. I'm so sorry. I didn't hear you come in." He took some earbuds from his ears. Ah. That explained it. From here, she could see the wires that connected to the laptop. On his screen was an image of water.

"I'm sorry to scare you. I rang the bell twice and I called you, but there was no answer. I was starting to fear you'd had a heart attack or something, so I barged in. I'm so sorry to interrupt..."

"No, I'm sorry." He pushed the space bar, and the image on his screen froze. Priscilla looked again and saw that it was not just water. It was a marina. And way out at the far edge of the screen, there was a boat. A houseboat. "I was absorbed in this, and I didn't hear a thing. I'm sorry."

"What is that?" Priscilla asked. But even as she said the words, she knew what it was.

Gerald didn't answer right away.

"Is that the security footage from the marina?" She moved closer to get a better look. There must have been some night vision technology that meant you could see what was happening even though the sky was dark. The houseboat was so far out in the marina that it was hard to see, but because there weren't many other boats moored in the marina at this time of year, it made it easier to make out. "You got it from Lloyd and Fisher?"

Gerald sighed. "Yes. The court order came through today. They released the footage. This is a copy."

Ah. That must have been why Officer Brown had been at the courthouse when Priscilla had called this afternoon.

"Anything interesting?"

"Not yet."

Priscilla knew Gerald wanted her to stay out of this. He'd made that abundantly clear. But they'd finally gotten the security camera footage that showed what had really happened that night.

"Well, don't let me interrupt. Feel free to keep watching."

Gerald looked from her, back to the screen, and then back at Priscilla. He wanted to keep watching, she could tell. And she wanted him to as well.

"I'll just sit here quietly," she said, lowering herself into the chair next to Gerald. She set her purse on the floor and scooted the chair forward. She kept a big smile pasted on her face.

Gerald was still hesitating. Then the lines in his face relaxed, and he seemed to make some sort of decision. "April Brown told me you came into the station today," he said. "She said you'd figured out that Bart Flask was not the guy's real name."

"That's right," she said. "That name was a dead end, I'm afraid."

Gerald nodded. "You were right about that." And then, without another word of explanation, he handed her one of the earbuds, put the other in his ear, and started the video.

Priscilla wanted to laugh. Just last night he'd been warning her to stay out of things, but it seemed that he was letting her watch the video with him because she hadn't stayed out of things after all. Well, whatever the reason, she was glad. She focused on the screen.

"What about Frank Ripley? How does this footage change what's happening with him?"

Gerald didn't answer for a moment. Then he said, "Frank was released today. They didn't have enough evidence to hold him."

"What?"

"Well, without a body or anything, they really couldn't hold him. But what we turn up here will obviously affect that. Or not, depending."

Priscilla nodded and watched the footage. The little white numbers at the top of the screen told her it was ten thirty on Thursday night. The marina was still. There was a light on in the houseboat, but there was no movement. The video was playing at triple speed, but there was nothing to see.

"Where is the camera mounted?" she asked.

"At the top of a wooden post at the edge of the dock," he answered. She nodded. That made sense. That was the farthest out it could get and still be attached to land.

The only sound in the video was the sped up noise of waves lapping against the dock.

"Has it been like this since the beginning?" she asked.

"Yes. The most exciting thing I've seen so far is a bird flying across the screen," he said.

She nodded and kept watching. For a while nothing else happened. There was no movement. Nothing. Then, at just past 11:10, a small boat appeared at the far left side of the screen.

"What's that?"

Gerald paused the video. All they could tell about the boat from here was that it was small.

"Where did it come from?" she asked.

Gerald shook his head. "Could be from one of the private boat slips," he said. "Or the public boat launch."

"Or from somewhere outside the marina altogether," she added. He nodded and started the video again.

The small boat slowly crossed the water of the marina. It had a motor and was some sort of fishing boat or other small craft. Those were common enough around here. There appeared to be one person inside, but it was so far off that she couldn't tell much about him.

They watched as, slowly but steadily, the small boat headed straight for the houseboat. There was no mistaking where it was going. Priscilla held her breath. Gerald slowed the footage, and they watched as the boat pulled up to the houseboat and tied up to the platform around it.

Whoever was in the small boat climbed out, carrying something bulky under one arm. He went to the door of the cabin, pushed it open, and disappeared inside.

Then the footage ended.

"Wait. What happened?" Priscilla asked.

Gerald was already moving his cursor around, trying to make sense of things. The bar at the bottom of the screen showed they were at the end of the video. "They didn't give us the whole night," he said. It was the closest to angry she'd ever heard him.

"That's it? That's all the video you have?" She couldn't believe it. How could the footage just cut off right when they needed it?

He had clicked over to the icon of the thumb drive the video had been saved on and looked through its folders. There was just this one video, and it ended here, right at the time when this mysterious man had boarded the houseboat.

Gerald muttered something under his breath and pulled out his phone. He dialed a number and started talking into the phone, expressing his frustration about the footage they'd been given. While he was doing that, Priscilla moved the bar under the video back again and took another look at the footage.

Whoever was on the other end of the line with Gerald also seemed to be up in arms about the footage they'd been given. They had not gotten the footage of the whole night like they had been promised. Gerald and whoever he was talking with were going back and forth about what to do next. Should they go back to Lloyd and Fisher and demand the rest of the footage? Or should they go straight to the judge first thing in the morning? She heard something about the lawyers already being on the case.

"I don't know who it is. Do you know who the man is?" Gerald said. "I don't see how anyone could make it out based on what we have. We need the whole video—"

Priscilla saw a little magnifying glass icon at the bottom of the screen and tried it out. She could use it to zoom in on a section of the footage, so she zoomed in on the image of the man tying up to the houseboat. She was surprised by how big you could make it. The image was grainy at this size, but you could still make out a fair amount.

"I agree with the counsel. I say we go straight to the judge. This is an obstruction of justice," Gerald was saying.

Priscilla froze the video and focused on the image of the person tying up to the houseboat. It was a man, she could see that clearly now. And the man looked kind of familiar. It was hard to tell, with the image so grainy. The night was dark and the camera far away. But still, she could see the distinct image of a man.

And if she wasn't mistaken, it was a man she knew.

She started the video again and watched as the man in the video tied up and stepped out of the boat again. Yes, she knew this man. She was sure of it.

"Gerald," she said. He'd gotten up and was pacing across the kitchen floor, arguing with whomever was on the other end of the line. "Gerald," she tried again.

This time he stopped pacing and looked at her.

She pointed at the screen, where the image of the familiar man was pushing open the door of the houseboat cab, a package tucked under one arm.

"I know who this man is."

CHAPTER FIFTEEN

Gerald squinted at the computer screen. "I'll have to call you back," he said into the phone. Then he ended the call, set the phone down, and turned back to the screen. "Oh my."

"That's Dan Galvin," Priscilla said. "Trudy's husband."

"Oh my," he repeated, shaking his head. "It *is* Dan, isn't it?"

The image on the screen was blurry and grainy, but his face was unmistakable. There were those chiseled cheeks, that pointy chin Priscilla had come to know in the few months she'd been here. But Dan was so soft-spoken. So well-mannered, if a bit, well, intellectual. He was a marine biologist, for goodness' sake. How could a scientist be responsible for all this? He couldn't be behind the disappearance on the houseboat, could he?

"What would Dan be doing on the boat the night this man disappeared?" she asked.

Gerald shook his head. "There's one obvious explanation."

"No way." Priscilla couldn't believe it. But there it was. Right there on the video. Dan approaching the boat in the dead of night, the same night the boat was cut loose and the man and dog vanished.

"I don't know," Gerald said. "But I can tell you one thing. We're going to find out."

Gerald went off to meet up with the police and discuss what they'd seen on the video, and Priscilla started toward town. She would be late for the meeting at church, but she could still make it in time for the end. But as she neared the little downtown area, passing Maypop Antiques and the St. Michael's Thrift Store and the Brown Jug, a neat little store with gourmet cheeses and condiments, she couldn't fathom sitting through a boring meeting about recruiting and training volunteers to set up the folding beds the shelter used. Her mind was far away, on a little boat in the marina. Could Dan really have been behind the man's disappearance? It seemed so crazy, and yet there he was, caught on the footage. Did he have an evil twin somewhere?

Instead of turning into the small parking lot at the side of the brick church building, Priscilla kept right on driving, and before she had even admitted to herself where she was headed, she had pulled up in front of Trudy and Dan's house. They lived in a two-story cottage painted a light gray. The house was in a nice area, with private neighborhood beach access and a well-run neighborhood organization, but the houses were all relatively modest. There was a stone wall in front of the lawn as it sloped down to the street, and phlox and hydrangeas lined the flagstone walkway. Lights were on inside the house. Priscilla hurried to the front door and knocked.

"Oh! Hi, Priscilla. Come in, come in." Trudy stepped back and ushered her inside. "What a nice surprise. What brings you here? Ooh, did you hear about the guy who went missing in the harbor? Isn't it crazy? Would you like some tea?"

Priscilla didn't even know where to start answering questions, but it didn't seem to matter because Trudy was already leading her into the kitchen and setting the kettle on.

"Chamomile, mint, or Earl Grey? Well, I guess you probably don't want Earl Grey at this time of night. Oh. And I have green tea too, but I can't stand the taste of the stuff myself. How about you?"

Trudy was looking at her expectantly, her smile wide. If she knew Dan was responsible for what had happened out there on that boat, she was very good at hiding it.

Trudy set a basket of tea bags on the granite counter. The kitchen had white cabinets and stainless steel appliances and was bright and open, like the rest of the house. A row of cobalt-blue glass vases lined one shelf, giving the room a pop of color.

"Chamomile, please." It was no use telling Trudy that she hadn't come for tea. It was usually best to just let Trudy do her thing. And truthfully, Priscilla hadn't really planned out what she was going to say, so she welcomed the few moments to gather her thoughts. She looked around and tried to figure out how to bring this up. She saw that the television was on, with the image of an English country house paused on the screen.

"I was just watching *Midsomer Murders*," Trudy said, following the direction of her gaze. "Have you ever watched the show? It's set in the English countryside, and it's really addicting."

"I'll have to check it out," Priscilla said. Then, as if it had just occurred to her, "Is Dan here?"

"No, he's in Florida at some conference for the next few days. Something about plankton or something. Sounds super boring to me, hence the reason I'm binge-watching the shows he doesn't have the patience for."

"Oh." He was gone? She hadn't prepared for that either. That was not going to sit well with the police or the Coast Guard, she knew that.

"What's wrong, Priscilla?"

Trudy may be preternaturally upbeat, but she wasn't dumb, and she must have picked up on the fact that Priscilla was nervous. Priscilla tried to figure out how to respond.

"Did something happen?"

"No. I mean, not today. Maybe not any day."

Trudy looked at her, her head tilted, her arms crossed over her chest.

"It's just that—has Dan been going out at night recently?"

"What?"

As soon as the words were out of her mouth, she regretted them. Hopefully Trudy wouldn't think she meant...

"You know that houseboat? The one that was in the harbor?"

"Yes...," Trudy said uncertainly. "What about it?"

Priscilla thought fast, but she couldn't come up with any good way to say this. She decided to just say it and get it out there.

"I was just at Gerald's. Since the Coast Guard found the boat, they've been investigating the disappearance along with the police. And they got ahold of some footage from the marina on the night the man disappeared."

"Okay…"

"I saw the footage, Trudy, and it's the strangest thing. You can see that at about eleven on Thursday night, the same night the guy disappeared and the houseboat was cut free, a small boat approaches the houseboat." She paused. "Dan has a boat, right?"

Trudy nodded warily. Dan commuted back and forth to Woods Hole on the ferry, but Priscilla knew he had a smaller boat that he used in his spare time. Trudy looked more scared than anything now. "He hasn't put it up for the season yet because he's still been fishing on the weekends. It's moored at the town docks."

Priscilla knew the spots at the town dock were hard to come by, as they almost never turned over from year to year. Only those who had been in Tisbury for many years had them—a benefit of being a longtime local, she supposed. Not that it mattered at the moment.

"The weird thing is, in that video you can see someone pull up to the houseboat that night. And it's Dan."

"What? What do you mean, it's Dan?"

Priscilla tried again. "You can see the man quite clearly in the footage. He ties his boat to the houseboat, gets off, and goes into the houseboat. And it's Dan."

"That's not possible." The kettle started whistling, but Trudy didn't seem to notice.

"I know it doesn't seem likely, which is why I wanted to come and say something about it. I'm sure the police are going to want to talk to him, and—"

"The police?" Trudy shook her head. "You've seen this video?"

Priscilla nodded then moved to turn off the kettle. "I wanted to warn you about it so it wasn't such a shock when they show up. But also, I figured there had to be some mistake. Like, does Dan have a twin or something that I don't know about?"

"No." Trudy shook her head. "He has a sister, but that's it. She lives in Worcester."

"But then, how—"

"Are you sure it was him?"

"It sure looked like him," Priscilla said. "The same cheeks, the same chin." She took a breath. "Were you with him at that time on Thursday night? Maybe there's some good excuse?"

Trudy sighed. "Until now, I would have sworn he was with me the whole time. But the truth is, I had a migraine Thursday night, so I took some medication that knocks me out. It helps with the headache, but I'm dead to the world."

"So you're saying Dan could have gone out, and you wouldn't have known?" Priscilla felt a sense of dread wash over her. She hadn't realized how much she'd been hoping she was wrong. But now that it seemed like it was really possible it had been Dan, she wasn't sure what to do.

Trudy's face had gone pale, and she was uncharacteristically quiet. But she nodded slowly.

Priscilla didn't know what to say.

"I'm calling him." Trudy reached for the cordless phone on the counter. Priscilla held her breath while she dialed, but the line rang and rang, and no one picked up. "Where is he?" Trudy muttered and tried the number again, but there was no answer.

"Trudy, I'm sorry, I . . ."

There was a knock at the door. Priscilla glanced out the kitchen window and saw a police car in the driveway.

"No. Thank you for warning me," Trudy said. "I would have had a heart attack if they'd shown up without any warning." She still looked pale, but she moved around the counter toward the front door.

"Hi, Ms. Galvin. I'm sorry to bother you, but I was hoping I could ask you a few questions." Priscilla recognized the voice of Officer Holmes, April Brown's partner. "Is your husband at home?"

"Come in." Trudy stepped back. Both Officer Holmes and Officer Brown stepped inside. Officer Brown saw Priscilla, and her eyes widened. "I'm afraid Dan isn't home at the moment. But you've met my cousin, Priscilla, I think," Trudy said as if this was the most normal conversation in the world.

Priscilla saw recognition in Officer Brown's eyes. She knew why Priscilla was here.

"Yes. Nice to see you again, Ms. Grant," Officer Brown said. "But I'm afraid we need to ask Ms. Galvin some questions."

"Of course." Priscilla understood. She needed to clear out so the police could do their work. As if she hadn't been the one to identify the man in the video and steer them all in the right direction. As if they would be able to get anything out of her cousin that Priscilla hadn't already gotten. "It's been lovely to see you, Trudy. Call me if you need anything."

She hitched up her purse and headed out, letting the front door fall closed behind her.

CHAPTER SIXTEEN

Priscilla slept badly, tossing and turning throughout the night as she worried about Dan, about Trudy, and about whatever had happened on the boat that night. Trudy had known nothing about Dan's visit to the boat; she was sure of that. The pained look on her face when Priscilla told her what she'd seen and the scared look in her eyes when the police showed up confirmed it. Whatever Dan had done, Trudy was innocent. But Priscilla also knew that didn't make it easier for Trudy, who now no doubt had all kinds of questions and suspicions about her husband.

Finally, when the gray light of a misty dawn broke through the curtains, Priscilla pushed herself out of bed and padded into the kitchen, knotting her bathrobe around her. She started the coffee then went out to get the newspaper. As the rich scent of coffee filled the kitchen, she paged through the paper. The hunt for the missing boater was still front-page news.

"Search for Missing Boater Continues; Time Is Running Out," the headline read.

Well, that was dire. But she supposed it was true. If the man was still alive somewhere, he could be in danger, and every day that passed, the situation no doubt got worse for him.

She sat down at the table with a cup of coffee and a bowl of oatmeal, and she read the article as she ate. It didn't mention that the suspect they'd held had been released, and there was no new information she could glean. She was grateful to see that news about Dan hadn't yet leaked to the press, but that was as much as she could learn.

When she was finished, she washed out her bowl and spent some time praying for the coming day, and then she reached for the phone. She was dying to call Trudy. Was it too early? She glanced at the clock and realized it was only seven thirty. Yes, too early. Trudy had probably been up late. But what could Priscilla do? She couldn't just sit here waiting to hear what had happened. Would Trudy have filled her sister in last night? She decided to send a text to Joan.

Have you talked to Trudy recently?

There. That looked innocuous. If Joan didn't know what she was talking about, it wouldn't be enough to make her suspicious. Priscilla hit Send and set the phone down on the counter. A moment later, it rang.

"Oh my goodness, Priscilla, I'm so glad you texted." It was Joan, and she was speaking really quickly. "I was waiting because I wasn't sure you would be up, but I am dying to hear what happened last night."

"I take that to mean you did hear from Trudy?"

"Gail and I both woke up to a strange text from her. She said the police came last night and asked her where Dan was Thursday night and that you came and warned her about it. She can't get ahold of Dan, and she's really worried."

"Oh dear." Priscilla bit her lip. "I'm so sorry."

"But what happened? She must have turned her phone off because she hasn't responded to my texts asking her what is going on."

Priscilla told Joan what had happened last night. "So the police haven't talked to Dan yet?"

"They don't know where he is. He's not answering his cell phone. Trudy says it's probably not picking up a signal, but who knows. They're trying to figure out where the conference is supposed to be but apparently haven't gotten ahold of him yet."

Joan said she had to work at the clinic that morning but would keep her phone on and would let Priscilla know what she heard.

Priscilla hung up and tried to figure out what else she could do. She was antsy. Now that Frank Ripley had been released from custody, maybe she could go talk to him. But he hadn't exactly responded well the first time she'd tried. Showing up now would hardly lead to a better result. Why would he suddenly confess to her when he hadn't to the police? She'd need to think a bit more and try to figure out how to get more out of Frank.

Well, she realized, she could start working on that quilt for Gerald. But in all the excitement last night, she had never actually gotten the fabric from him. He would no doubt be leaving for work soon, but if she caught him before he left, maybe she could grab at least some of the fabric and get started working on that today. That would give her something to do other than sit here and worry about Trudy.

She hopped in her car and drove the now-familiar route to Gerald's house. Just as she was stepping onto the porch, the door opened and he stepped out.

"Oh." He jumped back. "Priscilla. Hi."

"I'm sorry to startle you," she said. "And for coming over so early. I realized I didn't grab the fabric last night after all, and I was hoping I could get it now so I could start working today."

"Huh?" He looked lost for a moment, and then he nodded. "Oh, sure. Of course." He hesitated. "I'm really sorry, Priscilla. I have to run. We found the dog."

"What? You found Hawthorne?"

"Hawthorne?" Gerald blinked. "The dog's name is Hawthorne?"

"Yes. Didn't I tell you that?"

He sighed. "I'm not even going to ask how you knew that." There was something like amusement mixed with consternation on his face. "But yes, the missing dog has turned up in Woods Hole. The police in Falmouth called to report it just this morning."

"Really?" That was great news! "He was wearing the collar?"

Gerald hesitated. "I'm not sure about a collar. But they're sure this is the right dog."

"He had a collar when he was on the boat."

Gerald nodded. "We'll see when we get there."

"What about the owner?" Priscilla continued. "Did you find him?"

"No sign of him yet, but we're getting closer. I'm going now to meet with the police, and then we're heading over to Falmouth in a few minutes. So I have to run. But the fabric is in the living room. Go in and grab what you need. If you turn the lock on the handle, the door will lock behind you."

"Oh. Okay. Thank you."

With that, he saluted her and hurried off the porch. With uncertainty, she watched him drive off. Was he really going to let her just go into his house when he wasn't there? She felt flattered. And, if she were honest, a tad nervous.

But she turned and stepped inside, making her way into the living room uncertainly. There were the clothes, sorted into the bins they'd decided on. There was one with the clothes she didn't think they could use and two others full of clothes she thought might work, sorted by color.

She picked up the top bin. It wasn't very heavy, and she easily carried it to her car and plopped it into her trunk. She went back inside for the next bin but paused a moment in the hallway. His office was just down there. He wouldn't even know if she went in and looked around... But as quickly as the thought had come, she dismissed it. Gerald trusted her. She needed to be worthy of that trust. She grabbed the second bin, and on her way out, she turned the lock so the door would latch behind her.

As she loaded the second bin into her car, she ran through what Gerald had told her. They'd found the missing man's dog. This was great—truly it was.

But something about it still didn't add up for Priscilla.

She knew no one believed that she'd heard the dog barking out on the water, rounding the point, the night the man disappeared. And maybe they were right. Maybe she'd heard wrong.

But if she was right, if she had heard what she thought she'd heard, there was no way the dog should have ended up in Woods Hole.

Maybe she wasn't right. As they had already reminded her, they were the experts and she was not. But...

She thought for a moment. Something else was off.

Gerald hadn't known the dog's name. But Randy had said that he'd learned the dog's name by reading it on his collar. She didn't know if the dog that had been found in Woods Hole was wearing a collar.

Of course, even if it wasn't wearing one, it was possible that the collar had fallen off. Or been taken off. But it was also possible that this wasn't the same dog, wasn't it? It wasn't like golden retrievers were a rare breed. How could they be so sure this was the dog that had been living on the houseboat?

Priscilla slammed her trunk shut. She realized that she didn't know enough to say one way or the other, and she was sure the experts would get to the bottom of it. The fact that the dog had turned up in Woods Hole seemed to indicate that Gerald and the police were right. They now had the evidence that confirmed their suspicion.

But still, she couldn't help but wonder whether it was possible that the authorities were so sure the dog and its owner had left the island that they were reaching the wrong conclusions. Were they only seeing the clues that fit their accepted narrative?

Priscilla couldn't answer that. And she suspected talking with Dan might change things. But she did know that she had already figured out more than the experts at several points in this mystery so far. It was possible she was right about this too. What if she were right, and the dog—and owner—hadn't made it back to the mainland after all?

She knew she would have to wait to hear what they said about the dog when Gerald got back. But in the meantime…she didn't have to just sit around and wait. She might be wrong, but that didn't mean it wasn't worth checking out whether her suspicions were right.

Priscilla opened the car door and slipped into the driver's seat. She would get to work on the quilt later. First, there was a stop she had to make.

CHAPTER SEVENTEEN

Priscilla checked her phone to make sure she hadn't missed any calls from Joan or from Trudy. Nothing. Then she drove to Edgartown and parked in front of Micawber Books on a bustling stretch of Winter Street. The bookstore was nestled in a historic storefront and was flanked by a tea room that served the most delicious scones she'd ever tasted and a store that sold nothing but lanterns and address plates for the outside of homes. People took both seriously around these parts.

She stepped inside the bookstore and let the door fall closed behind her. Big windows at the front let in lots of natural light, and tables near the windows were piled with stacks of best sellers and staff recommendations. Toward the back of the store, comfy blue-and-white striped armchairs were arranged around a fireplace, and pictures of iconic book covers decorated the soothing bluish-gray walls. Wide-plank pine floors creaked as Priscilla walked, and long rows of rosewood shelves were filled with books of every kind. Fiction ran along one whole wall, and history and biographies took up the far wall. Cookbooks ran down one shelf, and Priscilla itched to go over and page through them. She had left most of her cookbooks back in Kansas, and she loved flipping through them, seeing the beautiful pictures and imagining the flavors. But on the front table was a new book by one of her favorite authors. She wrote big, dramatic, touching stories that always made you cry, and Priscilla had been wanting to read this one for a long time. She read the description on the front flap and then turned the book over and read through the endorsements on the back. Maybe she should just—

"Priscilla!"

She looked up and saw Sara smiling at her. "It's good to see you." Sara pointed at the book in Priscilla's hand. "That is phenomenal. Have you read her other books?"

Priscilla nodded. "I love the way her characters always seem so realistic, like they could be real people."

"Then you're going to love that one. It's her best yet."

Priscilla looked down at the book. It was a hardcover and not cheap... but then, the price wasn't really *all* that much, considering how many hours of enjoyment she would get out of reading it. And buying the book would benefit Sara.

"Okay," she said, tucking it under her arm. "Sold."

"Well, that was easy." Sara laughed. She started toward the register, and Priscilla followed. "Now, why do I have the feeling you didn't come in here just to buy a book?"

Priscilla set the book on the wooden counter. "It's true that wasn't my intention, but I can't say I'm disappointed."

Sara rang up the purchase.

"That's not the right price," Priscilla said. The total Sara had rung up was a good third off the price marked on the cover.

"It's the friends-and-family discount," Sara said. "Or, really, the discount I give to people I like."

"You can't beat that." Priscilla handed over her credit card. "Actually, I came to see if you had any news about that house across the street. They never responded to my phone call."

"I haven't heard back from Adam or Catherine either," she said, "but I did take Atticus out for a walk last night, and it's possible I might have let him roam around to the side of the house, where obviously I had to go back and get him."

Atticus was Sara's elderly teacup Chihuahua. Priscilla smiled, imagining the scenario.

"And I did see a light on at the back of the house, in what I assume is one of the second-floor bedrooms."

"And you're sure the Phillips family wouldn't have come back in the off-season?" Priscilla asked.

"I can't say I'm sure. All I can say is we've owned our house for ten years, and I've never once seen them here after August. But who knows?" Sara tucked the book into a paper bag marked with the Micawber Books logo. "I'll let you know if I hear anything from them," she said, handing the bag to Priscilla. "And if you want to swing by the house again, you're more than welcome to use my driveway as home base."

"Thanks so much."

"Sure thing."

Priscilla turned to go, but Sara said, "Oh, by the way, I talked to my mom a little while ago. She told me you talked to Aunt Trudy last night. She said they got ahold of Uncle Dan."

"Well, that's good news." Priscilla's heart raced. Maybe now they'd finally get answers about what he was doing in that video. "What did he have to say about what happened?"

"Nothing much so far, at least nothing we know about. He said he was on his way back from Florida and told Aunt Trudy he'd explain when he got home."

"Do they know when that will be?"

"I think today. I don't know. I didn't get any details. It sounds like Aunt Trudy doesn't have too many yet. But I'm sure we'll hear them as soon as they come out. That's how the grapevine works around these parts."

"Well, I'd sure love to be kept in the loop if you do hear what's going on," Priscilla said.

"Of course. You're friends and family, remember?"

Priscilla thanked her and walked out, her wallet a bit lighter but her heart full. Friends and family. This place was starting to feel more like home every day.

A few minutes later, she pulled up in front of Sara's place and studied the house across the street. It looked the same as it had Sunday. It was an attractive house, with its welcoming front porch and its symmetrical facade. It was daytime, so she couldn't tell if any lights were on, and she couldn't see anyone moving around inside. But that didn't mean no one was there.

She tried to think realistically. What were the chances that she'd managed to find the exact house where the missing man had been hiding out? She had to admit they seemed slim. Especially since Edgartown was to the east of her home, and it had sounded like she'd heard the dog on the west side of the point. But she couldn't shake the sound of that eerie, echoing barking that floated so strangely across the water. Maybe Gerald was right. Maybe the water had been doing weird things to the sound. What she did know was that she'd heard it, for sure.

Then again, maybe the dog that had turned up in Woods Hole really was Hawthorne. If that was true, she would have to admit that she'd been wrong.

But her gut was telling her she wasn't. It was the same sense of certainty she'd felt when she'd gone out to check on the barn after she'd heard lightning strike a little too close for comfort. Gary had insisted it hit a tree out in the windbreak, but Priscilla hadn't been so sure. Trusting her gut had meant they'd had time to get all the cows out before that section of the barn burned to the ground. It was that same sense that had told her something was terribly wrong with Gary and insisted he go to the doctor. Priscilla couldn't put her finger on what it was. Maybe it was intuition. Maybe it was God whispering. Whatever it was, it wouldn't leave her alone right now. It wouldn't let her sit back and trust that Gerald and the police would figure this out. Not when a man's life could very well be on the line.

Priscilla watched the house, but there was no movement. Nothing. But someone had been inside, she was sure of that. And there was a dog inside. She was sure of that too. And according to Sara, someone had been there as recently as last night. Should she go up and knock on the door? She'd tried that before, and it hadn't done any good. Still, it was worth trying again.

She climbed out and crossed the street then walked quickly up the porch steps. She knocked. She waited, but there was no answer. She tried again, but again, nothing. But there was no mail in the mailbox. Which meant that whatever mail had been delivered the past few days had been taken in.

Someone was here. They had to be. But was it the missing man? She could only think of one way to find out for sure.

The only pressing thing on her agenda for the day was working on that quilt, she thought as she crossed the street again. She opened the car door and settled in. She might as well wait here for a little while and see if she could learn anything else. At least she had a good book to keep her occupied while she waited.

Priscilla checked her phone one more time, but there was no news from her cousins, nor from Gerald. She set the phone on the console next to her, and then she pulled out her new novel and cracked open the cover. She lifted it and sniffed the clean, woody scent of a new book. Gary used to laugh at her when she did that, but to Priscilla, it was one of the best scents in the world.

Soon she was absorbed in the story. This book was about a French woman who rescued downed Allied pilots in Nazi-occupied France during World War II. She was totally sucked in, wandering the streets of Paris with the heroine, when a loud noise pierced the stillness of the car.

She was so absorbed in the story that it took her a moment to recognize the noise as her phone. Maybe there was news on Dan! Priscilla grabbed it and saw that the name on the screen was

Rachel. Well, it wasn't news about the mystery, but she was thrilled to hear from her daughter nonetheless.

"Hi, sweetie." Priscilla put the phone to her ear and checked the house. Nothing appeared to have changed.

"Hi, Mom. I'm just checking in to see how things are going."

"Just fine. It's beautiful here at this time of year. How are you?"

"Oh, things are fine. Work is busy but good."

"That's good. What else is going on? Anything fun outside of work?" Priscilla loved her daughter more than life itself and couldn't be prouder of all she had accomplished, but sometimes she worried the girl worked too hard. She never seemed to have time for other things. How was she going to meet a nice man if she was always looking at a computer screen?

"No boyfriend yet, Mom." Rachel laughed. "How's that handsome sea captain?"

"He's in the Coast Guard. My goodness, you make him sound like a character from a Dickens story. And he's just a friend, thank you very much."

"Uh-huh."

"Rachel. Your father has been gone less than a year." She sounded like a schoolmarm, but she didn't care.

"I know. Three hundred and six days."

Priscilla felt tears sting her eyes. Rachel knew the exact number of days since Gary had passed away. Sometimes, wrapped up in her own sense of loss, she forgot that while she had lost a husband, Rachel had lost a father. The most important man in her life was gone, just like that, and her grief was every bit as real as

Priscilla's own. And Rachel didn't have a new home and life to help distract her from that fact.

"I miss him, honey. I miss him every day."

"Me too."

Rachel was quiet for a moment. She sniffed. Was she fighting back tears?

"Mom, where are you?" Rachel finally said a few moments later.

"Huh?"

"It sounds like you're in the middle of an intersection or something."

"Oh. No. I'm just sitting in my car." She craned her neck and saw a UPS truck barreling down the street. "I guess a big truck did just go by though."

"Why are you sitting in your car?"

"I'm watching a house."

"Why?"

Why? Where did she even start trying to explain what she was doing here? "I think there might be somebody inside."

"Okay..." She could hear the skepticism in Rachel's voice.

"Somebody who shouldn't be there."

"Mom, are you staking out a house?"

"What?" That was not what she was doing. She was...

"Seriously, Mom, are you sitting in your car waiting for someone to come out?"

"I'm not...that's not..."

"Are you alone?"

"I am."

"Why in the world are you staking out a house in the first place, let alone by yourself?"

It was too hard to explain, so she didn't even try. "It's perfectly safe." She kept one eye on the house, but there was no movement inside.

"Does this have something to do with another mystery?"

"It might." There was no sense in arguing with her. Rachel was just trying her best to look out for her, she knew that.

"Mom, I don't know what the situation is, but I really think you should get out of there. Finding the history behind old antiques is one thing, but staking out someone's house is a whole other level entirely. Call the police and let them handle it."

"I'm perfectly safe, honey." She needed to change the topic and quickly. "Hey, how is your training going for the half marathon?"

Rachel wasn't easily distracted at first, but then she started telling Priscilla about the long runs she was doing to train for the thirteen-mile race she was planning to run next month, and they chatted for another ten minutes. Priscilla kept her eye on the house the whole time, and when Rachel said she had to get back to work, Priscilla hung up. She studied the quiet house for a few more moments then turned back to her book.

But she couldn't concentrate. Was Rachel right? Was what she was doing dangerous? How could it be? She was just sitting here in her car. If there was any danger, she'd just drive away. And was it really any different from the mysteries she'd solved before? If anything, those had been more dangerous. Someone had actually broken into her house trying to find that old British gold. This wasn't anything to worry about. She was just sitting here...

Priscilla's nerves were suddenly on fire. She'd seen something. Her subconscious recognized it several seconds before her mind caught up with what was happening.

The front door was slowly swinging open.

Priscilla held her breath and watched as a figure stepped through the doorway. No. It couldn't be...

But even as she was thinking it, the person looked around uncertainly and then stepped out onto the porch.

Priscilla pulled out her phone and dialed 911.

CHAPTER EIGHTEEN

9 11, what is your emergency?"

"Hi. I'm outside of—oh, I don't know. I'm on High Street. The shingled house with the porch." Even as the words came out, she knew they would do no good. Half the houses on this block were covered in shingles. "Anyway, it's about halfway down the block. And a girl just came out of the house!"

"Um...okay..." The woman's voice on the other end of the line was skeptical. "And what exactly is the emergency?"

"The house is supposed to be empty. But a girl came out. She's walking down the street now."

"Is this girl threatening you? Or anyone else?"

"No, she's..." Priscilla realized she sounded ridiculous. "She's just a girl. Young, maybe early twenties." The girl was now crossing the front yard in long strides. She was thin and young. Probably younger than early twenties. "She has a hat on, and it's not even cold out. And big sunglasses. It's cloudy out!"

"I'm sorry, ma'am. I'm having a hard time understanding. Is it your property? Or is there anything about the girl in particular that makes you feel like she's a threat?"

"She's not supposed to be there, and now she's getting away. Send someone quick!"

"All right. It's okay." The woman on the line was using a soothing tone of voice. "We'll send someone to check it out. Can you describe the location a bit better?"

"It's the middle of the block."

Priscilla watched as the girl walked away, and she felt adrenaline course through her. By the time the police got here, she would be gone. She couldn't wait. Should she get out and go after her? Rachel's warnings ran through her mind, but this girl couldn't possibly be dangerous. She couldn't weigh a hundred pounds soaking wet. Were there other more dangerous people still in the house? Or was the man on the houseboat inside, tied up and hurt? Priscilla had no way to know. But the one thing she did know was that she was watching the only break she'd had in this case in days walk away.

She squinted at the house. There. In brass, above the door. "It's number 24 High Street. The girl is walking toward School Street. Send someone soon!"

And with that, she hung up and tossed her phone in her purse then slung it over her arm and jumped out of the car. She couldn't just sit here. She wouldn't forgive herself if she let the only clue she had vanish because she was too chicken to act. Lives could be on the line.

She slammed the door behind her and hurried down the block on the opposite side of the street from the girl, who was about to turn onto School Street. Priscilla crossed the street and followed her. She was just a few steps behind her now. What should she do?

Priscilla hesitated, but only for a moment. She knew exactly what to do. She would just be herself. A Kansas farmer's wife, far from home. Lost and confused and out of her depth.

"Excuse me?" Priscilla let the Midwestern twang she'd learned to hide come out.

The girl stopped and turned around. Priscilla let out a gasp. She was younger than Priscilla had realized. She couldn't be more than sixteen or seventeen, and she was wearing shorts—in this weather?—and an Exeter sweatshirt.

"I'm sorry to bother you, but I'm a little lost. I'm trying to find 16 High Street," Priscilla said.

"Oh." Up close, Priscilla could see that there were dark circles under her eyes, and the whites were rimmed with red. Her legs had that too-skinny look where her knees knocked together. "I don't know. I guess it would be that way."

The girl's voice was high and uncertain, but she pointed down the lane the way she'd come.

"Thank you so much." Priscilla pretended to turn to go but then stopped. "Wait a minute. Didn't I just see you come out of number 24?"

The girl froze. Priscilla feared she might run. For a moment, the girl looked like she was about to take off down the street. But then she did something else entirely.

She started to cry.

CHAPTER NINETEEN

The girl was crying so hard it took Priscilla some time to get anything out of her. Was she in danger? Was someone keeping here there against her will? Priscilla didn't know. She just held the girl in her arms and let her cry.

Finally the girl calmed down enough to start making a bit of sense. Priscilla dug a packet of tissues out of her purse—once a mom, always a mom—and handed one to her.

"Amber," the girl said when Priscilla asked her name again. She swiped the tissue across her eyes.

"Amber. That's a pretty name."

The only response to that was more tears. But that was okay because it gave Priscilla time to think. She'd heard that name recently. And, with a sinking feeling, she realized where.

"I'm Priscilla." She put one hand on each of the girl's shoulders. "Amber, your parents own the house you're staying in, right?"

Amber nodded.

That was where she'd heard the name. In the pictures Catherine Phillips had posted on Facebook. In those perfect photos of that perfect family. Priscilla saw that this was indeed the same girl who had been in those photos, though she looked smaller and younger than she'd appeared online.

"Do they know you're here?"

Amber hiccupped and then shook her head. "No."

"You've been here since Thursday?" Priscilla saw her hopes of finding answers about the missing man draining away. She suddenly understood what was going on here—or at least, she understood part of it.

Amber nodded. "How did you know?"

"My niece lives across the street. She mentioned there was someone inside the house."

"Oh. Mrs. Kestner?"

"Exactly. She thought it was odd since there's usually no one here at this time of year."

"She knocked on the door. But I didn't answer because I knew she would tell my parents where I am."

Priscilla wanted to tread carefully. As a parent, she knew Amber's mother and father must be frantic if they hadn't seen or heard from their daughter in six days. But she didn't know the situation or what kind of trouble might have caused Amber to flee to the family's summer house. It was difficult to judge someone else's situation. She wanted to help, but she didn't want to scare Amber away. She tried to figure out what to say. The girl looked so thin. Priscilla knew that was the look kids tried for these days, but she couldn't help but think Amber could use a sandwich.

"Have you eaten recently?"

Amber didn't move for a few moments, and then she shook her head. "I used all my money getting here. There was some food in the pantry but not much. I didn't really think about what I would do once I got here. I just…I needed to get away, so I ran. I finally found some cash in my dad's dresser, so I was heading out to get something now."

She was so young. So young and so foolish. But who wasn't shortsighted at that age? And who knew what she was running from?

"No need to rob your dad's piggy bank. Can I get you something to eat?"

Amber hesitated, but as she looked up at Priscilla, something in her face changed. She nodded. "Can I bring my dog?"

Priscilla steered her back toward her car, thanking God that she'd found her.

CHAPTER TWENTY

A few hours later, Priscilla was cleaning up the kitchen while Amber napped in her spare bedroom. Ziggy, her mini Australian shepherd, had greedily eaten the chunks of chicken Priscilla had fed him, and now he was running around the yard. She'd called the police and told them not to come after all; she'd been mistaken.

She'd also gotten the full story from Amber. Her parents had recently fired the nanny, who had basically raised Amber, saying she was old enough that she didn't need a nanny anymore. It had been like losing a member of the family, the only one who really paid attention to her. And then just last week, Amber had had a big fight with her mom, who was traveling for work but was supposed to make it home in time for an art show opening Amber had some work featured in. Her father was technically around, but he worked so many hours that she basically never saw him, and no one expected him to come. When her mom said she couldn't make it home, Amber had let all the hurt and frustration of so many previous cancellations overcome her, and she'd run away and taken Ziggy, both to get some space and to hurt them. But she had come to realize over the next few days that she hadn't hurt them. In fact, they hadn't even noticed she was gone.

Priscilla's heart ached for the girl, desperately seeking the attention of her parents. The most tragic part was that her cry for help had fallen on deaf ears.

After a good meal, Amber had given Priscilla her dad's cell phone number, and Priscilla had called Adam at work and let him know that his daughter was in Martha's Vineyard. He had been shocked, that much was clear. Priscilla couldn't help but wonder how he hadn't even noticed his daughter was gone for six nights, but she didn't say that. For now all she said was that his daughter was safe. And to his credit, he promised to be there to retrieve her as soon as possible.

It was a sad story, and Priscilla's heart ached for the girl. She was glad she'd been able to play some small part in making Amber's life a little better, even if it was just a bowl of soup and a sandwich and a soft bed. But a small, selfish part of her also couldn't help but feel disappointment. If the missing man wasn't in the house, where was he? Could he be in Woods Hole after all?

Priscilla jumped when the doorbell rang. Had Amber's father made it here already? She pulled open the door. "Trudy."

"Hi, Priscilla." Her cousin gave her a tired smile.

"Come in, come in."

"Thank you." She stepped inside, and Priscilla gestured for her to follow her into the living room.

"Can I get you some tea? Or anything to eat or drink?"

"I'm all right, thank you. I just wanted to stop in and give you a quick update." She lowered herself down onto the couch. She was subdued, and her skin was pale.

"Thank you. I've been so worried." Priscilla sat in the armchair across from the couch. "Have you been in touch with Dan?"

Trudy nodded. "He made it home a little while ago. When the police demanded he return right away, he was able to cut his trip short and make it back in record time." She adjusted the throw pillow behind her back. "I let them know as soon as he was back on the island, and I talked to him while we were waiting for the police to show up at our house."

Priscilla's heart ached for her cousin. "I'm surprised they let you speak with him first."

"I am too actually. But I guess he's officially just being called for questioning, not an actual suspect at this point. Plus, well, I've known Hank for two decades. We used to go to school together."

"Hank?"

"The head of the police department. We grew up together, so he did me a favor."

"Well, that's a small blessing."

Trudy shrugged. "It is what it is. Anyway, Dan told me what the story was. You want to hear it?"

"If it's all right to tell."

"I don't see how they can stop me." Trudy smiled, and Priscilla saw a glimmer of the cousin she knew. "I guess back when that houseboat showed up in town, Dan noticed like everyone else, though he didn't say anything to me about it. But while I thought the guy had just stayed out there on his boat and didn't talk to anyone the whole time, apparently he came into town to go to the store at least once."

Priscilla nodded. That was when Joan had seen him.

"Well, I guess Dan was down at the marina when that happened, coming in from a day of fishing, and he stopped in at that little store to pick up some milk on the way home, which was the one thing I'd asked him to do. And apparently when he was there, he saw the houseboat guy and realized he knew him."

"He did?"

"He's apparently a guy named Mitchell Meagher. An old friend from Southie."

At Priscilla's confused look, Trudy explained. "Boston. They grew up together in Boston."

"Wow." Priscilla thought about this for a moment. "That was quite a coincidence."

"Not as much as you'd think. Half the people on this island have lived in Boston at some point." Trudy shrugged. "In any case, Dan was glad to see his old friend, and I guess they got to talking, and Dan went out to see the houseboat. And then he found out that Mitchell was trying to lay low and didn't want to go back to the store if he could avoid it, so Dan started bringing him groceries late at night."

Priscilla processed this for a moment. Something didn't add up.

"But why? Did he find out why Mitchell was trying to lay low or why he didn't like going in to the store?"

Trudy sighed. "Dan says he didn't ask."

"Do you believe him?"

"Yes." Trudy shook her head. "First off, he's a guy, and not just any guy. I don't know if you've noticed, but Dan is a bit...quirky."

Priscilla smiled. Yes. She'd noticed that he was super smart but a bit hopeless in social situations.

"He genuinely likes people, but I have never seen a creature less curious about the whys of the way people behave. He'll go to a party, and afterward I'll ask about what everyone is up to, and he won't know a thing, but he can tell me the details of the new engine the host put in his car. He just doesn't think like that, no matter how infuriating I find it."

She sighed and stretched out her legs. "But beyond that, I've seen him with some of his friends from Southie before. It wasn't the best neighborhood, from what I understand. Solidly middle class, hardworking people, and the kids that grew up there, they stuck together. They covered for each other. When he gets together with his old friends from the neighborhood, they still have that bond, even today. They were more like brothers than anything.

"So I don't know. As incredible as it seems, I guess I do believe that he might not have asked. I can see that if his buddy needed something, he could have just gone along with it without asking too much about it."

Priscilla thought about this for a moment. On the one hand, it seemed completely implausible. He was bringing his friend supplies late at night so his buddy could "lay low," and he never once asked why he was hiding? On the other hand, she knew friendship could be powerful. Priscilla had been close with so many of the women at her church back home, and for her close circle of friends—especially her best friend, Ruth—she probably would have done anything they asked, possibly without asking why. She trusted them enough to know that if they asked, they needed it, end of story.

"But why a houseboat? If he was trying to lay low, why not rent a hotel room or something? Why get something that was going to attract so much attention?"

"I don't know."

"How long was he planning on staying?"

"I don't know that either." Trudy toyed with the fringe on one of the pillows. "I also don't know what he was hiding from or anything about his life. I've never met him—he's not one of the guys from the neighborhood that Dan kept up with. But Dan swears that he's a good guy."

"So that's what he was doing on Thursday night then? Bringing this guy supplies so he didn't have to come in to buy them himself?"

"That's what Dan said. After I'd gone to bed, he went out again, drove over to the marina, and took the boat out to bring him some food."

"What time was this?"

"He says it was right after ten that he left, and around eleven when he got to the houseboat."

That matched the timing on the video. "Did he say why he had to do all this under the cover of night?"

"I'm not sure he did have to, except that was when I wouldn't ask what he was doing since I was asleep."

"So he didn't want even you to know he was helping his old friend."

"I guess not." She shrugged. "I'm trying not to be too upset about all of this. With mixed success."

"Of course." Priscilla nodded. "What time did he leave the houseboat that night?"

"He swears he only stayed five minutes or so. Just long enough to drop everything off. He had to leave for the conference in Florida the next day, so he didn't really stick around to chat."

"Is there any way to prove that?"

"I guess to get the rest of that video," Trudy said.

Priscilla nodded. She knew the police were working on that. "I'm sure they'll get it soon." She was dying to see the rest of it. "And I'm sure it will clear Dan once they do get ahold of it," Priscilla added.

"Thanks, Priscilla." Trudy sighed again and pushed herself up. "I should get going. I need to stop by Gail's and Joan's before I head home."

"Thank you for stopping by. Please send them my love."

"I will."

"And keep me posted."

"Of course."

Priscilla waved goodbye to her cousin and closed the door. Then she went immediately to her computer. She now had the man's real name. Mitchell Meagher. She opened her laptop, typed in the name, and ran a search.

The name Mitchell Meagher turned up thousands of results, but she quickly narrowed in on the ones that seemed like the right guy. Interesting. He was a lawyer and lived in Boston. He'd attended Boston College and then Notre Dame for law school and had returned to Boston to practice immigration law. A recent piece in an online trade journal mentioned that he'd recently left his job but didn't specify why. She found a picture of him. He had graying brown hair and blue eyes, and he still retained the strong jawline that must have made him quite handsome at one point. And—oh dear. The next link Priscilla clicked on was an obituary for a Kelly Meagher. Scanning the piece, she saw that Kelly had been his wife and had passed away not even six months ago. Just before he'd left his job at the law firm.

Did this have something to do with why he was hiding out in a houseboat anchored off Martha's Vineyard? Was whatever he was scared of related to his wife's death? Or the abrupt end to his legal career?

Theories were already swirling in Priscilla's head. What had his wife died from? She scanned the article again. Natural causes, it said. That could mean any number of things—and it wasn't that hard to make a death look like it had come about by natural causes, if all the television shows and mystery novels these days were correct. Or did his sudden mysterious appearance in the area have anything to do with the end of his tenure at his law firm? It hadn't said why he was leaving—could there be some cloud over the end of his employment there?

A sharp knock at her door startled her. Priscilla set the laptop aside and hurried to the door, opening it to reveal a man dressed in a sharp business suit and starched button-down. She recognized him immediately.

"You must be Adam Phillips." Amber's father. He had dark hair and a suit that she was sure cost more than her car. It just had that look. He looked just like the picture on his company's website, right down to the smug countenance. How had he gotten here so quickly? It had been just over two hours since she'd reached him at his desk in Manhattan. She saw that there was a black livery car idling in the driveway.

"That's right. Is she here?" He was already trying to push his way past her into the house.

Priscilla wasn't sure what made her do it. Maybe she was tired of having her ideas pushed aside. Maybe it was indignation on behalf of that poor little girl curled up in her guest room, who had made a cry for help in running away and whose parents hadn't even noticed she was gone. Maybe it had just been a long couple of days. But Priscilla moved to block his entry into her house.

"Wait." She would never have been this bold back in Kansas. A powerful man like this? She would have been so intimidated, she would have let him bowl right past her. Maybe she was changing since she'd come to this island. Trusting herself more. "Just wait a second."

This was her home, after all. She decided who came inside and when.

Adam stopped, but a dark look crossed his face. "My daughter is inside, right?"

She nodded, but she didn't move.

"Then please move so I can get to her." He started to push past her again. Priscilla stayed right where she was.

"She's sleeping right now. Before I wake her up, I want to make sure that she's going to be okay going back with you."

"Excuse me?" She could see that this man was not used to being questioned. "She's my daughter. I think she will be perfectly safe coming home with me."

"How was it that no one even realized she was gone for six days?" Priscilla knew she was treading in dangerous territory. A few hours ago, Amber had been a total stranger. But after finding her so broken down and hurt, she felt very protective of the young girl.

"Look, not that it's any of your business, but I've been working late on a big project. And my wife is out of town. I assumed she was in her bed sleeping, where she was supposed to be, when I came home from work and still there when I left in the morning. The school didn't tell us she'd been absent." He shrugged, like this made everything obvious. "As soon as you called, I got on a jet and came as soon as I could."

Priscilla couldn't believe it. What kind of parent thought it was normal that he hadn't seen his daughter for six days? Was this so common that it didn't seem strange to him?

"Amber needs help. She needs attention from her parents. She needs supervision. She is too young to be fending for herself. She needs someone who knows when she comes and when she goes, and who cares enough to make sure she's all right. Ideally, it would be one of her parents. The people who are supposed to care for her first. Failing that, you could hire the nanny back again. I know she was just an employee to you, but I'm not sure if you realize it was like losing a member of the family for your daughter."

He straightened, squaring his shoulders, making himself taller. "Who are you anyway? What makes you think you get to lecture me about my own daughter?"

Once again, Priscilla didn't know what had changed inside of her. Back on the farm, she never would have had the courage to stand up for herself like this. But now, here, it just came out.

"I'm Priscilla Latham Grant. My family has been on this island for generations. I own this place and that historic lighthouse. And I'm the one who found and cared for the teenage daughter you hadn't even realized was missing."

He seemed to be considering how to respond; he apparently settled on condescension. "Just let me have my daughter so I can get out of here and let you go back to your historic lighthouse."

But Priscilla didn't move.

"Dad?"

Priscilla turned and saw Amber in the hallway behind her. She had tears in her eyes.

"Sweetie. There you are." He moved toward the door again, and this time Priscilla stepped aside so he could come in. He went right to Amber, who threw her arms around him.

Priscilla felt a tightness at the back of her throat. Girls loved their daddies—even terrible, arrogant, absent daddies. She felt tears sting her eyes and fought them. Things clearly weren't rosy in the Phillips household. Big changes needed to happen, in Priscilla's mind. It was simply inexcusable that Amber had been missing for six days and no one even noticed.

But as soon as Priscilla had called, he'd come for her. She had to give him that. He had come as fast as he could—on a private plane, no less—to rescue his daughter as soon as he'd learned the news. And judging by the way he was holding her now, he loved her. He loved her imperfectly, sure, but then didn't everyone love imperfectly?

"Thank you, Priscilla," Amber said when she finally pulled back. "Thank you for your help. And for…well, standing up for me."

How long had Amber been standing there? Had she heard what Priscilla had said to her father? Judging by the way Amber was looking at her, she had heard every word. Suddenly, Priscilla was glad she'd had the courage to say it.

"I'm glad I was able to help. You have my number now, right? You let me know if you need anything."

Adam cleared his throat. "Are you ready to go?" he asked his daughter.

Amber nodded, and he turned and led her out. She followed him, her hair falling in front of her face. But as they were making their way down the path, Amber turned back to Priscilla and smiled one more time.

Priscilla closed the door, trying to make sense of it all. She felt bad for Amber, but she almost felt worse for her parents. They didn't seem to realize they were missing out on the most precious time of their lives. In just a few years, Amber would be grown and out of their home, and they would never get these years back.

Priscilla would give anything to be able to go back to when Rachel was young and enjoy watching her grow up all over again.

Well, hopefully this had been a wake-up call for the family. She didn't know what else she could do except pray for them. And she would do that.

She headed into the kitchen and set the kettle on. She needed a cup of tea to clear her head. She tucked a bag of Earl Grey into a delicate china cup, and as the water heated, she thought about what had just happened. While she was glad to have been able to reunite father and daughter, it did leave her with one problem. She now knew that Mitchell Meagher wasn't hiding in the house on High Street.

So where was he? If he hadn't made it to the mainland, he had to be here on the island somewhere. Where would she look next? How would she even begin to figure out where he might be?

She decided that she needed to learn more about Mitchell. She'd go back to searching for whatever she could learn online, but she'd probably need to dig beyond that. Property records were public documents, as were marriage, birth, and death certificates. Maybe there would be some clue in one of those documents that would point her in the right direction. She could also call his old law firm and talk to his former coworkers to find out what they thought about him.

The kettle started whistling, and she turned off the heat and poured water into the cup. She watched the steam rise up from the surface in curling wisps. She could track down people who had known Mitchell's wife, she realized. See what they said about her.

All of those things would be a good start. But would they get her any closer to finding where he was now?

Her thoughts were interrupted by another knock at her door. This place was just Grand Central Station today. Who could it be now?

She walked to the door and opened it to find Gerald on her doorstep.

"Well, hello there," she said. She couldn't help the smile that spread across her face.

"Hi, Priscilla. I wanted to say I'm sorry for the way I rushed out this morning."

"That's all right." A thousand questions ran through her mind. What had they found when they got to Woods Hole? Was it the right dog? "I understand."

"And I wondered... I know you're working on the quilt, but I never intended to stick you with all the work. I thought maybe I could help?" He looked down at the ground, sheepish.

"The quilt." Priscilla laughed. She hadn't had a chance to even take the fabric out of her car. This day had not gone according to plan. "I would love that."

After he helped her carry the bins inside, she spread out piles of dresses across the dining room table and laid out her rotary cutters, mats, and rulers and showed him how to cut a perfect square. Gerald started working on a blue cotton dress, and Priscilla started cutting pieces from a pink-and-white button-down. Late-afternoon sunlight streamed in through the windows, and they worked in companionable silence for a few minutes.

"We found that dog in Woods Hole," Gerald said.

Priscilla looked up. She'd been dying to ask him how the trip had gone but hadn't found the right way to ask.

"Oh?" She tried to sound only mildly interested, but inside she was dying to know what they'd found.

"It was a golden retriever all right, about the right age, male. A stray, obviously in bad shape. By the time we got there, the dog had been taken to a vet. They found a microchip in his ear."

"Oh good! I was hoping there would be one." Now that Priscilla knew how they worked, she knew how useful they could be.

"Well, they scanned it."

"Was it Hawthorne?"

"Nope." He used the rotary cutter to cleanly slice the fabric. "We found out he was named Snickers and belonged to a family in New Bedford. They were very relieved to find him. They'd been so worried."

"Wow." Priscilla processed this. First, she felt a pang of dismay. They hadn't found him then. If he was still out there somewhere, every day that passed meant he could be in more trouble, or at least farther away. But after that, she felt a surge of triumph. It wasn't Hawthorne after all. Which didn't mean their theory about Mitchell going back to the mainland was wrong, necessarily. But it didn't prove it was right either.

"How did he get to Woods Hole from New Bedford?"

"It's one of those crazy stories." Gerald shook his head. "The family had vacationed in Nantucket over the summer, and apparently the dog had become friends with a female dog in the house next door. Somehow he got out and made his way back to Woods Hole."

"And he obviously couldn't figure out which ferry to take from there," Priscilla said.

Gerald laughed. "Apparently not."

"The things we do for love."

Gerald laughed again and turned the fabric in front of him, lining up his ruler.

Priscilla finished cutting another square and set it onto her pile. "That's crazy. I've heard stories about dogs following some kind of internal compass and making long journeys like that, but I've never known if they were real."

"Apparently they are. This dog made it almost fifty miles, including over the bridge to Cape Cod. I'll never figure out how he knew exactly where to go, but he sure did."

"Wow." Priscilla had so many questions about this, but none of them had answers. How did dogs navigate mysteriously? And the fact that they did it in the first place—did that mean they had complex relationships like humans did? Had Snickers really gone all that way hoping to reunite with his doggy girlfriend? "When I get to heaven, I'm going to ask God all about how that works."

"Me too." Gerald had gotten all the squares he could out of the blue dress, and he set it aside and reached for a frilly yellow infant dress. Maybe from Aggie's first Easter, Priscilla guessed.

She laughed, and they worked in quiet for a few more minutes, each lost in their thoughts. It was nice not to have to fill every moment with chatter.

Priscilla thought through the fact that there was still no proof Mitchell—and Hawthorne—had made it back to the mainland. She now knew that he wasn't hiding out—or being held—in the house in Edgartown, but that didn't mean he wasn't on the island somewhere.

"Have you had any luck getting the rest of the security camera footage from Lloyd and Fisher?" she asked.

"We're working on it. The company rep said it was a mistake, but who knows? They promised they're working on getting us the rest of the footage from that night, but I don't see how it could possibly take this long. If they don't hand it over in the morning, we're going back to the judge. She wasn't in today, but she's about to get an earful tomorrow."

"What could the judge do?"

"Issue a search warrant, for one thing. That would give us permission to go in and find the footage ourselves, assuming it hasn't been destroyed."

"Wow. And if it has been destroyed?" She hadn't considered that possibility.

"They're already possibly looking at obstruction of justice charges. That would certainly be grounds. Hopefully we'll find what we need though."

She nodded. Hopefully getting the rest of that footage would make a lot of things clear.

"Have there been any other leads about where Mitchell is?" Priscilla asked.

Gerald looked up from his cutting and paused and then sighed and set the rotary cutter down. "I guess I shouldn't be surprised that you know his name, should I? You seem to figure out every piece of this puzzle right alongside us."

"Sometimes before you," Priscilla couldn't help adding with a smile. "Though in this case, you can't really blame me. I didn't go looking for that bit. Trudy told me."

Gerald nodded. He was quiet for a moment, looking down at the yellow fabric. Then he sighed and said, "I probably shouldn't tell you this."

That got her attention. She set down the piece she was cutting and waited.

"But since you're probably going to find out somehow anyway, I suppose I might as well save us all time and tell you that the police got access to the laptop left behind in the houseboat. Their IT department was finally able to unlock the password and get inside."

"Was the password his birthday?"

Gerald sighed. "Yes, it was."

Priscilla had to force herself to suppress a smile. She tried to keep her voice even when she asked, "Did they find anything useful on it?"

"It's too early to say." He reached for the next thing on the pile, pink corduroy pants, and set them in front of him. "They're looking through his recent search history and bank records stored on the hard drive and such." He turned the corduroy pants over in his hands.

Priscilla had the impression there was more he could say, so she waited. Sometimes if you just gave people a minute of quiet, they would rush to fill the silence. He'd already told her more than he probably technically should have. There might be more coming.

"There is one thing that's kind of interesting," he said, smoothing the fabric out in front of him.

"Oh?" Priscilla tried to affect a tone of polite interest, but inside her heart was pounding.

"There's a folder on his desktop. Inside are lots of newspaper articles about a recent theft at an art museum in Boston."

"Really?" Well, that was interesting. The man was an artist; they knew that much. Why was he so interested in the theft at the art museum? "Which museum?"

He hesitated for a moment. "It's called the Martin Museum. A small place."

"And what was stolen?"

He hesitated again. "I've already told you more than I should have. My guess is that, given the things you've already found out, you'll be able to uncover this too. But I could get in trouble for what I've already shared." With that, he picked up the shears and cut along the seam of the pants to flatten them out.

"Got it."

While Gerald went back to cutting out fabric squares, Priscilla's mind raced. A theft at an art museum in Boston. Was Mitchell Meagher an art thief?

"What about the key? Any luck on that?"

The scissors hummed as they sliced cleanly through the fabric. "Nothing solid." She could tell he wanted to say more but couldn't.

Priscilla nodded, but her mind was spinning. Mitchell had a file of information about a painting that had gone missing right around the time the houseboat had shown up in the harbor, not long after his wife died and he quit his job. She needed to figure out how all the pieces fit together. But she was certain they did.

CHAPTER TWENTY-ONE

Rain spattered against the windows as Priscilla sat down with a mug of tea and her laptop. Gerald had stayed for dinner, and Priscilla had enjoyed having the company. But still, she was secretly relieved when he finally went out to his car and headed home because it meant she could turn her attention to finding out more about this art museum robbery.

She typed the phrase *Boston art museum theft* into her browser and held her breath while it returned her results.

A few articles came up, and she clicked on the first one. It was from the *Boston Globe* and reported a painting being stolen just a few weeks earlier from the Martin Museum in Boston. But she could only read the first hundred words. To read more, she had to log in with her subscription information. She didn't have a subscription, so she went back to the main search and tried again. She couldn't find anything more, so she realized she would have to go to the library in the morning and hope she could find the article on microfiche.

Priscilla had never heard of the Martin Museum, but a quick search revealed that the museum was housed in an old mansion on Society Hill and had started as the private collection of Isabella Martin, an art lover married to Boston Brahmin Ralph Martin. Over the years the collection had grown, and the home had become a private museum dedicated to collecting and preserving art from local artists and works from "an eclectic variety of old masters," according to the website. She saw that they had paintings by some names she recognized—Degas, Velázquez, Hopper, Rothko—and many more she did not. But what painting had been stolen? The museum's website didn't say, and it didn't mention anything about a recent break-in. She supposed that was understandable, but it meant she would have to wait until the morning to find out more.

And she would, first thing.

For now she went to bed, her mind swirling.

A storm blew through Wednesday night, but Thursday dawned clear and bright, and the world looked clean and fresh. Priscilla got up and had her coffee and devotions, and then she took a look at the newspaper. The story was still front-page news—and Frank Ripley was now mentioned as well. Priscilla scanned the article and saw that he'd been arrested and released, though the evidence the police had against him wasn't mentioned. Priscilla was pretty sure he would not be happy about this. But short of showing up to ask him questions herself—which she was still pretty sure would not go over well—she had no way of finding out how his finger-prints got on those knives.

Priscilla cleaned up the kitchen and headed to the library. She got there a few minutes before it opened and stood on the front step, peering in through the glass door.

"Some people just can't wait to get their hands on great books," Clara said when she opened the door. She laughed as she let Priscilla in.

"Actually, I'm here to look for newspapers. I was hoping I could find what I need using microfiche."

"Sure thing. How old is the newspaper you're looking for?"

"A few weeks."

"*Hmm.*" Clara hesitated as the front door fell closed. "That's recent enough that we may not have it on microfiche yet."

"Oh." Priscilla felt all her excitement vanish.

"But what newspaper is it? We may have a subscription for online access."

"The *Boston Globe*."

"Ah. That helps. You should be able to access the online archives easily enough. Come on. Let's get you set up."

A few minutes later, Priscilla was seated at one of the computer terminals and logged into the newspaper archives using the library's credentials. She ran a search for the missing painting at the museum, and the full article she'd started last night came up.

Priscilla scanned it quickly. The theft had occurred late at night after the museum was closed, and the museum's security was still trying to ascertain exactly how the thieves had gotten in undetected. The museum's security system had been disabled, they were quick to point out. No doubt they were going to be making some changes there, Priscilla thought. She read on.

The painting that had been taken, she learned, was a newly acquired work by an artist named Sean Meagher.

Wait a minute. That last name. That couldn't be an accident, could it?

The article included a photo of the missing painting, which depicted a woman shown from the back, standing at the edge of a cliff and gazing out at sea. To the left side of the painting was a small wooden cabin, and off to the right, you could see the top of a lighthouse rising above the bluff. It wasn't Priscilla's lighthouse—it was brick, and it didn't have the familiar black stripe at the top—but it was definitely a lighthouse. The main focus of the painting seemed to be the woman, who had long brown hair and was wearing tight black pants and an oversized man's shirt.

The painting, she read, had been made in the early 1970s and was important because it was the earliest example of the photo-realistic style Sean would come to be known for. The woman in the painting was rumored to be his wife, Molly. Because of its historical significance, the painting was valued at over a million dollars.

Priscilla's phone started to ring, and she quickly silenced it. Joan, the screen read. Well, she couldn't talk here. She'd call her cousin back as soon as she was done.

Thoughts and ideas swirled through her head. A million dollars? For a painting?

Who was Sean Meagher, and how was he related to Mitchell? Why had the painting been stolen, and why did Mitchell have a folder about it on his laptop?

The one question that stood out most clearly was also the most simple: had Mitchell Meagher been an art thief?

Priscilla needed to learn more. She went back to the main search page and found several follow-up articles that filled in some of the holes the first article hadn't answered. The museum had determined that the security system had been disabled remotely, by accessing the museum's server. Priscilla hadn't even known that was possible. She was only vaguely familiar with what a server was and hadn't realized someone could hack in and turn off a security system with it.

There had been no physical evidence left behind, the article continued, but police suspected the robbery was done by someone familiar not only with the computer systems, but also the layout of the museum, as from the time the system went down to the time a car was seen speeding away from the museum was no more than a couple of minutes.

She also learned that the painting, a recent addition to the museum's collection, had been given as part of a bequest of the artist's son Robert. The crime, she determined, had not been solved.

Well, that was interesting. Priscilla opened a new browser window and went to the genealogy site she'd mentioned to Officer Brown. She typed in the name Sean Meagher, and once she sorted through to find what she was pretty sure was the right one, his family tree appeared.

Sean had been married to Molly Meagher, née Simons. They'd had three children, a daughter Susan, son Robert, and a third son Peter, who had passed away as a child. Priscilla felt her heart ache for Molly, whoever she was. She couldn't imagine anything worse. But she forced herself to focus and narrowed in on Robert, the son mentioned in the newspaper article. The painting had been donated six months ago as part of a bequest, she knew, and there—sure enough, he was marked as deceased, as was his wife, Karen. They had two sons, Justin and—Priscilla's heart pounded—Mitchell.

There he was. The grandson of the famous painter. Who had suddenly quit his job and holed up in a houseboat in the harbor just about the time his grandfather's valuable painting had been stolen from a museum.

That didn't mean he'd stolen it, Priscilla reminded herself. Not necessarily, anyway. She thought back through what she'd seen on that houseboat. Mitchell was a painter—or he was trying to be one. How was that related to all this? The paintings he'd been working on were abstract and very different from what his grandfather's paintings had been, at least based on the little she knew about Sean Meagher's work.

She needed to find out more about Sean Meagher's paintings, she realized. She needed to see if there was some connection in the paintings Mitchell had been doing to Sean's work. How could she find out more about Sean's work?

She looked around and instantly felt like a dolt. If she wanted to find out more about Sean's work, she was in a pretty good place to do so. She quickly navigated to the library's catalog and then, Dewey decimal number in hand, easily found the books on contemporary art.

The library had filled up. Toddlers were being chased by harried young moms, and the computer terminals were filled with people staring at screens. She'd been so engrossed in her research, she hadn't even noticed.

She found a volume that profiled several dozen artists and saw that Sean was included. She'd take it home and read it carefully there.

She checked out the book and exited the library. She dug her phone out of her purse. Joan had left a voice mail.

"Hi Priscilla, this is Joan. I'm finishing up at the clinic in a little bit and wondered if you wanted to grab lunch. Let me know if you're free."

Well. Nothing sounded better right now than lunch with her cousin. She called Joan back, and Joan was just finishing up. They agreed to meet at the Colonial Inn in fifteen minutes.

It was such a nice day that Priscilla decided to leave her car where it was and walk to the inn, which was only a few blocks away on Main Street. The sidewalks were busy with people ducking in and out of shops and cafés, and Priscilla had to remind herself that this was real. This was where she lived now.

She stepped up onto the porch of the inn, which had lovely hanging baskets and a stunning view of the harbor. There were tables outside, but the bite in the air meant only a few brave souls were seated out here. Priscilla opened the heavy door and stepped inside.

"Hello, Priscilla." Tilly Snyder greeted her, quickly giving her a once-over. Priscilla immediately felt self-conscious. Tilly was known for being very particular about decorum and the way her patrons presented themselves, and Priscilla hadn't known she was coming here, so she hadn't exactly dressed up. But her khakis and sweater must have passed muster because Tilly grudgingly nodded. "How many?"

"Two please," Priscilla said. "Inside."

"Right this way." Tilly led Priscilla to a small table next to one of the windows in the front room. Priscilla loved the inn's Victorian decor, from the beautifully painted wall coverings to the burled oak tables to the thick, heavy damask drapery. Soft classical music played over some hidden sound system. Priscilla perused the menu, but she already knew what she was going to get. The inn was famous for its shrimp salad.

"Hey there!" Joan said, appearing at the table.

Priscilla stood and gave Joan a hug, and then Joan peeled off her light jacket and scarf and hung them over the back of the chair before she sat down.

"How are you?" Joan asked.

"I'm all right. How are you?"

"Oh, you know." Joan laughed. She moved her menu aside without even glancing at it. "It's been a strange couple of days."

"I should say so. How's Trudy?"

"I talked with her this morning. She's all right," Joan said. "Dan came home last night, so thankfully he doesn't seem to be under arrest. I gather they didn't have enough evidence to hold him. Or they believe his story. One or the other, I guess."

"Why wouldn't they believe his story? Don't you?"

"Oh, of course—100 percent. You just never know what the police will do or think."

Hilda, a waitress Priscilla had met in the past, showed up and poured ice water into their glasses and took their order, and then Joan continued.

"Dan is a stand-up guy," she said. "It's too bad that he's mixed up in all this. It sounds like he was just trying to help a friend and somehow got caught up in something he had no idea about."

"So you don't think there's any way he could have been involved?" Priscilla didn't believe it herself, but she wanted to make sure.

"Let's just say that I would be very, very surprised. According to Trudy, he's really worried about his friend. They still haven't found out what happened to him, have they?"

"No. Not that I know of." Priscilla thought for a moment. Could she tell Joan what she had learned? She didn't think she could mention anything about the folder on Mitchell's laptop, but she supposed there was no harm in mentioning the things she had discovered on her own. "But guess what I did find out."

Priscilla filled Joan in on the stolen painting and how Mitchell was connected to the artist.

"Oh my goodness." Joan's mouth hung open. "Are you saying that guy who was living out on the houseboat was an art thief? That he was hanging out there on the water hiding a stolen painting?"

"I don't know," Priscilla said. "But it does seem like someone thought the stolen painting was on that boat. That must have been what they were looking for when they trashed the place."

Hilda set plates of shrimp salad down in front of them and quietly turned to go without interrupting.

"*Hmm.*" Joan scooped up a bit of the salad with her fork. "It does explain why the place was trashed, I guess." She took a bite and chewed. The creases on her forehead told Priscilla she was thinking.

"The question in my mind is did whoever break in looking for the painting find it?"

"Maybe." Joan nodded and chewed a bit longer, and then she set down her fork. "That's certainly a question. But maybe it's not *the* question."

"What do you mean?" Priscilla took a bite. It was delicious—shrimp mixed with a creamy dressing, sprinkled with dill.

"I guess I'm suggesting that maybe you're looking at this all wrong," Joan said. "I mean, sure, maybe someone did come onboard the boat at some point after Dan left Thursday night. Maybe someone did ransack the place, looking for a hidden painting. But a couple of things don't add up."

"Like what?" Priscilla hadn't realized how hungry she was. She tried to keep herself from shoveling the salad in. Tilly would certainly not approve of that.

"Well, for one thing, if this Mitchell guy really was trying to hide, why do it on a boat in the middle of the harbor, where everyone could see him?"

"I've wondered that myself."

"It doesn't make any sense. If you were trying to hide on Martha's Vineyard, wouldn't you get a room in some hotel with a reputation for discretion or rent a house somewhere? There are hundreds of places you could rent at this time of year."

"I agree. It does seem strange."

"He could have even just gotten a regular old sailboat and lived in that if he wanted to be on the water. But no, he picked a houseboat, the only one anywhere near here, and parked it out where everyone could see it. It's almost like he wanted to be noticed."

Priscilla nodded. She could see Joan's point.

"Then there's the fact that a houseboat in Martha's Vineyard is a terrible place to hide a valuable painting. Between the humidity and the sun and the potential for storms, why would you take a million-dollar painting out there? It's still hurricane season, you know."

"Don't remind me."

"Don't worry. They're extremely rare here." Joan used her fork to wave the concern away. "But still. My point is, it doesn't make any sense that he would have hidden the painting on a houseboat in the Atlantic."

"It's only the marina, technically."

"Whatever. It's not smart."

"Fair enough. But maybe he didn't. We don't know that whoever went looking for the painting found it."

In fact, now that she thought about it, she realized that Joan was right. Why would Mitchell hide the stolen painting on the boat? Wouldn't it make more sense to lock it up somewhere safe?

To lock it up and . . .

Priscilla wanted to smack her forehead. She couldn't believe she hadn't figured it out before. If you had a valuable painting, wouldn't it make sense to lock it up . . . and hide the key?

"The key. The one I found on the boat. I bet it opens whatever place he stashed the painting."

"What?"

Priscilla filled Joan in on the key she'd found and how it had a strange shape. "Not like a regular key."

"Oh. More squarish?" Joan asked.

When Priscilla nodded, Joan said, "It's probably for a safe-deposit box then. That's what most of them look like."

"So whoever ransacked the boat was looking for the key," Priscilla said. Once again, she couldn't believe she'd missed it. It was so obvious. All they had to do was figure out which bank held the box that key opened, and they would find the painting. Whoever had ransacked the place clearly hadn't found it, so the painting should still be there. Maybe they'd somehow find some clue about Mitchell's whereabouts inside too.

"Maybe." Joan still looked dubious.

"What do you mean? What else could they have been looking for?"

"That's my point. I don't know that there was someone looking for it."

"Huh?" Now Joan had lost her.

"It's just an idea. But what if no one came onboard after Dan that night? What if no one really ransacked the houseboat?"

"But I saw it. Someone did ransack it."

"Right." Joan took a sip of her water. "But what I'm getting at is, maybe it wasn't someone who was coming after Mitchell looking for the missing painting. Maybe it was Mitchell himself."

Understanding washed over her slowly. She saw what Joan was getting at now. She'd even had that idea herself early on.

"You're suggesting that maybe Mitchell faked it."

"I'm suggesting that it seemed like he wanted to be noticed. And then he disappeared in a very public way. In a way that immediately made it seem like he was a victim."

"Faking his own disappearance would throw the suspicion off him, in other words." Priscilla rolled this around in her mind. Maybe Mitchell had ransacked his own place, made everyone think he'd been kidnapped or worse, and then set the boat loose and escaped somewhere where no one would ever think to look for him. It was definitely possible.

"It's just a theory." Joan took a bite of her salad.

"But a good one." Priscilla ran through the scenario in her mind. "But would he do that?"

"I have no idea," Joan said. "I have no clue what kind of person he was or what he wanted."

Priscilla nodded. She had no way to know that either.

"But luckily for us, we do know someone who knew Mitchell quite well."

"Good point." Priscilla felt a smile spreading across her face. "How do you feel about paying Trudy and Dan a visit after lunch?"

"I think it sounds like a good idea." Joan took another bite of her salad and nodded, a knowing look in her eyes.

CHAPTER TWENTY-TWO

Joan called ahead on the way over, so when they showed up at Trudy and Dan's house, Trudy welcomed them inside.

"You're sure it's all right that we're barging in?" Priscilla asked as they stepped into the living room. Trudy's living room was bright and airy, with big windows that let in lots of light, and though the couch and the rug were a neutral dark blue, there were bright accent pillow pops of color everywhere you looked.

"Trust me, it's fine. It will be good for Dan to come up from the office and get some sunlight. He's not allowed to leave the island at the moment, so he's been hidden away in the basement working all day." She gestured for them to sit on the couch and headed down to the basement.

Priscilla looked at Joan as they heard her footsteps disappear down the stairs. She wasn't sure what to say to Dan. Could she just come out and ask if his friend was an art thief who had faked his own disappearance to get away? She wasn't sure how to phrase that, and the last thing she wanted to do was say the wrong thing and mess up the relationship with her newfound cousin. Joan had known Dan for decades, and her sisterly bond with Trudy meant she could get away with saying things Priscilla would never feel comfortable asking.

For a moment, she felt a pang of—was it loneliness? Not exactly. She didn't have any siblings, and she had never had anything like what Joan, Trudy, and Gail had.

"It's okay. He doesn't bite," Joan said.

Priscilla gave her a weak smile.

The footsteps came back up the stairs, two sets this time, and then Dan came into the living room and stood in the doorway.

"Greetings," he said and then hovered in the doorway for another moment before seeming to realize he should come in and sit down. Priscilla had noticed before that Dan was a tiny bit awkward—overly formal, shy, seemingly unsure about how to navigate some social situations. But he was always warm and polite and seemed to genuinely enjoy people, even if he didn't always know how to act around them. She guessed his work as a scientist suited him pretty well.

"How are you doing?" Joan asked as he lowered himself into a chair. He was wearing khakis and a button-down shirt—his standard "relaxing at home" attire, from what Priscilla had seen.

"It's been a strange few days," he admitted. "I've never been hauled back to the island and detained by the police before."

"I would imagine that's not a fun situation," Priscilla said.

"It was not my favorite thing I've ever done." He ran his hand through his beard, which was dark brown but edged with white. "But fortunately, I am innocent, and I think the police know it, so I have that in my favor. Still, I wish they'd spend less time interrogating me and more time finding Mitchell. He's in trouble somewhere, and they're wasting time hunting me down at a phytoplankton conference."

The police had hunted him down because they thought he might lead them to Mitchell, but she didn't point that out.

"Can you tell us what you know about what happened?" Joan asked. "Or about the man who was living on the boat?"

"I don't know much at all about what happened that night, but I can tell you about Mitchell," Dan said. "We grew up together in South Boston. He was always a nice guy. When I ran into him in town a couple of weeks ago, we reconnected."

"What was he like, growing up?"

"Quiet. Studious." Dan shifted in his seat. "He and I always got along because we were two of the only kids around who cared about school. Most of the guys were too busy chasing girls and looking for how to make a quick buck to study, but I was fascinated by science, and Mitchell, well, you could just tell early on he was going somewhere."

Trudy came in and set a tray of cookies and a stack of linen napkins on the ottoman between them. Dan reached for a cookie as she settled down on the couch next to Joan.

"His family had been in the neighborhood a long time, back before it started going downhill. They were always a little different. No one else had an artist in the family. They traveled. They even had a cottage here on Martha's Vineyard when we were kids. He brought me once. We couldn't have been more than ten or eleven. That was the first time I ever came to Martha's Vineyard, and that's when I fell in love with it. With sea life too, now that I think about it. We spent hours down at the shore, poking around in the tide pools and examining what we found."

"Did you keep in touch with him as you grew up?"

"As much as I could. He went off to a private high school and then off to some fancy college, and I went public the whole way. But we kept in touch, as much as you do."

"I exchanged Christmas cards with his wife," Trudy added. "She was wonderful. It was so awful when she passed."

Priscilla reached for a cookie. It had cranberries and walnuts and big chunks of white chocolate in it. She took a bite. It was delicious, with just a touch of salty to balance out the sweet.

"Did he say why he was living on a houseboat out here?" Joan asked.

"Not really. I didn't really ask, not in so many words. But his wife had recently passed away, and his dad died not long before that. He never had kids. He was a lawyer, and when I saw him a few years back, he mentioned that he didn't really love it. Too many hours, soul-sucking work, that kind of thing. So I figured he just needed a change."

Could it be that simple? He just wanted a change of scenery, and living on a boat sounded nice? If his reasoning was as innocent as that and he wasn't really hiding, then it made a bit more sense why he'd chosen to live on the houseboat in public view.

But was it that simple? If it were, how had his boat ended up trashed and adrift? And what about the stolen painting and the key?

"But why was he reluctant to come to land to buy groceries? Why were you bringing him supplies?" Joan asked.

Right. There was that. That didn't seem like someone just hanging out enjoying the view.

"I think he really just wanted to disconnect from the world, and going in and facing people made that hard."

"How did you end up bringing him supplies?"

Dan shrugged. "I offered. It was clear he didn't want to be doing it, that he just wanted to stay on his boat, and I wanted to help him out."

"I don't like grocery shopping either, but that doesn't mean I get my friends to do it for me," Joan said.

Dan hesitated. He seemed to be trying to think about how to respond. For a long, awkward moment, Priscilla thought he wasn't going to say anything, but then he finally spoke.

"Have you ever lost someone you really cared about?" he asked. Trudy reached out and rubbed his forearm gently.

Joan didn't respond, but Priscilla felt her throat close up. She understood what Dan was getting at. Right after Gary died, she'd gone into this other world of grief. She'd been completely unable to function for the first few weeks, sometimes barely getting out of bed. Her good friends and church family had carried her through that time, cooking for her and cleaning for her and making sure the laundry got done. Making sure she ate. Praying with her. Picking her up off the floor when all she could do was cry. She'd been too lost in her own grief to even understand how much they were carrying her at the time, but looking back now, she couldn't be more grateful. Grief could do that to you. It could knock you flat. It could paralyze you, make you incapable of performing the most basic functions.

"My little sister Monica drowned when we were kids. In this little pond behind my grandparents' house. My mom didn't get out of bed for weeks after the funeral. I hadn't even realized how much it was possible to cry before that, but it changed things for our family. I mean, obviously. But…yeah." Dan looked down at his hands. He seemed to be struggling for words.

"Losing someone you care about can change everything," Trudy said gently.

He nodded. "I don't know. He'd lost his father and his wife in six months. I guess it seemed to make sense to me, Mitchell wanting some peace, some place to just *be* for a while without distraction. So I offered to help."

Priscilla was quiet for a moment. She certainly hadn't expected such sensitivity from Dan, the guy who had to be reminded to tie his shoes. It was a good reminder that people had many layers.

Was that all Mitchell had been doing in the harbor then? Grieving? It did make sense, once Dan explained it that way. Could it be that he'd been painting because it was something he'd always wanted to try, not because there was some secret message hidden in his paintings?

"But why did you deliver the supplies so late at night? Under the cover of darkness?" Joan asked.

"I had no control over the darkness. That's just what happens at that time of night."

At first Priscilla thought he was joking, but then she realized he was just stating the facts.

"I went at that time of night because that was when I had time. It wasn't some nefarious plan to avoid detection. I was just busy all day and couldn't get away until ten p.m."

From anyone else, this explanation might have seemed fishy. But she knew Dan well enough to know that this sort of logic made perfect sense to him. Listening to him, all the things that had seemed so damning now appeared to have perfectly logical explanations. Had she been looking at this all wrong? Seeing ghosts where none existed?

But then again, something *had* happened out there on that houseboat Thursday night. No matter what Mitchell had been doing out there before that night, something had happened. And that was still a mystery.

"So you didn't get the impression that Mitchell was... hiding from something?" Joan asked.

Dan gave her a strange look. "Hiding? If he were hiding, he picked a strange place to do it. Everyone could see what he was doing there." He took a bite of his cookie, and then he continued. "He'd been stuck in this job he hated, and his grandfather had been an artist, and it was something he'd always wanted to try his hand at, so he found a way to make it happen."

It made sense. But there was still that matter of the stolen painting and that hidden key.

"Did you notice anything Thursday night that indicated he might be planning to make a change of any kind?" Priscilla asked. "Or did he seem scared at all?"

"No. Not that I noticed."

That didn't necessarily mean there hadn't been any signs, Priscilla reminded herself. Again, Dan wasn't always the most intuitive when it came to stuff like that.

"What do you think happened to him then?" Joan asked. Priscilla was surprised by the bluntness of the question, but Dan didn't seem to mind.

"I don't know." He looked down again.

"Maybe Frank Ripley knows," Trudy said. "That's what they said in the newspaper, right?"

Priscilla looked at Joan, who was nodding. "They must have had some evidence to arrest him," Joan said.

"I don't think so," Dan said. "The police asked me about that."

"About what?" How could Dan know about Frank and the knives?

"About how the knives got inside the boat." Dan was looking down at his hands.

"What are you talking about?" Trudy was getting exasperated.

"They found Frank's fingerprints inside the boat," Priscilla said. "On a kitchen knife. That's why he was arrested."

Joan and Trudy looked stunned, but Dan just shook his head. "So naturally they asked me about it when I talked with them because Frank had told them I gave the knife to Mitchell."

"But why would he tell them that?" Joan asked.

"Because it's the truth. I know how Frank's fingerprints got on those knives. They were Frank's knives. Mitch told me he needed better kitchen knives, and I picked those up at Frank's yard sale last week. They were in the bag I brought on Thursday night."

Priscilla couldn't believe it. Was it really that simple? "Are you serious?"

"Do I seem like a jokester to you?" Dan said.

Priscilla had to crack a smile at that. No, Dan wasn't really one to crack a lot of jokes. So that explained why the police had released Frank then. She felt frustration rise. If it hadn't been Frank, who had done this to Mitchell? Or was it all a ruse, a trick to make them think something horrible had happened after all?

"So what do you think happened?" Priscilla asked again.

"I sure wish I knew, but I don't," Dan said. "He's gone, and his boat was destroyed, and I sure hope they find whoever did it."

He was quiet for a moment, and then he continued.

"Someone came onto that boat and turned it inside out, but I don't know who. Maybe it was just random. Maybe someone had it out for him. I don't know. But I can't help but wonder what might have happened if I'd come out a little bit later. Maybe I could have stopped whatever it was."

Priscilla imagined middle-aged Dan, with his paunch and his Dockers, intervening in a confrontation, and smiled.

"Do you think he could have been in some trouble with the law?" Joan asked.

"I seriously doubt it. He's not like that."

Of course Dan would be inclined to think well of his old friend. But how well did he know Mitchell at this point?

Priscilla decided to change the direction of the conversation. "You mentioned that his grandfather was a painter. I read that he was quite a successful one at that."

"Yes, I believe that he was an artist of some note. Art isn't really my thing, so I couldn't say much about it beyond that."

"I read that one of his grandfather's pieces was recently donated to a museum in Boston and was stolen from the museum shortly thereafter."

"Really?" His eyes widened. He looked surprised. Genuinely surprised. Something about the slight flare of his nostrils, the disbelief that passed over his face. Priscilla believed that he hadn't known this.

"It was just about three weeks ago. It turns out the painting was worth quite a bit of money. Seven figures, they said."

"*Really?*" Stronger this time, with more confusion than disbelief. "For a painting?" He shook his head.

"The timing seems a bit convenient, doesn't it? The painting by his grandfather is stolen from a museum in Boston, where Mitchell lives. He shows up here right after that, hiding from the world..." Priscilla let her voice trail off.

Dan shook his head. "No. Absolutely not. I see what you're insinuating, and you're dead wrong. Mitchell did not steal that painting. I don't care how much it was worth. He would never do something like that."

Priscilla looked over at Joan. Joan nodded. Dan believed what he was saying. He didn't believe his friend could have stolen the painting. But that didn't make him correct. People did all kinds of things you wouldn't expect them to.

"Is there anyone else who might have had reason to want that picture?" Joan asked.

"You just told me it was worth at least a million dollars. I can name any number of people who would like to have a million dollars."

Fair enough. Priscilla tried a different tactic. "Can you think of anyone who might have some personal connection to the painting?"

"I don't know." He shrugged. "If you're suggesting the fact that it was his grandfather's painting is relevant, I guess you need to look at everyone in Mitchell's family. I know his parents are both gone, but he had a brother a few years older. Justin, I think. Maybe he knows something." He shrugged. "I couldn't say. I lost touch with him many years ago. He was always a little...different than Mitchell."

"Different how?"

He shrugged again. "Just more like the rest of the boys in the neighborhood. Not so studious."

"Did he ever get into trouble?"

"Oh sure. But who didn't?" He reached for another cookie. "I haven't talked with him in decades, so I don't really know what else to say about him. Maybe he wanted the painting. But he didn't seem like much of an art enthusiast to me."

Priscilla smiled. Maybe not an art enthusiast, but he was certainly interested in what the painting was worth. Anyone would be. She decided she would look into him.

"A million dollars?" Dan was shaking his head. "For a picture?"

"I'm sure it was a beautiful picture," Trudy said, patting his hand.

"I think it was more because it was the earliest known example of the characteristic photorealistic style he would come to be known for."

Priscilla got the uncomfortable sensation that everyone in the room was staring at her.

"I mean, that's what it said in the newspaper article," she added.

"Photorealistic style?" Joan repeated. "What in the world does that mean?"

"It looks real," Priscilla said quickly. "He painted it so it looks like a photo. Here." She reached into her purse and pulled out her phone. She used a browser to pull up a picture of the painting. "Here. See?" She enlarged the image and held the phone out. "This is the painting that was stolen. See how he's painted it to make it look like a photograph?"

Joan and Trudy were nodding. "I see," Joan said, and Trudy reached out and used two fingers to enlarge the painting even more.

"I like that house," she said.

Priscilla noticed that Dan had gone still, and something in his face showed…confusion? Recognition? He was squinting at the screen.

"What's the matter?" Priscilla asked.

"Can I see that?"

She handed him the phone, and he stared down at the picture of the painting.

"I know this cabin," Dan finally said. "This is their family's cabin, here on Martha's Vineyard. I've been there before."

Priscilla was immediately interested. "Do you know where it is?" Maybe this was where Mitchell was hiding out, either by choice or by force.

"It's got to be Aquinnah," Trudy said as she reached over to the phone and used her fingers to zoom closer.

"Definitely," Joan added.

Priscilla looked up, questioning. She had been to Aquinnah herself, but how did they know that so certainly? "Are you sure?"

"Those cliffs are unmistakable," Trudy said with a smile.

"The cabin *was* in Aquinnah. I remember that," Dan added.

Priscilla imagined the map of Martha's Vineyard in her head. Aquinnah was up-island, on the far southwest tip. From Tisbury, a boat would have had to travel past her place to get to it. Which would explain the barking she'd heard Thursday night.

"Do you remember where in Aquinnah?" She tried to keep her voice calm. The painting had been done more than forty years ago. Even if the cabin were still standing, there was no guarantee the Meagher family had anything to do with it anymore.

Dan shook his head. "I don't remember. I'm sorry. It was so long ago."

"That's all right." Priscilla didn't know how, but if this cabin still existed, she would find it.

CHAPTER TWENTY-THREE

As soon as Priscilla got home, she sat down at her laptop and ran a search on Justin Meagher. There was a social media profile that had been inactive for years, and a few mentions in posts made by other people, but the most interesting link that came up was an article in a Boston newspaper from four years ago. The headline read "Suspects Arrested in String of Robberies". She clicked on the link and read the story.

Two men were arrested in connection with a series of armed robberies in South Boston last night, police reported. The string of robberies started two weeks ago, when a house on East 8th Street was burglarized in the middle of the night while the owners slept in the next room. Cash, electronics, and other valuables were taken. Similar robberies were reported in the following weeks, including one encounter in which a woman woke up and interrupted the two men, who threatened her with a gun. The bold nature of the crimes have led to panic in the neighborhood, and stores report that sales of home security systems are up sharply. Authorities report that the men were arrested last night when they tripped a silent alarm that had been recently installed, and police arrived to catch the men in the act. The men were identified as cousins Justin Meagher and Scott Mackenzie, both of South Boston. Mackenzie has a long history of crimes, including petty theft, assault and battery, and benefit fraud. Meagher has been previously arrested for cyber crimes, including hacking into the databases of several local businesses to gain access to customers' banking and credit card information. The men were denied bail and will face trial later this month.

Interesting. So Justin had a criminal record—and for armed robbery, no less. And he had experience hacking into systems. Could he have hacked into the museum's security system and turned the cameras off? Priscilla thought it was distinctly possible. This cast things in a different light. Was he still in jail? If so, then he had an ironclad alibi. If not . . . well, she'd just have to find out.

How could she learn that? Was that the kind of thing that was public? She had no idea, so she did what she usually did when she had no idea where to start: she typed it into Google. *How do I find out if someone is in prison?*

The search engine immediately returned the result she was looking for—a site called VINElink, which, as far as she could tell, was intended for victims of crimes to be able to keep tabs on the people who had hurt them. You could search by state and find where any inmate was housed and when they were moved or released. Priscilla selected Massachusetts and typed in the name Justin Meagher.

Wow. It really was that simple. Priscilla was able to see that he'd served time in the Massachusetts state correctional facility in Cedar Junction before being released on parole less than two months ago.

Which meant that he had been free when the painting was stolen. Had he and Mitchell worked together to steal the picture then? She knew Dan didn't think it was possible, but she knew better than to assume you knew what someone would or wouldn't do. Two years ago, she would have laughed at the idea that she—a Kansas farm wife—would be living on Martha's Vineyard. Yet here she was.

Mitchell could have been drawn in to Justin's plan for all sorts of reasons. But what were they? Why had they broken into a museum to steal the painting? Was it just the money they'd been after? The museum had a number of Sean Meagher paintings, she knew. Why had they stolen just this one, the most recent addition to the collection? And what had happened to the painting? Had it been on Mitchell's boat after all? Or was it locked away in a safe-deposit box somewhere? Was the key, not the painting, what the person had been looking for all along? Or had Mitchell indeed faked his own disappearance, giving him a chance to escape without detection?

Her mind was swirling. She had so many questions and so few answers. But she knew she needed to find Justin or Scott. They would lead her to Mitchell. She couldn't explain the certainty she felt, but she knew this.

She also needed the rest of that video footage. She needed to see what had really happened on the houseboat that night.

She set her laptop to the side and reached for her phone. Gerald answered a few minutes later.

"Hi, Priscilla. Hang on." He was whispering, and then she heard some vague noises she couldn't make out. Then, a moment later, he came back on the line. "Sorry about that. I wanted to get somewhere I could talk."

"That's quite all right. Where are you?"

"I'm at the courthouse, waiting to speak with the judge."

"Well, I guess that answers my question. I was hoping you'd already gotten the video footage from Lloyd and Fisher."

"Not yet. Since they haven't turned it over, we're waiting to go in and ask the judge for a search warrant."

"Well, I hope you get it."

"Thanks, Priscilla. Look, I can't really chat right now. But I'll talk to you later."

"Good luck." She hung up and set the phone down. She leaned back against the couch cushions and closed her eyes. What if the mooring company had destroyed the footage? Why would they do that? Was someone from Lloyd and Fisher guilty? Would they be implicated by whatever was on that footage? Or was this just an honest mistake? Somehow she doubted it.

She was jumpy. She wanted to see what was on the footage. What else could she do?

Priscilla thought back through her conversation with Dan earlier this afternoon. He'd said that the cabin in the Sean Meagher painting had been the family cabin, where he'd gone with Mitchell when they were boys. That had been forty years ago though.

Chances were, it probably didn't even exist anymore. A lot of those old fisherman shacks had been destroyed to make way for larger homes. And if the family still owned the cabin, why would Mitchell buy a houseboat and camp out in the harbor? A remote cabin on the cliffs of Aquinnah seemed exactly like the kind of place one would go to get some peace.

Most likely, the fishing shack was not related to anything.

But then again, it could be something. And trying to find that out would be better than sitting here getting more anxious about that footage. How could she find out more?

Could she just go to Aquinnah and drive around until she found the cabin? That seemed like foolishness. She could search property records, but she would need to know the address for that. Unless...

Something tickled at the back of her mind. She set her laptop down and went to her bedroom to grab the book she'd checked out with the entry on Sean Meagher. She flipped to the section that had his biography and career highlights, and, sure enough, there was a paragraph about the painting with the cabin. There was also a picture of this, his most famous painting. She saw the woman, the cliffs, the tip of the lighthouse. She read the paragraph, which said that the cabin, originally built as a fishing shack in 1952, had overlooked something called Dogfish Bar, referred to by many people as the end of the world. Rising over the horizon was the top of Gay Head Light.

Priscilla got up and dug through the junk drawer in the kitchen. She knew she had a map of the island in here some-where—yes. There it was. She pulled out the map and spread it out over the dining table. She found Aquinnah, the little bit of land at the far western end of the Vineyard. It was connected only by a spit of land. She put one finger where Gay Head Light stood, at the far west shore, and then traced her finger along the curve of the northern shore. It had to have been along here somewhere. Where was Dogfish Bar? There were not many roads along here, but she wished she could see what was on them.

Then she realized she could. She set the map down and grabbed her laptop. It only took a moment for her to open Google Maps and pull up a map of Aquinnah.

On the surface of it, there was no reason to believe this cabin had anything to do with Mitchell's disappearance. But her gut was telling her this was at least worth investigating. So far in this mystery, it was when she'd trusted her gut that she'd had the best results. She may not be a professional, but she was better at this than anyone had believed possible. And if she was right about this—about the fact that she'd heard that dog out on the water last Thursday night—then the cabin being located on the northern shore of Aquinnah made perfect sense.

She looked at the online map in front of her. She narrowed in on the northern shore then opened a second window and searched for the term Dogfish Bar. There was an entry on the Massachusetts Department of Energy and Environmental Affairs page that listed Dogfish Bar as a fishing spot open to the public, with directions on how to get there.

Take State Road past Menemsha and Squibnocket Ponds, she read. Sometimes she had to laugh at the names places had around here. *Take a right onto Lobsterville Road and then a left onto Lighthouse Road. Then take a right onto unpaved Oxcart Road, which parallels the beach.*

This sounded promising. A remote fishing cabin would very likely be off an unpaved road near a known fishing spot. Her heart was pounding as she traced her finger along the paper map, following the route. This had to be it. But where on Oxcart Road would the cabin be?

She went back to the online map and switched over to the Earth view. This allowed her to see what the land looked like from above. Using this view, it was easy to see how remote this area was. There were only a few houses out this way. She zoomed in on one, but she could quickly see that it was too large to be the small fishing cabin she was looking for. She went down the sparse row of houses that lined Oxcart Road, facing the northern shore of Aquinnah, but none of them seemed right until she found one significantly smaller than the others. From overhead, the narrow driveway was overgrown and the house was a small square. Could this be the fishing cabin made famous by the painting?

She clicked over to Street View, and immediately it was as if she were standing there in person. For a moment, Priscilla thought about how creepy it was that technology allowed her to basically look at any location in the world as if she were standing there, but she brushed it aside. No matter how creepy it was, it had its uses. She manipulated the view she had, rotating away from the beach and toward the house.

And then she gasped. There it was. The cabin from the painting. The small wooden frame, the off-center door, the weathered clapboard siding—it was there. It looked different. Someone had painted the trim around the windows and built a deck and added an outdoor shower. But it was unmistakably the same place. And Google conveniently told her that the address was 24 Oxcart Road.

A remote fishing cabin along an unpaved dirt road would be a very good place to hide a stolen painting. Was that what was out there?

She didn't know if the Meagher family still owned the house, however. If not, then it seemed unlikely it was tied up in this. But if so...

She needed to find out who owned the cabin now. She thought for a moment and realized she knew how she could figure that out.

Priscilla grabbed her purse and her coat and headed out.

CHAPTER TWENTY-FOUR

Priscilla headed toward the Dukes County Registry of Deeds in Edgartown, the county seat. This was where all the property records for Martha's Vineyard were kept. She'd had to go there to finalize some paperwork when she'd inherited the house, so she knew that the records housed there went back hundreds of years and were open to the public.

As she made her way down Main through Tisbury, her eyes kept drifting toward the marina. What had happened out there? Had someone boarded the houseboat, invited or not? Had there really been a struggle? Where had Mitchell gone? She tapped her fingers on the steering wheel. She hoped they would find answers when they saw that video footage.

It was a short drive to Main Street in Edgartown, and she found the stately red brick building that housed the Registry of Deeds easily. She parked in the small lot and went inside. The wood floors were old and creaky but polished to a high sheen, and the walls here hung with black-and-white historical pictures from different periods in Martha's Vineyard history. She approached the front desk. A woman in her forties with a helmet of brown hair looked up at her and smiled.

"How may I help you?" She was soft-spoken and had a slight Midwestern twang that made Priscilla a teeny bit homesick. Behind her was a wall with a huge portrait of a man with a long beard, a pointy mustache, and a white frilly collar. The brass plate beneath it said it was Bartholomew Gosnold, the British explorer who'd discovered Martha's Vineyard. The Bart who'd inspired Mitchell's fake name. Would he now lead her to Mitchell? To the left and the right were hallways that branched off toward the back of the building, and Priscilla could see the base of a wooden staircase to the left.

"I was hoping I could look up some property records," Priscilla said.

"Then you've come to the right place." The woman beamed. "You want to use the electronic search system, right?"

Did she? Priscilla didn't have a clue. She had hoped they would tell her what she needed to know. "Is that the easiest way?"

"It sure is."

"Then yes. That's what I want to do."

The woman laughed. "Perfect. I'll show you where the terminals are."

Priscilla followed her down the hallway that branched off to the left and into a small room with three computer terminals set up along a long wooden table. Heavy wooden chairs—all empty— sat in front of each monitor.

"Here you go." The woman indicated the first chair and shook the mouse to wake up the screen. Priscilla lowered herself into the chair while the woman clicked on the icon for a computer program. It opened a window with fields where she could enter an address, a town, or a ZIP code. "Let me know if you have any questions!"

Priscilla typed in the address she'd found for the old fishing cabin: 24 Oxcart Road. A little wheel spun for a few moments, and then the information appeared on the screen.

The deed for the house was first registered in 1952 by Sean Meagher. It remained in his name until it passed to Susan Mackenzie in 1998. That was the year Sean Meagher died, Priscilla knew. Priscilla knew from her research that Susan had been Sean's daughter, and the cabin must have been left to her in his will. Mackenzie must be her married name. This would make her Justin and Mitchell's aunt and the mother of Scott, the cousin Justin had been arrested alongside.

Then just last year—had Susan died?—the cabin had passed to…oh my.

The cabin had passed to Scott Mackenzie.

Priscilla took in a long, slow breath. She suspected she had a very good idea where Mitchell Meagher might be hiding.

CHAPTER TWENTY-FIVE

A s soon as she got back to her car, Priscilla called Gerald. He
didn't pick up. Well, he was probably still at the courthouse
or else very busy with the investigation.

But she couldn't just sit on this information. She knew this
was important. She could feel it in her gut. She'd been right. She
had heard that dog out on the water. Mitchell had stayed on
Martha's Vineyard after the houseboat was set free—either by
choice or by force. He was in Aquinnah. Should she just drive out
to the cabin herself and check it out? But if he really was there—
and she was sure he was—she still didn't know if he'd faked his
own disappearance or if someone had taken him there against his
will. She wasn't sure it would be safe.

Well, if she couldn't get ahold of Gerald, she would tell Officer
Brown. With that decided, Priscilla turned her car back toward
Tisbury, and a few minutes later she pulled up in front of the
police building. As soon as she walked inside, she knew something
was going on. There was a sense of excitement in the air, and she
could see people scurrying around in the main area behind the
reception desk.

"You're back," the receptionist said. Gabrielle, Priscilla reminded
herself.

"I am. And I'm hoping to see Officer Brown again."

Gabrielle nodded. "Let me see if I can get her attention. There's kind of a lot going on at the moment, but I'll see."

"Please tell her it's important."

Gabrielle nodded and went to the back. Priscilla waited, looking around the small lobby area, with its padded seats and some sort of tree-like plant in the corner.

Gabrielle returned a few moments later. "Officer Brown will be out shortly," she said and then gestured toward the chairs. Priscilla nodded and smiled, but she was jumpy and nervous with excitement, and she couldn't sit still.

Finally, after what seemed like an hour but the clock on the wall told her was only five minutes, April Brown's familiar face appeared in the doorway.

"Hi, Priscilla." She smiled, but it didn't reach her eyes, and it was clear from the way her eyes darted around that she was distracted. "Gabrielle tells me you have some news for us?"

Was Priscilla imagining it, or was there a note of annoyance in her voice?

"Yes, I found out something that I'm sure is important."

"Come on back." Officer Brown led her into the same small office as before. On the way, Priscilla could see that several of the other officers were gathered around a computer on a desk in the middle of the open work space. They were staring at something on the screen. Was that the rest of the footage from Lloyd and Fisher? Had they finally gotten it?

Priscilla sat in the chair across the desk from Officer Brown. The police officer left the door open, and Priscilla noted that she could still see what was going on at the desk the other officers were huddled around. She looked across the desk at Priscilla. "So what have you found?"

"Well, you know how all along I've believed Mitchell was still on the island because of that dog I heard barking from a boat headed west Thursday night?"

Officer Brown nodded, but she kept glancing out at the desk where the officers were staring at the screen.

"Well, I did some research into the Meagher family," Priscilla said, a touch louder. Officer Brown looked back at her, waiting for her to go on. "And I discovered that the family still owns a cabin out in Aquinnah. It seems it's not much more than an old fishing shack really, but it's definitely owned by Scott Mackenzie, who was arrested along with Mitchell's brother Justin for an armed robbery a few years back."

Officer Brown was just looking at her blankly. Was she even hearing what Priscilla was saying? She decided to try a different approach.

"I know you all found a file on Mitchell's laptop with articles about a theft—"

There was a commotion outside the office. The men gathered around the computer were gasping in excitement.

"Excuse me," Officer Brown said. "I'll be right back."

Priscilla was left alone in the office, waiting. She could hear an officer instruct another to back the footage up and another say to write down the number. Priscilla scooted her chair over so she could see what all the excitement was about. She couldn't see the actual screen they were gathered around, just a bunch of backs hunched over the computer.

"That's him," Officer Holmes was saying. "That's got to be our man."

"There's two of them."

Priscilla understood that they had gotten the footage and had finally seen something interesting.

"Get that number." She recognized the police chief pointing at the screen.

"Got it." Another was writing down whatever the number was.

"Run it through the Boat, OHV, and Snowmobile Registration Bureau system, stat," the chief said, and the second officer scurried off, clutching a piece of paper.

Priscilla guessed it wasn't a snowmobile they had seen. They'd gotten the registration number off the boat that had approached the houseboat then.

She craned her neck, hoping to catch a glimpse of what they were seeing on the screen, but it was too far away, and there were too many people crowded around it. She looked around. No one seemed to remember she was here. Would they even notice if she got up to take a peek?

"Whoa. How did he get that open so fast?"

"Breaking and entering," the chief said.

"The other guy is right behind him. And . . . they're inside."

Did that mean the visitor had just picked the lock on the door? Or gotten in some other way? It was driving her nuts, not being able to see what was on the screen. She looked around again. Maybe if she just stood up... She pushed herself up and moved toward the doorway. No one seemed to notice.

"What are they doing in there?" the first officer said.

"This must be when he was ripping the place apart," Officer Brown said. Priscilla tried to imagine it. The camera was a good ways from the houseboat, and she doubted you could see much of what was going on inside the boat. She stepped out of the office and moved a little bit closer. The officers were all so focused on the screen that they didn't see her.

"Yep. Look, that's when he tossed the table over," Officer Holmes was saying.

"But where's Mitchell? What's he doing while all this was going on?"

"Is that him?" Someone was pointing at something on the screen.

"Can't say," Officer Brown said, squinting at the screen.

Priscilla took another step, and then she shifted over to the side a bit. There. She could see a corner of the screen now. It was the same grainy black-and-white footage she'd seen before, and the houseboat was so far out into the marina that it was difficult to tell much of anything. But—she moved over a bit—there was a small fishing boat tied up at the houseboat's platform, and from what she could tell, there was movement inside the houseboat, though she couldn't see much beyond moving shadows.

"The first one is out," Officer Brown said.

"The second one's out, and he's got Mitchell with him," the police chief said. Priscilla sucked in a breath. There he was. Mitchell, slumped over the intruder's shoulder, ropes around his wrists. He hadn't faked his disappearance then. He'd been kidnapped.

"Who is he?" Officer Holmes was saying, but no one knew, so no one answered.

She moved a step closer as, on the screen, the intruder tossed a bound Mitchell into the waiting fishing boat. She was only a few feet away from the officers now, but they still hadn't even noticed she was there. No one was looking at anything but the screen.

"Pause it," the chief said. The man closest to the computer tapped the space bar to stop the footage. "He's looking right at the camera just a few frames before this. Back it up."

They backed the footage up and played it again, painstakingly slowly, and then paused it again when they got to the frame where one of the intruders had, indeed, looked directly toward the camera.

"We have a visual. Austin, can you enlarge it so we can get a better view?" The chief was squinting at the screen.

The officer named Austin zoomed in so the man's face took up most of the screen.

"Anyone recognize him?" Officer Holmes was saying.

Was that . . . Priscilla angled her body a little closer. She thought it could be . . .

"I ran the registration number through the system." The man who'd scurried off with the paper was back, but his face was dour.

"The boat is registered to a man named Nick Black in Hyannis. The boat was reported stolen almost two weeks ago."

Priscilla was focused on the screen. She thought she knew that face. But the image was so grainy, so pixilated, that it was hard to tell for sure.

"So this isn't Nick," Officer Brown was saying.

"Most likely not."

The officers seemed momentarily stunned. That avenue was not going to help them identify the man in the footage. But if she could only...

"Zoom out again," Officer Holmes said. The image on the screen shrunk again, and as the suspect's face got smaller, Priscilla felt recognition wash over her, followed by a small thrill of excitement.

"Who is he?" the police chief said, his voice getting more agitated.

Did she just come out and say it? Would she get in trouble? Priscilla knew she wasn't supposed to be standing here, watching this. Then again, they didn't know who the man was. It was clear from the silence that none of them understood what they were looking at.

But she did. Now that the image had zoomed out some, the image was smoother, less grainy. The face was smaller, but she could see it more clearly. And as the face sharpened, a few other things came into focus as well.

"We need a name. We need to find out who this man is," the police chief was saying.

Priscilla knew she could get in trouble if she spoke up. But she also knew that they needed to hear what she knew. She had to say something, and she couldn't let them ignore her or brush her ideas aside this time.

She took a deep breath, and then in a strong, clear voice, she said, "I know who that man is."

CHAPTER TWENTY-SIX

All eyes in the room turned and looked at her. Most seemed confused about who she was and why she was standing there, but a few of the faces showed curiosity too.

"Priscilla?" Officer Holmes narrowed his eyes. He hadn't even seen her come into the station then.

Officer Brown spoke up. "I asked you to wait in the office—"

"I know." Priscilla held up her hand. "You did ask me to wait there, and I came out anyway. I was curious what you were looking at. But listen to me. I know who that man on the screen is."

How did they *not* know? Hadn't they done research on Mitchell like she had? Hadn't they dug into his background, learned about his family, looked for information from the people who knew him best?

But the blank look on their faces showed that they hadn't. So she felt a bit of triumph as she declared, "That's Justin Meagher, Mitchell's brother. And his cousin Scott Mackenzie. They must have been looking for the painting they stole."

What followed was a flurry of activity. Some officers went off to research Justin, while Priscilla ended up back in the small office with Officer Brown, Officer Holmes, and the police chief. She recounted everything she'd learned about Justin, about Scott, and about the painting, and what led her to the conclusion that they had stolen the painting. She explained how they both had criminal records and that the painting had been stolen just after Justin had been released from prison. And she explained what she'd come here to tell them in the first place—that she believed Mitchell was hiding out in the cabin in Aquinnah. Though now that she'd seen the footage, she realized he wasn't hiding out after all. He'd been kidnapped by his brother and cousin.

"But if Justin stole the painting, why would he ransack Mitchell's houseboat looking for it?" Officer Brown asked. She toyed with her wedding ring as she spoke.

"Did they break into the museum together?" Officer Holmes asked.

"And then Mitchell ran off with it, and Justin wanted it back?"

"No, I don't think Mitchell had anything to do with stealing the painting," Priscilla said.

"But then what is all this about?" The chief gestured toward the screen of the laptop, where they'd watched the footage again a few minutes before. His large frame looked almost comical, stuffed into one of the padded chairs.

Priscilla didn't yet understand *why* it all happened, but she had a pretty good idea *what* had happened.

"Sean Meagher, Justin and Mitchell's grandfather, was a painter of some note. Most of his pieces are in museums, but one, his earliest work in the style he's most known for, had been in the collection of his son Robert."

"Right. But Robert died, and the painting was donated to the Martin Museum," Officer Holmes said. "We know all that."

"My guess is that at least one of Robert's sons was not happy about the painting being donated to the museum."

"We're not interested in guesses, Ms. Grant."

Priscilla tried not to let that sting. Didn't they realize she was trying to help them? "Well, I'm not guessing about this. Justin Meagher was a hacker. The robbery at the museum was successful because the museum's security system—cameras, alarm, the whole works—was disabled remotely."

"Meaning?" The chief looked at her over arched eyebrows. Outside the office, officers were scurrying about, shouting pieces of information and hustling paperwork back and forth.

"Someone hacked into the system and shut it off."

None of the officers said anything for a moment, but Officer Brown was making notes on her yellow legal pad.

"Okay," the police chief said. "Say he did steal the painting. Say Mitchell wasn't involved. Let's assume you're right about all of that. Then what in the world happened out there on the water? Why would Justin come out here and attack and kidnap his brother? Why trash his boat and set it adrift?"

Priscilla had some ideas, but she knew he was only interested in facts.

"Mitchell must have gotten the painting somehow," Officer Holmes said, filling in the gap.

"Or Justin thought he did," Officer Brown added.

"But *did* he have it?" Holmes pressed.

"I suspect he probably did at one point," Priscilla said. "There's no other reason I can think of for Justin to ransack the boat looking for it."

"But he didn't have it any longer." Officer Brown nodded. "We know that because we know where it is."

"The key," Priscilla said. "I believe it opens a safe-deposit box. My guess is the painting is in there."

All of the officers were nodding. "Call the judge. Get that search warrant now," the police chief said. Officer Holmes nodded and scurried out of the room, and the chief started looking at something on his phone.

"We knew it was a safe-deposit box key," Officer Brown explained. "And by searching his computer files, we know what bank it belongs to. We just haven't gotten permission to open the box yet."

"Wait. You knew what that key was?" Priscilla felt—inexplicably, she knew—left out. How had they known but she hadn't?

Officer Brown laughed. "There are a few things we figured out on our own."

The chief looked up from his phone. "Do we have that address for Justin Meagher yet?" he yelled to no one in particular.

"Just getting it now," a woman's voice called, and a moment later a young woman appeared in the doorway in a police uniform. Priscilla hadn't seen her before and wasn't sure where she'd been earlier, but the police chief just grabbed the paper and looked down.

"Southie." He muttered something under his breath and then shouted into the hallways again. "Smith, get the boats ready. We're going to the mainland. Rogers, call the precinct over there. Tell them what's going on and that we're on our way. Michaels—"

Priscilla listened to all this, her mind reeling. They were going to look for him in *Boston*? "He's not there," she said, shaking her head.

The police chief and Officer Brown were already heading out the door, ready to get moving. But Officer Brown paused and looked at Priscilla. "Why do you say that?"

"He's got Mitchell at the cabin in Aquinnah. The one I came in here to tell you about." Priscilla tried to keep the indignation out of her voice.

Officer Brown looked torn. "Do you have any evidence? Any reason at all to believe that might be the case?"

"No, no evidence exactly, but I know he's there. I heard that dog—"

"Brown! Let's go!" the chief called from the hallway.

Officer Brown hesitated. Then she turned back to Priscilla and shook her head. "I'm sorry, Priscilla. We're headed to Boston to investigate there. If that doesn't pan out—"

"It might be too late!" Priscilla felt herself getting shrill, and she took a deep breath before she spoke again. They were not going to listen to her if they thought she was acting hysterical. "You saw what happened in that video. He was tied up. Shoved into a boat. Every moment that passes—"

"I get it," Officer Brown said but not unkindly. "Look. I don't know about this cabin idea. It seems pretty far-fetched to me. But you've gotten a few things right so far, so I'm willing to check it out if this doesn't pan out. But right now, we're headed to Boston."

With that, she grabbed a wool coat that was hanging on a coat rack, and then she turned and headed out the door.

Priscilla sat there for a moment, listening and watching as the officers rushed about, getting ready for their trip to Boston.

She couldn't believe it. They still didn't believe her. They were headed straight into what Priscilla knew was a dead end and were ignoring what she'd given them once again.

But what could she do about it? She wasn't a police officer or the Coast Guard. She couldn't go out to Aquinnah and investigate herself. Justin and Scott were no doubt armed. She couldn't put herself in that kind of danger.

Then again, if she was right, Mitchell was in danger this very moment. Every moment he wasn't turning over the painting, he stood between his brother and cousin and what they wanted. Would Justin really hurt Mitchell to get to the painting? She hated to think it—but then, he'd already kidnapped him and destroyed the houseboat looking for it. There was no telling what he'd do.

And every moment she sat here—every moment the cops were off chasing answers in a place they wouldn't find them—Mitchell was still in danger. But what could she do? She couldn't exactly go in, guns blazing, and demand that he be set free.

Priscilla felt the cold, hard plastic of the police chair beneath her.

Maybe she couldn't spring Mitchell from his captors. But she could go by the cabin and verify that he was there so that when the police returned from Boston, clueless and unsure what to do next, she would have evidence to make them go check it out.

That was what she'd do, Priscilla decided. No one else may believe her, but Priscilla Grant trusted her gut, and she knew she was right.

Now all she had to do was prove it.

CHAPTER TWENTY-SEVEN

The sun hung low in the sky as she made her way toward Aquinnah. The sea was choppy but sparkled like bits of broken glass in the sun. Normally Priscilla would be totally taken with the scenery, but right now all she could think about was what lay ahead. If there was anything at the cabin, she would find it. She would find it, and when the police got back from their fruitless search in Boston, she would be here to point them in the right direction.

As she drove, she thought about how much she'd changed in the few months she'd lived on Martha's Vineyard. Back in Kansas, she wouldn't have had the guts to contradict a police officer. She wouldn't have thought it was her place; they were the professionals after all. They probably knew more than she did. But for some reason, being here had helped her see things a little differently.

They *were* professionals. They had tools she didn't have. But that didn't mean they were infallible. She had experience and knowledge they didn't have, and when her gut was telling her something, she had come to see that it was worth listening.

She wondered what Rachel would say if she could see her mother now, racing off to a remote fishing cabin, hoping to find evidence of a kidnapping. Rachel would lose her mind. She'd probably warn Priscilla to stay out of it. She'd tell her she was being reckless. Well, she'd be careful then. Somehow it felt good to do something she knew would drive Rachel nuts.

Still, it probably wasn't a bad idea to check in with someone so they'd know where to look for her if something went wrong. She grabbed her phone from the console and plugged in her headset. She could call one of her cousins, but they would only worry. She decided to call Gerald. The phone rang and rang, but he didn't pick up. Strange. Why wasn't he answering?

She left a message, explaining what she was doing and where she was going, mentioning the address 24 Oxcart Road. Just in case.

She tried not to think about how crazy it was to be leaving the address *just in case*, but still heading that way nonetheless. Was she driving into a disaster? Well, it was too late now. She had to see for herself. She had to know she could trust her gut. She returned the phone to the console and focused on the drive.

It took almost a half hour to drive to Aquinnah, but it passed quickly, and Priscilla was surprised to find herself driving past Menemsha and Squibnocket ponds and onto the wooded road that wound through this desolate landscape. Aquinnah was a world apart from Tisbury—largely unpopulated, with only a few shops and restaurants. Nature still reigned in this corner of the world.

Her GPS led her along the same route she'd read on the Dogfish Bar website. She turned left onto Lighthouse Road and drove past a small inn and past the turnoff for Lobsterville Beach to the narrow dirt road labeled Oxcart Road. If she hadn't been looking for it, she wouldn't have spotted it. She slowed as her wheels hit the rutted, hard-packed dirt. Every so often, a driveway branched off, but for the most part this road was desolate. Finally, just when she'd decided she was going the wrong way, her GPS told her to turn right, and she found herself at a narrow little break in the trees. A dirt path branched off. This must be it.

Priscilla took a deep breath and turned into the driveway. It ran under the trees for a moment, and then they thinned out and gave way to a clearing. The house was just beyond that, perched at the edge of the land before it began to slope down toward the sea. She could see the water just a few hundred yards beyond the little house. It was small—it couldn't be more than a couple of rooms. But it was unmistakably the same cabin from the Sean Meagher painting.

There was a light on inside.

Priscilla slowed down and parked a ways back from the house. There were no cars parked around it. But the light meant someone had to be inside—didn't it?

Priscilla knew she should turn around and go back. She'd verified there was someone at the cabin. That should be enough to get the police to come out here and investigate.

But she couldn't just turn around and run. Something in her wouldn't allow it. She had to see if Mitchell really was here. After all this, she didn't want to trust the police or the Coast Guard to find the answers. She had put this puzzle together, and she would find its conclusion.

Priscilla turned off the car, slipped her phone into her pocket, said a prayer for protection, and then stepped out onto the dirt driveway. The sun was setting now, and in the twilight, the shadows seemed to gather around her, but she just put one foot in front of the other and moved toward the house. There was no noise coming from inside, just the low rumble of the waves pounding against the shore beyond.

At the back of the house was a door, but she wasn't about to just walk inside. She moved around, trying to keep her footsteps as quiet as possible, until she came to a window. She took a deep breath, and then she leaned forward and peered through the dirty glass. It looked in on a bedroom. The light in this room was off, but she could see clothing scattered across two single beds, and a few duffel bags sat open on the floor. There was no one inside the room. She looked for a moment longer and then moved along, toward the front of the cabin where the light was.

She stepped up onto a wooden deck in front of a sliding glass door. She passed a set of rusted wrought-iron deck furniture and moved toward the door, which looked out over the beach. At the back of her mind, she registered a high-pitched whine underneath the sound of the waves, but she was too focused on creeping quietly across the deck to really notice. She crept closer then pressed her face against the glass. There was no one in the room, but there were dirty dishes on an old wooden table, and she could see the cabinets of a small kitchen crowded with cans and boxes of pasta. Whoever was staying here wasn't much for housekeeping.

She stepped off the deck and made her way around to the final side of the house, where she found another window. She put her face to the glass and peered in. This must be another small bedroom. The light was off, but...

Oh my. Instinctively, Priscilla put her hand to her throat. Was that...?

There was a body on the narrow bed. It wasn't moving. Was that Mitchell? She leaned in, trying to see more in the dim light in the room. She was looking at the man's back. His hair was brown, like Mitchell's. But then, a lot of people had brown hair. But there—was that rope? She squinted and was pretty sure she saw rope around his ankles. His hands were out of sight, but she guessed they too were bound. Then Priscilla noticed that a blond dog slept next to the bed. Was this Hawthorne?

The man was tied up, whoever he was. But he wasn't moving. She couldn't even see his back rise and fall with breath.

They wouldn't have—his own brother.

But then...was he...

She knew she shouldn't do it, but she couldn't help it. She had to see if this man, whoever he was, was alive. She rapped on the glass. And then she held her breath.

The dog lifted its head and looked up at her.

The man in the bed turned his head, and she felt relief course through her. There was something over his mouth—a gag of some kind—but he had moved. He was alive. His eyes widened when he saw her. In that instant, she recognized him.

It was Mitchell. She'd found Mitchell!

She realized this just a second before she was grabbed from behind. A hand closed over her mouth, blocking her scream. It only took a fraction of a second for her to realize she was in very deep trouble.

CHAPTER TWENTY-EIGHT

The man kept one hand over Priscilla's mouth, and with the other he held her close to his body. She screamed, but the sound vanished into his hand.

"Who are you?" he hissed. "What are you doing here?"

Where had he come from? She hadn't heard a car drive up. She couldn't see his face, but he was big, and judging by his grip on her, he was strong too. Considering the fact that his hand covered her mouth, she assumed the question he'd asked was rhetorical.

"I got the rope here," another man said from behind them. She had a sinking suspicion she knew who they were.

"Get her feet first," said the man holding her. She guessed it was Justin, though maybe it was Scott. From this angle, she couldn't tell who was who. A moment later, the other man was wrapping her feet in thick nylon rope. It gouged into her flesh, but when she shouted, the sound once again went nowhere. A moment later, her hands were bound too, and the big man let her go. He stepped back, and she saw that he was Justin. Scott must be the one currently folding a handkerchief—to cover her mouth, if she had to guess. She gulped for air, suddenly starved for breath.

"Who are you?" Justin asked again.

Should she make up some story? Convince him the police were hot on their tails? In the end, she decided to just stick with the truth.

"I'm Priscilla Grant." Her heart was beating like she'd just run a marathon. "I live in Tisbury."

"What are you doing here?" Scott asked.

"I was looking for Mitchell." She inclined her head toward the window.

"You police?" Justin asked.

If she hadn't been scared out of her mind, she might have found this funny. She was an unarmed fifty-something woman in slacks, a sweater, and comfortable flats. Did she look like she worked for the police?

"She doesn't look like police to me," Scott said.

"I'm not. I'm just someone who was interested in finding out what happened to Mitchell." She had to work very hard to keep her voice calm and level when all she wanted to do was scream for help or break down in tears. Either one of those would get her gagged instantly, she was sure, and she needed to keep that from happening.

"How did you find us?" Scott asked.

Before she could answer, Justin was asking, "Who knows you're here?"

She tried to decide whether it would be better to make them think a large fleet of armed officers was on its way or whether the truth—that it was possible no one knew she was here—would work out better for her.

"Well?" Justin moved closer to her again.

"No one knows I'm here," she said. Above them, the sky was darkening into night, and stars had started to appear.

"Can't be for long," Scott said, looking at Justin. "Someone will track her here."

Justin nodded. "We have to move."

Scott started cursing under his breath but said, "I'll go get our stuff."

"Grab Mitch too. We're clearing out."

Justin took the gag and wrapped it around Priscilla's mouth. It dug into her gums, and she couldn't talk, but she could breathe. Justin picked up the rope and marched her toward the back patio. With her feet bound, she had to take teeny tiny steps, but she could move a bit. He sat her down on one of the wrought-iron chairs and used the rope to tie her to it.

As soon as she was secure, Justin vanished inside, and she was left alone on the deck. The last light of sunset was just vanishing over the horizon. Under different circumstances, she would have found this view peaceful, but now all she could do was try to think of how to get out of this mess.

"What do we do about this dog?" one of them asked.

"Leave it here." Something banged against a wall inside.

She adjusted in the seat and tried to grab her phone. Her bound hands made it difficult, but there was enough give in the rope that she could move them some. In his rush, Justin must not have tied the rope as well as he could. She wiggled her way to a place where she could just barely reach into her pocket. Her fingers brushed the edge of the plastic, and then, twisting her whole body, she was able to grab the phone. She was so jumpy she could barely hold it. She knew she only had a few moments, so she tried to get this right. Her hands, bound at the wrist, were shaking so much it took two tries to type in her password, and she was not used to working at such a difficult angle, but she finally got the phone unlocked and then navigated to the phone app.

She heard the sliding door swish open. Someone was about to come out. She fumbled with the screen. She had intended to call 911, but there was no time. A list of her recent calls was on the screen, and she hit the top one.

"Hey." It was Scott, his arms loaded down with bags, stepping out onto the deck. The blueish light from the phone was a beacon in the darkness. "Drop it."

Priscilla didn't know what else to do, so she dropped the phone on the deck. She held her breath. Scott nodded, and then he continued past her, carrying the bags down a narrow little path that led toward the water. She got a sinking feeling in her stomach. She understood now where the two men had come from so suddenly. They'd come in on a boat. That was why she hadn't heard a car drive up; they'd approached the house from the water. Between the distance from the shoreline and the fact that she'd been focused on what she was doing, she hadn't recognized the sound of the motor on the boat as they approached.

And now, she knew, they were about to leave in a boat as well. They were going to leave the cabin for good. And who knew where they'd end up.

The phone continued to ring as Scott disappeared down the shore, and finally, Gerald's voice mail picked up. She knew the voice mail was recording, so she tried her best to scream, but she knew it wasn't enough. Gerald would never be able to understand what was going on.

A moment later, Justin came out of the house with Mitchell slung over his shoulder. "I'll be back for you," he said, nodding at Priscilla.

She saw that Mitchell's arms and feet were bound just as hers were, and his mouth was gagged too. He met her eye as Justin carried him past. He looked tired, and he looked scared.

She sat in the darkness, waiting for whatever was coming next. Was Gerald's voice mail still recording? She didn't have any way to know, but the screen had gone dark.

A few minutes later, Scott returned. "Ready to get in the boat?" he said, grinning grotesquely.

She tried to scream again, but it came out as nothing more than a moan. He hoisted her up, balancing her over his shoulder. The world spun beneath her as she bounced the whole way down the narrow sandy path to the beach. A fishing boat—the one that had been in the security footage, she felt sure—had been dragged onto the sand. He leaned over and dropped her into it, and she landed in the bottom roughly. Mitchell, still tied up, was next to her, and Justin stood next to the boat.

Once both prisoners were inside, Scott and Justin grasped the edge, leaned into the boat, and pushed it down the sloping sand toward the water. As the buoyant water lifted it, they both hopped in, the motor screamed, and they were off.

Wind whipped around the boat, and she was suddenly cold. Where were they going? What would wait for them there? Priscilla didn't have a clue, and as the land receded behind them, all she could think to do was pray. She asked God for His protection, for His mercy, and that help would come soon. She also prayed that He would keep their little boat safe—she had noticed they were flying through the water with no lights on. She was sure this was both illegal and dangerous, but what could she do?

There had to be something she could do. She looked around the boat and took stock of the situation. She didn't know much about boats, but she had heard the police refer to this as a fishing boat when they saw it on the video. There were two seats, leather or something like it, perched high behind the windshield, and behind them—where she and Mitchell had been tossed—was an open space surrounded by narrow benches for perching around the edges of the boat. She supposed this was where you'd keep coolers to put the fish you caught. The bottom and inside of the boat were made of some sort of fiberglass, and at the rear—the bow or the stern? She couldn't remember—was a very large and very loud outboard motor.

Built into the walls were several recessed storage areas. She could see life vests tucked into the one on the far side of the boat. She shifted as much as she could and pushed herself up on her elbows so she could look into the storage area closest to her. She saw what looked like lengths of rope, a first-aid kit, an air horn, and an orange bag of some kind. She shifted a bit more and realized what it was. A flare kit. For sending out distress signals. And—she couldn't believe it. A knife. There was a knife for cutting marine rope in there.

Her mind raced. She had to get her hands on those distress signals. If she could get them out, and if she could set them off, would anyone be around to see them? And what would happen to her if she did? She couldn't imagine Justin and Scott would take that well. Would they toss her overboard? She wouldn't survive that, not with her hands and feet bound. Still, she knew she had to try. She'd worry about the consequences later.

First, she wiggled her hands. There was still give in the rope, and, as she'd discovered earlier, it wasn't tied as tightly as she would have thought. No doubt an oversight because of the rush. She tried to work the rope off. The boat lurched over the waves, speeding away from shore, and they were tossed around in the back, but she kept working. There. Was that loosening? The rope burned her wrists, but she bit her lip and kept wriggling her hands, trying to get one out.

Finally, she managed to slip one hand out of the rope. She almost laughed in triumph—though of course, she couldn't actually make any sound. Once she had one hand free, the other slipped out easily.

Priscilla used her hands to push herself up. She glanced at the front of the boat. The two men were focused on the water ahead of them. She reached behind her head and yanked the gag off. Then she reached into the storage compartment, took out the knife, and used it to cut the rope that bound her feet.

She leaned over and cut the rope that bound Mitchell and removed his gag. He seemed stunned, his eyes wide. Now that the gag was off, she could see that he was gaunt.

"Who are you?" he whispered.

She used her hands to shush him. She would explain later. Even over the roaring of the outboard motor, she didn't want to risk the men hearing them. She indicated Mitchell should reach behind him. He moved slowly, like every move was painful, but he rolled himself over and nodded when he saw the life vests tucked into the storage compartment next to him.

She hoisted herself up so she could peer over the edge of the boat and look around. They were way out in the middle of nowhere. She could still see some lights back on shore as Martha's Vineyard receded behind them but could see nothing but black water ahead.

Wait! There. Off to the left side. Starboard? She didn't know. But there were lights moving. A boat, racing through the water. A few other boats were just behind it. Three in all? They were moving fast. Was there any chance...?

It didn't matter who it was. With the lights on this boat off, they would never see it—and even if they did, why would they pay attention to it? But if she could set off a flare...

What had Gerald said? A flare would only work if someone was looking for your location. It would be best to use a marine radio— set to the special Coast Guard station—first so that someone would be looking for you in the first place.

Well, she didn't have a marine radio. There probably was one on this boat attached to the steering console, but she knew she wasn't going to be able to get to that. But if she could set off the flares...

Gerald had said that a series of flares would be taken as a distress signal. Priscilla reached into the storage area and pulled out the orange kit. Her hands were shaking, as much with cold as fear. She unzipped the pouch and saw that it contained half a dozen handheld flares, which were basically like the glow sticks Rachel played with as a kid. There was also a flare gun, as well as six cartridges to be inserted into the gun. God bless whatever fisherman they stole this boat from.

Priscilla checked the men in the front, but they were still absorbed in navigating to wherever they were headed. They paid no attention to the prisoners in the back.

She knew this was risky. She reached for the life vest Mitchell was handing to her and, her hands shaking, clipped it on. Was she really going to do this? Would this be better than waiting and seeing what would happen to her on the other end? She thought for half a second and realized that whatever would happen once they got to the mainland, or wherever they were headed, it was not going to be good. She also knew that if she went ahead with this insane idea, there was a very real chance she was going overboard.

She didn't know how long she could hold on in the cold water, but she knew a life vest would help. She tucked a few of the handheld flares into the life vest and also tossed a few toward Mitchell. He nodded and took them silently.

Then, glancing forward once again, Priscilla fired the flare gun. The two men in the seats jumped and started cursing, but Priscilla watched the bright red light rise high into the sky and then arc back down toward the water. The air was filled with the sulfurous smell of burning ozone.

Was she imagining it or did the boats she'd seen change direction? She couldn't be sure, but she quickly reloaded the gun and shot it up once again. By this time, Scott had launched out of his seat and was trying to grab the gun from her. She managed to get one more flare launched before he wrenched the gun from her hands and tossed it overboard.

"What are you doing?" he shrieked, his face twisted in anger.

Priscilla didn't try to answer.

"Scott!" Justin called, but Scott didn't seem to hear.

"How did you get free?" Scott was shouting now.

"Scott!" Justin yelled, louder this time.

Scott lunged toward Priscilla, letting out a string of curses as he wrestled her arms behind her back.

"*Scott!*" Justin was screaming now. "We've got company. We have to go."

Scott froze, and then he turned and looked back behind them. He uttered another profanity.

"We have to lighten the load," Justin screamed.

Scott didn't hesitate. He reached down and grabbed Priscilla. She fought him, kicking and biting and punching, but it was no use. He was too strong, and before she knew it, he had hefted her up over the side of the boat and tossed her in.

The frigid water hit her like a train, and she sank down under the surface. She couldn't move, her system so shocked by the water.

She knew she needed to get to the surface, but the water was black and so cold all around her. She held her breath and fought her way up, and after what felt like minutes but was probably no more than a few seconds, the buoyant life vest carried her to the surface. She gasped for air, but even breathing was hard. She was shivering, shuddering. She was so cold, and the boat was roaring away. She turned and watched it go. Watched as Scott hoisted Mitchell up.

Was he really going to do it? Was he really going to toss his cousin overboard? Priscilla couldn't believe it. Would Justin really allow Scott to toss his brother into the sea? Scott hesitated, looked down at Mitchell, but then tossed him over the side.

A splash rose up as the boat sped away. Priscilla did her best to swim toward the splash, but it was so cold and so hard. How long could they survive out here? She was glad she didn't really know.

But she knew she wasn't imagining it now. They had been tossed overboard because the boats she'd seen on the horizon really were coming toward them. Priscilla knew they'd never find them unless she got the handheld flares out and lit. She was shaking, but she grabbed a flare from where she'd strapped it on her life vest, bent it until it lit, and tucked it into a loop on her life vest. She grabbed another one and did the same thing, and then she started swimming toward where Mitchell had landed again. Had he surfaced? Where was he? All she could see around her was black water.

"Mitchell?" she called out. "Where are you?"

What else was in this water? Were there sharks around here? She knew the movie *Jaws* had been set on Martha's Vineyard. That must mean…

No. She couldn't think about that.

She focused on the boats. They were coming this direction now, she was almost sure of it. They were headed toward where the flares had appeared. But would they see her, even with these hand-held lights? The Sound was so big, and she was such a tiny speck. How could they possibly see the flares?

"Mitchell?"

It was so dark and so quiet out here. She heard splashing behind her to the right, but when she looked in that direction, she couldn't see anything.

"Mitchell?"

Was he gone? Was she alone out here, floating in the middle of the sea?

Then, just as she was losing hope, she saw it. A flash of light. A phosphorescent stick was being held up, maybe fifty yards from her.

"Mitchell!" she yelled and started swimming in that direction. Another light appeared. She just kept moving, swimming toward the lights. Every stroke was difficult. It felt like she was running a marathon as she used her frigid arms to pull her closer to him. Finally, gasping and sputtering, she found him.

"Mitchell," she said. He was floating on his back, looking up at the sky, holding his glow stick in the air above him.

"Are you some kind of superhero?" he asked, righting himself and turning toward her.

Despite it all, she laughed. "No. I'm Priscilla Grant."

"Well, I don't know who you are, Priscilla Grant, but thank you for coming to my rescue." His teeth were chattering, and his lips were turning a pale blue, Priscilla could see in the light of their flares.

"Don't thank me yet. So far all I've done is landed us both in the middle of the Sound," she said.

"Those boats are headed this way. Let's hope they find us." He lifted his glow sticks above his head and started waving them. Priscilla did the same.

Now that the first wave of panic was subsiding, she understood fully how much trouble they were in. Floating on the Sound. Nighttime. Their life jackets their only means of support. Would anyone ever find them? Would a shark or some other sea creature find them first? A swell passed, lifting them up and dropping them back down.

The boats were closer now. She and Mitchell waved the glowing sticks above their heads. Could the boats see them? Were they coming for them?

At some point, Priscilla's shaking stilled. Either she had gotten used to the water, or her body was starting to shut down. She had a thousand questions to ask Mitchell, but forming words seemed too hard. Was this what it was like to freeze to death?

Soon she could hear the roar of the motors as the boats approached them. Who would be on the boats, and what would they find? Priscilla had no idea, but she hoped they would be able to help. She glanced at Mitchell. He was still shaking, and his lips were now darker blue. He seemed to be having trouble keeping his eyes focused. After a week tied up, he was no doubt weak and malnourished. How long would he survive out here?

"Look," he said. He used his stick to point toward the approaching boats.

She squinted and saw what he had noticed. The approaching boat had a dark stripe around the top and, beneath that, a familiar white logo. Priscilla felt her body go weak with relief. "It's the Coast Guard," she whispered.

They watched silently as the three Coast Guard boats approached and then slowed as they got close. The first boat navigated close enough to toss down a chain ladder, and a cadet she recognized stepped down to pull her onboard.

"Seeley," she said, tears of relief spilling over.

"Ms. Grant. We thought that might be you." He held her with one arm and pulled her up the ladder.

As soon as she was over the rim and onboard, one of the other officers climbed down the ladder to pull Mitchell up. She found herself wrapped in a heavy blanket and brought down a few steps to a small cabin under the steering area.

"Priscilla!" Gerald appeared just as the other officer brought Mitchell down the steps. "And"—his eyes widened—"is this…?"

"Hi, Gerald." Priscilla was shivering again, but she gave him a weak smile. "I believe this is Mitchell. Though we haven't been formally introduced."

Mitchell looked ghostly white, and his whole body was shaking, but he gave her a weak smile. "Yes," he said. "I'm Mitchell Meagher." He turned to Gerald and the other officers gathered in the small cabin. "And Priscilla Grant just saved my life."

CHAPTER TWENTY-NINE

A s they cruised back to land, the two other boats were dispatched to search for the one that carried Justin and Scott, and a police crew was already on its way to the cabin to search for clues and rescue the dog stranded there. Priscilla sat on the Coast Guard boat, a heavy blanket wrapped around her shoulders and a space heater aimed at her, and shared what had happened. She explained how she'd found the cabin and tried to get the police to investigate but how the officers had gone to Boston instead. How she'd decided to check the cabin out herself and how she'd been grabbed. How she and Mitchell had both been tossed in a boat and how she managed to work her hands free and grab the flares.

"She was like MacGyver," Mitchell said, shaking his head. "I was watching her, and I don't know how she was able to do it."

Even though she was shivering, she felt warmth spread through her.

"And it's a very good thing you did," Gerald said. He sat next to her on the low bench, a little closer than was strictly necessary, but she certainly didn't mind. "I was in meetings all afternoon. Strategy meetings," he said, glancing at Mitchell, "for how to find you." He looked at Priscilla and shook his head. "Turns out I should have just taken the calls from Priscilla. I sure wish I had.

When I got your voice mail saying that you were at the cabin, I freaked out a bit."

"He did," Seeley said. He was taking notes on a steno pad, but he looked up and nodded. "I was trying to talk to him, and when he played the message, he got up and started to run out of the office before it even finished playing."

"I was worried. It was a really stupid thing to do," Gerald said, leveling his gaze at Priscilla.

"Well, yeah. I know that now," she muttered.

"Luckily I stopped him," Seeley said, "because the new message started playing. That was when he really lost it."

"All I could hear was what sounded like you screaming, but really far away, followed by this gruff voice saying something about getting in the boat."

His voice mail had recorded that exchange on the patio then.

"That was when we knew you were in trouble and headed for the boats," Gerald said. "But we never would have found you if you hadn't sent off those flares."

"I was just glad you were there to see them," Priscilla said.

"So am I." He touched her leg.

"But the question still remains," Seeley said from the other bench. "How did *you* come to be at that cabin?"

He was looking at Mitchell, who seemed to be a bit steadier now. He was drinking a Gatorade and had eaten a banana, and a bit of color was starting to come back into his cheeks.

"Yes," Priscilla said. "I figured out some of it, but there are several things I haven't been able to put together." She took the cup of tea one of the officers was holding out to her. "Like, did you have anything to do with stealing that painting?"

Mitchell shook his head and then explained everything that had led up to this moment. How his grandfather's most important work had been in his father's possession, and it was supposed to have been passed down to the eldest son, Justin, when he died. How his father had changed his mind, and his will, after deciding that Justin, who had spent his adulthood going in and out of prison, would simply sell it to the highest bidder—a plan Justin had espoused many times. Robert considered leaving it to Mitchell, but in the end decided that his father's legacy would be better protected by having the painting hang in a museum. Mitchell had agreed with the decision, but Justin, with whom Mitchell had strained relations, didn't take it so well. He felt cheated, and there was a big to-do. He'd contested the will but lost his case, as their father's wishes had been perfectly clear. Mitchell had been the executor of the estate, so Justin blamed him as much as their father for cheating him out of his inheritance.

"I had nothing to do with it," Mitchell said, pulling the heavy wool blanket tighter around his shoulders. His hair was a bit darker and threaded with more gray than in the picture she'd seen online. "I didn't disagree, but I didn't have anything to do with it."

Mitchell, Priscilla was learning, was soft-spoken and gentle, and the learned way he spoke, even with his teeth chattering, made it clear he was very intelligent.

When Mitchell had read about the painting vanishing from the museum, he continued, he knew what Justin had done. He had the technical skills and the greed to pull off something like that. He suspected—and later confirmed—that their cousin Scott, who had gotten in trouble with Justin in the past, had been involved too. He'd no doubt been promised a cut of the profits when they sold the painting. Mitchell had gone to Justin's apartment to confront him about it and had found the priceless painting lying on his kitchen counter, next to cups of coffee and bottles of ketchup. Mitchell had been so enraged that when his brother left the room, Mitchell had swiped the painting and run.

"Of course, as soon as I had the painting in my possession, I realized what a bad position I was in," Mitchell said.

"What were you planning to do with it?" Gerald asked.

Priscilla had stopped shaking, but in her wet clothes, she was chilled to the bone. Nothing sounded better than dry clothes and a hot shower.

"I'll admit I hadn't really thought that through. My initial thought had been to return it to the museum, but I quickly came to see the problems with that plan."

"Like what?" Priscilla asked.

"Well, they would no doubt wonder where I got it." Mitchell laughed, but it sounded hollow. "Right after the painting had vanished, the police came to talk with me, but they quickly realized I didn't do it.

"And though I was not proud of my brother, when the moment came, I realized I didn't want to send him to prison for life. No matter how badly he messed up, he was still my brother, and I couldn't face the idea of being responsible for sending him away for life."

Priscilla didn't respond. This was the brother who had repaid Mitchell's compassion by kidnapping him, ransacking his home, tying him up for a week, and tossing him overboard into the frigid water of Vineyard Sound. Priscilla didn't have any brothers or sisters, but she knew relationships with siblings could be complicated. Still, she doubted the Meagher brothers would recover at this point. She was sure Mitchell would be grieving that for years.

"So what did you do with the painting?" Priscilla asked. The whine of the outboard motor powering them toward shore meant they all had to speak a bit louder than usual. Gerald had decided to take Mitchell and Priscilla directly to Martha's Vineyard Hospital, which was in Oak Bluffs, on the east side of the island.

"I took out a safe-deposit box to keep it in while I figured out what to do," Mitchell said.

Priscilla nodded. She'd been right about that then.

"And I knew I wasn't safe. I knew Justin would be looking for me and the painting. I was pretty sure he wouldn't hurt me to get to the painting, but I didn't want to take any chances." He laughed again, but this time it just came out sounding bitter. "I was wrong about that, obviously."

No one said anything for a moment. The pain in his words was clear, and she couldn't blame him. He'd recently lost his father, and now he had lost his relationship with his brother too.

"How did you decide to come to Martha's Vineyard?" Priscilla asked.

"Well, I knew I needed to disappear, and fast. And to be honest, I was ready for a change. In addition to my father passing, my wife passed away last year, and I was...I was untethered. Adrift."

Priscilla knew the feeling.

"I had enough money to make it a few years without working, and I was still mourning, still processing. The idea of going off the grid for a while was welcome actually. Just me and my dog on the open waves." He shrugged. "It sounded nice. I've always loved Martha's Vineyard. We came here a lot as kids—it was my grandfather's cabin at that point—and it has always felt like home."

Priscilla understood that feeling too. The way this island called to you. The way it was in your blood. But something about this didn't make sense.

"But surely you knew that the cabin now belonged to Scott. Why would you come so close to it?"

"Scott never really used the cabin," Mitchell said. "He hadn't been here in years. I knew I couldn't go there, but I thought I would be safe enough on the far side of the island."

"But why a houseboat? Why not just rent a house somewhere where you wouldn't be so noticeable?" Priscilla asked.

"For one thing, I hadn't realized what a stir it would cause." He shrugged again. "I would not have done it if I'd realized that. Who would have guessed that a boat in the harbor would make so many people upset?"

Seeley laughed. "People around here can always find things to get upset about."

"It was as much because they hadn't seen one before as anything," Gerald said. "And because it was so visible."

"I hadn't counted on that." Mitchell shook his head. "That was one of several major miscalculations I made. At the time, I was just thinking that it sounded like a nice way to be out of sight. Surrounded by water, no neighbors to disturb me, just me and my dog. I'd always had an interest in art, and I wanted to paint, but I'd always had to focus on work. This seemed like a good way to find some uninterrupted time and space to try that."

"How long did you plan to stay there?" Priscilla asked.

He tipped his head. "A few weeks. Months, if I could. I knew that with winter coming, I couldn't stay there forever, but I wasn't really thinking that far ahead, to be honest. I just needed a place to disappear, and quickly, and I went for it and figured I'd work out the details later. I mean, I was in possession of a stolen painting worth a million dollars. I was just trying to disappear as quickly as possible."

Given the situation he was in, Priscilla found this plausible enough.

"Is that why you gave everyone a false name?"

He shrugged. "I thought Bart Flask was pretty clever myself."

"It certainly threw us off." Gerald's gruff demeanor had melted away as they spoke, and he realized Mitchell wasn't a threat. "Priscilla was the one who figured that out as well."

Mitchell drank his gatorade and gave her a smile. "Seems like maybe you should get a job with these guys."

Priscilla laughed. "No thanks. I've had enough adventures at sea to last me a lifetime." She took a sip of her tea. "But maybe I'll put in an application at the police station."

Gerald smiled, and then he said to Mitchell, "Tell us about your relationship with Dan Galvin."

"He's just an old friend. He was totally innocent in all this. He had nothing to do with anything."

"Did you plan to contact him when you came here?"

"No. I didn't really think about it." Mitchell looked down at his drink for a moment. "I mean, I guess I knew he lived here. Our wives exchanged Christmas cards. You know how that goes. But I hadn't really thought about it. I wasn't here for social reasons, after all. My plan was to talk to as few people as possible. But we ran into each other at the market and reconnected. It was a fun surprise."

"When did he start visiting you on the boat?" Gerald asked.

Mitchell smiled. "That started shortly after we reconnected. I'd mentioned I didn't like going in from the boat, and he offered to bring me things. He always was a really nice guy."

He truly was, Priscilla knew. But she had other things she wanted to understand.

"How did Justin find you?"

Mitchell stared down at the bottle in his hands. "I said I made a number of miscalculations, right? Well, one of them was underestimating Justin. He is very good at computer stuff."

"I read he was a hacker," Priscilla said.

Mitchell nodded. "I didn't realize he would be able to use my phone to find my location. It was silly, in retrospect. I knew the police could use data from the phone company to pinpoint your location based on cell phone usage. But I was pretty sure the police weren't looking for me, and I hadn't thought about Justin using that same technology to find me."

"He used your phone to find you?" Priscilla tried to make sense of this. How was that possible?

"It's not that uncommon," Gerald said. "We can use information about which cell phone towers any activity on the phone activates, and that gives us a pretty good general idea of someone's location."

Priscilla couldn't decide whether to be impressed or scared by this. What didn't the authorities know about people's personal lives these days?

"So your brother just showed up and demanded the painting back?"

"That's about the gist of it," Mitchell said. "My cousin was there for good measure. They were not happy when I said I didn't have it."

"We saw what they did to the boat," Gerald said.

"They looked everywhere. And when they didn't find it, they tied me up and brought me out to the cabin."

"How did they think that would help?" Priscilla felt the velocity of the boat slow some. They must be getting close to their destination.

"I guess they thought maybe I would change my mind and tell them where the painting was."

"Did you?"

"No. As it turns out, treating someone badly is not a good way to get them to cooperate." He took a sip of his Gatorade. "Even if I had wanted to, there was no way I could have gotten it for them. The key for the safe-deposit box was still on the boat, which they'd cut free and sent out to sea."

Priscilla nodded. "It was taped under the drawer."

He looked up. "You all found that?"

"Priscilla found it." Gerald gave her a fond look. "We haven't been able to get the box open yet, but now that we have you, I'm sure we'll be able to return the painting to its rightful place at the museum shortly."

"Captain O'Bannon?" A Coast Guard officer came down the steps and stood at the entrance to the little space. "We just got word from the other boats. They've found the boat carrying the suspects and apprehended them."

Priscilla hadn't realized how much anxiety she'd been carrying until she felt it melt away at that news. They'd been caught. The bad guys had been arrested. Mitchell was safe. The painting would be returned to its home.

There would still be a lot of healing, Priscilla knew. Mitchell would bear the scars from this past week for years—physically and otherwise. She didn't know how he could recover from being kidnapped and left for dead by his own brother. But she knew that with God, all things were possible.

It would take some time for Priscilla to recover too. Floating out there in that water tonight, she'd thought her time was up.

She'd never been so afraid. She knew that it would take time and a lot of prayer for her to recover from the events of the evening as well. But again, she believed that God could make all things new. The God who had created the waves had saved her from them. He would be her anchor now and in the coming days.

Priscilla felt the boat slow even further, and a moment later, she felt it bump gently against the dock. She had never been so thankful for dry land. She knew ambulances would be waiting to take them both to the hospital, but for the moment, she simply relished the idea of standing on solid ground.

Gerald helped her to her feet, holding on to her arm a moment longer than he really needed to. Priscilla didn't mind at all.

"Ready?" he asked.

Priscilla nodded. She was certainly ready to get off this boat. And she was also ready for whatever came next. Priscilla didn't know what the future held, but she knew that God was in control. And she also knew, with a certainty she couldn't explain, that she belonged here in Martha's Vineyard. She couldn't wait to see what happened next.

CHAPTER THIRTY

Priscilla had just unplugged the iron when the doorbell rang. She looked down and surveyed their work one more time and nodded. Pressed and ready to go, the quilt looked even better than she'd imagined. She carried it into the living room, draped it over the couch, and then walked to the front door.

"Hi there." She opened the door, and all three of her cousins trouped in. "My goodness. You all came together."

"Gail insisted on driving because she thinks I'm too careless," Trudy said, wiping her feet on the mat.

"We thought it made sense to carpool," Joan explained, stepping in behind her sister.

"And Trudy really is a terrible driver," Gail added. "She once crashed into a building."

"I just tapped the outside of the building, thank you very much. And I swear they moved that wall. It wasn't there before."

Priscilla could only laugh. She was so glad to have them all here.

"So where is this quilt?" Joan asked, looking around. "I want to see it."

"I'll bring it out when Gerald gets here. For now, go on out back. I'll bring out snacks."

"You don't have to tell me twice," Gail said. She headed through the kitchen and out the back door, Trudy and Joan a few steps behind. Priscilla stopped in the kitchen to grab a tray of sliced baguette and runny, tangy cheese and roasted almonds, and then she stepped outside as well.

She had lit a fire in the fire pit and laid out a variety of drinks on the picnic table. Strings of white lights brightened the area. Her cousins were already helping themselves to tea and sparkling water when she set the snacks down.

"This is just gorgeous." Trudy had a glass of sparkling water in one hand and had moved away from the table to look over the cliff and out toward the sea. "I don't see how you manage to get anything done. I would just stand here and look out at the sea all day."

"It really is nice," Priscilla agreed. The sun was setting, bathing the sky in brilliant orange and pink, and the water reflected that light back up into the heavens. It was hard to believe she'd thought that water might be the end of her just a couple of days ago. It was so peaceful and calm and gorgeous now. "Especially at this time of day."

"It's nice any time of day," Joan insisted. She was loading up a small paper plate with baguette and cheese. "And we're so lucky you share it with us."

"So. Where is it? I want to see this quilt." Gail had settled into one of the Adirondack chairs gathered around the fire. Priscilla had set out heavy blankets in case it got cold, but between the fire and the warm night, they didn't need them.

"I want to wait until Gerald gets here," Priscilla said. "And then I'll show you all at once. But this gathering isn't just about the quilt. It's my way of saying thanks."

"Thanks for what?" Joan took a bite of the bread and cheese. "Oh my goodness. This is delicious. What is this cheese?"

Priscilla laughed. "It's a triple cream sheep's milk cheese I got at the Brown Jug. I'm glad you like it." She grabbed a plate and took a piece of bread for herself. "And I'm saying thanks for making this place feel like home."

"Knock, knock." Gerald stepped out onto the patio. "I rang the doorbell but no one answered, so I came in. I hope that's all right."

"That's great. Come on back." Priscilla ushered him into the yard.

He looked around. "This is really nice."

"I figured this might be one of the last times I can host out here this season, so I wanted to take advantage of it."

Gerald said hello to each of her cousins, and while he filled his plate, Priscilla went inside and grabbed the quilt. Then she stepped back outside and held it up.

"What do you think?" she said.

"Oh my." Gerald set down his plate. His mouth hung open.

No one said anything for a moment, and the only sound was the roar of the waves pounding away at the rocks beneath them.

"It's stunning," Joan eventually said.

"Really, Priscilla. It's gorgeous," Trudy said.

Priscilla looked up and saw that Gerald was surreptitiously wiping away tears.

She had stitched the fabric triangles into little squares that she'd lined up to form individual stars. Each star had the same basic structure, with pinks and purples being the dominant colors in each, but each was unique in its own way.

"How did you do that?" Gail asked.

"It's just a bunch of fabric cut into triangles," Priscilla said. And it was true. It was that. But it was so much more too. It was hours of work and hundreds of scraps of fabric individually pieced together. It was many different pieces of fabric lovingly arranged and pulled together to form a beautiful design. Priscilla had taken hundreds of different pieces and brought them together into one.

"Aggie is going to love it," Gerald said.

That was all she needed to hear to know it had all been worth it.

Priscilla handed him the quilt, and he took it carefully, draping it over one arm. "She'll be wrapping your granddaughter in it in no time."

"Thank you, Priscilla." Gerald held her eye for a moment, and then Priscilla forced herself to look away.

"Yay!" Trudy clapped her hands. It was so uninhibited and free, and Priscilla was grateful for something to interrupt the serious moment. "A beautiful quilt on a beautiful night with beautiful people. What could be better than this?"

She raised her glass in a toast, and Priscilla and Gerald and the others did the same. As they all stood there together, watching the sun set, Priscilla thanked God for bringing them all here. They were each individuals, unique in their own ways. And God had brought them into her life and was stitching them together in a way Priscilla could only begin to imagine. She knew that out of the pieces of her life, He was creating something beautiful. Priscilla could not wait to see how it all turned out.

AUTHOR LETTER

Dear Reader,

Though I haven't spent much time on Martha's Vineyard, my parents live in Cape Cod, so in many ways, writing this book felt like coming home. The narrow cobblestone streets and colonial-era buildings are so vivid in my mind, as are the craggy cliffs and the bobbing boats and the salty tang of the seaside air. This is a part of the world that I could visit again and again, and I loved getting to visit it in the pages of this book.

And I also loved exploring the marina and the world of boating in this story. I will admit, this is not something I have much experience with, but my dad grew up sailing, and it was fun getting to ask him for help as I wrote. He explained the difference between a mooring and a boat slip and how people got from their moored boats to the land (something I'd always wondered!) and how the system of finding a place to park your sailboat works. It was fun to get his help on this. If any of the details are wrong, that's my fault!

Getting to write for any Guideposts fiction series is a treat, but this one has it all—a beautiful setting, characters with whom you want to spend time, intriguing mysteries, and a lighthouse!—and I think it just may be my favorite one yet.

Best wishes,
Beth Adams

ABOUT THE AUTHOR

Beth Adams lives in Brooklyn, New York, with her husband and two young daughters. When she's not writing, she spends her time cleaning up after two devious cats and trying to find time to read mysteries.

AN ARMCHAIR TOUR OF
MARTHA'S VINEYARD

Aquinnah

When most people picture Martha's Vineyard, they imagine charming streets, beautiful historic homes, quaint boutiques, and miles of beaches crowded with bathers. You'll certainly find all of that here, but if you get out of the more populated sections and head up-island (that is, west), you'll find a place that still feels natural and open. Aquinnah, the section at the far southwestern tip of Martha's Vineyard, feels like a whole different world from the bustling heart of Tisbury.

Aquinnah is a tiny town (311 residents at the last census), but the area is known mostly for the stunning clay cliffs and pristine beaches. Gay Head Light—the one that appears in Sean Meagher's painting in our story—is there, and that and the beaches are the main draw for tourists. But this part of the island is also valued for its peaceful feel and some great fishing spots. Aquinnah is also the home of the only federally recognized Native American tribe in the Commonwealth of Massachusetts, the Wampanoag tribe.

If you ever make it out to Martha's Vineyard, be sure to check out this unique part of the island.

SOMETHING DELICIOUS FROM
OUR SEASIDE FRIENDS

Priscilla's Red Lentil Soup
(Perfect on a chilly autumn night!)

2 tablespoons extra-virgin
  olive oil
1 onion, chopped
2 shallots, chopped
½ teaspoon red-pepper
  flakes

6 cups vegetable or chicken
  stock
1⅓ cup red lentils
½ cup brown rice
Sea salt, to taste

Combine the oil, onion, shallots, and red-pepper flakes in a large pot over medium heat. Cook until the onions soften and caramelize a bit, then add the stock, the lentils, and the rice. Simmer for about thirty minutes or until the rice has cooked through, and the lentils have collapsed. Season with salt, and adjust until it tastes good. Priscilla likes to top this soup with a big splash of olive oil, some salty feta cheese, almonds sliced thin, and some good black olives.

Read on for a sneak peek of another exciting book
in the series Mysteries of Martha's Vineyard!

Maiden of the Mist
by Nancy Mehl

Priscilla Grant walked down the street with her cousins, Joan, Trudy, and Gail. Martha's Vineyard was bustling with locals and tourists in town for the annual Fall for the Arts Festival. Creations from local artists filled the shops and galleries, and displays spilled out onto the sidewalks. Paintings, crafts, needlework, carvings…there was something to suit everyone's artistic taste.

Priscilla was still trying to process the recent revelation that mild, quiet, mousy Joan had been hiding a secret talent. Her love of flowers and gardens was well known to everyone, but she hadn't told anyone she'd been painting. When Joan finally admitted to it, Priscilla was impressed with her still-life floral paintings. Trudy had insisted that Joan show her artwork during the festival. At first Joan had refused, but after goading by Trudy, Gail, and Priscilla, she'd finally, albeit grudgingly, agreed. A local store that sold handmade items, the Art Attack, had accepted four of Joan's paintings to show.

After stopping for some coffee at a local coffee shop, the women stepped out into a beautiful evening in Martha's Vineyard.

Although the air was a little chilly, a light jacket was sufficient. Since the shop displaying Joan's paintings was just a couple of blocks away, the women had decided to walk.

They entered the Art Attack to find it packed with people. It didn't take them long to find Joan's paintings. There were three of them, all lined up together.

"I was told they were going to display all four of them," Joan said under her breath.

"I wouldn't worry about it," Gail said. "Looks like they ran out of space. I don't see anyone else with this many paintings on the wall, Joan. You should be proud."

"Aren't they lovely?"

Aleeta Armbruster, the owner of the Art Attack, stood behind them, smiling at the paintings. Her lithe figure was covered by a clingy black dress accented with silver jewelry and a shiny silver ribbon braided through her long white hair. Priscilla suddenly felt dumpy in her black slacks and light blue sweater.

"We've had so many people ask about them, Joan. I think you could easily sell them if you wanted to."

Joan blushed. "I...I don't know. I don't think I want to do that."

"Up to you, dear, but they're really popular." Someone called Aleeta's name. "Excuse me," she said, rushing off to another part of the shop.

"They really are beautiful," Priscilla told Joan. Each painting portrayed a different flower. One showed a bunch of wildflowers in a blue-and-white jar. The next one displayed purple irises lying on a white lace tablecloth. The third painting featured yellow roses in a clear vase with a yellow-and-green butterfly sitting on the edge of the vase. "Which one isn't here?"

"The lilies of the valley." Joan looked around, probably trying to locate Aleeta.

"Maybe you should ask Aleeta about it later," Gail said. "She's really busy tonight."

Priscilla was about to agree when someone bumped her from behind. Priscilla had to grab Joan's arm to keep from stumbling. She turned around to find a teenage boy with large brown eyes and shaggy dark hair staring at her.

"Sorry, lady," he said. His two friends snorted and shoved him as if they found his apology funny. He looked embarrassed, and the three teens walked quickly away.

"Those boys are always causing trouble in town," Trudy said, her soft blonde curls bouncing as she shook her head. "They created a lot of mayhem last year on Halloween. The boy who ran into you is a sad case. I'll tell you about him later."

Priscilla nodded. Over Trudy's shoulder she noticed a woman and a man staring at her. They seemed to be talking about her. The woman was thin with dyed red hair, a sharp face, and black eyebrows that looked as if someone had drawn them on in the dark. The man was balding, portly, and had a florid face. Dressed nicely, he looked more like a businessman than a tourist or a local out to enjoy the festival.

Priscilla turned away. Were they really looking at her, or was she being paranoid? She tried to focus on the other paintings displayed on the wall. One right next to Joan's caught her eye immediately.

"Oh my," she said, grabbing Trudy's arm and pulling her over to look at it. "That's my lighthouse."

"You're right," Trudy said. "How cool!"

The painting was done in shades of blue, gray, and gold. It was night, and the light from the lighthouse cut through the black sky, highlighting the dark ocean with a sparkling golden beam.

"Look at that," Priscilla said, pointing to a single figure standing on the edge of the cliff outside her cottage. It was a woman in a glowing blue dress. Her head was turned away as she gazed out at the sea. Long black hair flowed down her back. Priscilla stared down at the title typed on a card below the painting. It read, *The Weeping Woman.* She turned to Trudy. "Who is the weeping woman?" she asked.

"I have no idea," Trudy said, frowning. "It's a new one to me. Who's the artist?"

"Maryane Davis-Rathvell," Priscilla read. "What an odd name." She opened her purse and took out a piece of paper. She quickly wrote down the artist's name.

Gail came over to them. "I need to get going. Work in the morning."

"Sure," Trudy said. "Come on, Priscilla."

Priscilla wanted to ask Aleeta about the painting, but she seemed to be having a deep conversation with someone interested in buying a large seascape on the other side of the shop. Priscilla decided to come back tomorrow and see what she could find out. Who had painted her lighthouse, and who was the weeping woman?

She tried to put it out of her mind as they prepared to leave. She was almost to the door when a woman stepped right in front of her. Priscilla had seen her at church, but she couldn't remember her name.

Priscilla smiled at her. "Hello, nice to see you," she said.

The woman didn't respond, just scowled at her. "Is Captain O'Bannon here?" she asked, her voice nasally and rather unpleasant. She wasn't unattractive. Short, with a tight figure and nicely coiffed blonde hair piled on top of her head. Her makeup was a little overdone, making her look a little older than she probably was.

"I...I'm sorry. I have no idea," Priscilla said, confused by her question. "I haven't seen him."

The woman stared at Priscilla for a few seconds, making her feel distinctly uncomfortable. Finally, the strange woman turned on her heel and strode quickly away.

"Well, what in the world was that about?" she whispered to Joan who stood next to her.

"Let's get outside, and I'll tell you."

When they stepped outside onto the sidewalk, Joan pulled Priscilla aside. "That woman is Eleanor Gufstead."

"I've seen her at church, but I couldn't remember her name," Priscilla said.

"Well, she knows *your* name."

Trudy and Gail came up next to them. "We should have told you about her before, but we assumed she'd given up."

Priscilla frowned at her. "Given up on what?"

Gail grabbed Priscilla's arm. "Gerald O'Bannon."

"I don't understand..."

Joan sighed. "Eleanor has had her sights set on the captain for a long time."

Priscilla's mouth dropped open. "What does that have to do with me? He's not interested in me. I barely know him."

Trudy shrugged. "I guess Eleanor thinks there's something going on between the two of you."

"Well, I can guarantee her it's not true. For crying out loud..." Priscilla took off walking toward their car. Of all the silly things. Why would this woman think she had an interest in Gerald O'Bannon? It was ridiculous. She was still grieving for Gary. The very idea...

"Hey, Cuz," Joan said, catching up to Priscilla. "Don't be upset. Eleanor's just a lonely woman. She lost her husband ten years ago, and she's been trying to find a replacement ever since. Don't be offended."

"I...I'm not offended. It's just..."

"I know. You still feel married to Gary. You'll probably feel that way for quite a while. Trust me, I understand. Alan has been gone a long time, but that connection is still there." Priscilla turned to see all three women looking at her, compassion on each face. For some reason, it made tears wash into her eyes. "I'm sorry. Let's just forget it, okay? I need to get home and so does Gail."

The women walked silently to the car. By the time Priscilla dropped everyone off and got home, it was dark. Jake was sitting by the door, ready to go out. Priscilla put a leash on him, and they walked around outside until he did his business.

As Priscilla was headed back to the house, Jake suddenly began to bark. Before she could stop him, he pulled the leash out of her hand. Then he ran toward the cliff where a woman dressed in a glowing blue dress stood, looking out to the sea. Just before he reached her, the woman stepped off the cliff and disappeared.

A NOTE FROM THE EDITORS

We hope you enjoyed Mysteries of Martha's Vineyard, published by the Books and Inspirational Media Division of Guideposts, a nonprofit organization that touches millions of lives every day through products and services that inspire, encourage, help you grow in your faith, and celebrate God's love.

Thank you for making a difference with your purchase of this book, which helps fund our many outreach programs to military personnel, prisons, hospitals, nursing homes, and educational institutions.

We also create many useful and uplifting online resources. Visit Guideposts.org to read true stories of hope and inspiration, access OurPrayer network, sign up for free newsletters, download free e-books, join our Facebook community, and follow our stimulating blogs.

To learn about other Guideposts publications, including the best-selling devotional *Daily Guideposts*, go to Guideposts.org/Shop, call (800) 932-2145, or write to Guideposts, PO Box 5815, Harlan, Iowa 51593.

Sign up for the
Guideposts Fiction Newsletter
and stay up-to-date on the books you love!

You'll get sneak peeks of new releases, recommendations from other Guideposts readers, and special offers just for you . . .
and it's FREE!

Just go to Guideposts.org/Newsletters today to sign up.

Guideposts®

Visit Guideposts.org/Shop
or call (800) 932-2145

Find more inspiring fiction in these best-loved Guideposts series!

Mysteries of Martha's Vineyard

Come to the shores of this quaint and historic island and dig into a cozy mystery. When a recent widow inherits a lighthouse just off the coast of Massachusetts, she finds exciting adventures, new friends, and renewed hope.

Tearoom Mysteries

Mix one stately Victorian home, a charming lakeside town in Maine, and two adventurous cousins with a passion for tea and hospitality. Add a large scoop of intriguing mystery and sprinkle generously with faith, family, and friends, and you have the recipe for Tearoom Mysteries.

Sugarcreek Amish Mysteries

Be intrigued by the suspense and joyful "aha!" moments in these delightful stories. Each book in the series brings together two women of vastly different backgrounds and traditions, who realize there's much more to the "simple life" than meets the eye.

Mysteries of Silver Peak

Escape to the historic mining town of Silver Peak, Colorado, and discover how one woman's love of antiques helps her solve mysteries buried deep in the town's checkered past.

Patchwork Mysteries

Discover that life's little mysteries often have a common thread in a series where every novel contains an intriguing whodunit centered around a quilt located in a beautiful New England town.

**To learn more about these books,
visit Guideposts.org/Shop**